The Choice

The Chase Runner Series

Book 1: The Chase
Book 2 The Choice

The Choice

The Chase Runner Series

By
Bradley Caffee

MOUNTAINBROOKFIRE

The Choice
Published by Mountain Brook Ink
White Salmon, WA U.S.A.

The website addresses shown in this book are not intended in any way to be or imply an endorsement on the part of Mountain Brook Ink, nor do we vouch for their content.

This story is a work of fiction. All characters and events are the product of the author's imagination. Any resemblance to any person, living or dead, is coincidental.

Scripture quotations are taken from the King James Version of the Bible. Public domain.
ISBN 978-1953957-15-3

The Team: Miralee Ferrell, Alyssa Roat, Kristen Johnson, Cindy Jackson
Cover Design: Lynnette Bonner

Mountain Brook Ink is an inspirational publisher offering fiction you can believe in.
Printed in the United States of America

To Samantha and Hunter,
who never doubted their dad could become a writer

Acknowledgments

To simply say that "God is good" would not be enough to describe the blessings I have experienced from my Lord and Savior, Jesus Christ. Life has dealt some hard blows, and yet I am still standing by the grace of my God. Thank you, Jesus, for saving this flawed man and gifting him a life in your blessing. I pray this simple book is an offering pleasing to you.

Thanks also to: Tirzah, my rockstar wife, who has made it her personal mission to see that I never give up on my publishing dreams. You have given me those healthy pushes to keep pursuing this goal, and I am so grateful for your love and patience as I continue to learn to become a writer. Thank you also for the celebration. 2020 was a difficult year to celebrate anything, but you insisted we take moments to smile and be grateful with each milestone.

Sami and Hunter, to whom this book is dedicated. Sami, you are my first fan, and I love that you include me among your favorite authors and cannot wait for my next book. Hunter, you are an endless encourager to your mom and me, and I love that you believe in me (and one day I'll write a book you are interested in reading. I promise.).

Miralee Ferrell, my editor, who has become my 'Yoda' as I improve my writing craft, thank you. You have taught me a great deal as we've edited these projects together. I am grateful for your influence to help this story be so much better.

The team at Mountain Brook Fire, you are the silent ninjas making this book transform into its final version. Thank you for all your hard work.

Sarah Freese, my agent, for cheering from the sidelines as each of these installments of the Chase Runner series launches.

Lauren, my first-reader, Willis, Perryn, and Sheila owe so much of who they are to your input. You have applauded my efforts and redirected my missteps. Thank you for being a friend through this and making sure that first read is juiced for everything it's worth.

Becca, Greg, Kyla, Lauren, and Nikayla, my beta-team who gave their time to pour over the first completed manuscript. Thank you for challenging me to broaden the emotions of the characters. You helped make them far more human. You all are amazing!

To my fellow writers at Realm Makers, it was shortly after finishing the first draft of this manuscript that I met you for the first time and you inspired me to take my writing to the next level and put it out there. I have loved being part of your community. Live long and prosper, my fellow writing nerds!

To all of you who have been harassing me for this second installment of Willis and Perryn's journey, thank you! There were more than a few moments where knowing your desire to read the next book kept me going. Many of you love these characters almost as much as I do. It's been a long wait between books. I hope you love it!

Chapter One

Truth has a way of being dangerous in the World Coalition. As Sheila's fingers flew over the keyboard, she ignored the knot in her stomach that slowly crawled its way up into her throat. More than once, she had to inhale deeply to keep from revisiting her in-flight meal. Her words were illegal. At least they had been hours earlier. Glancing around the plane, she wondered how many of her fellow travelers understood what Jaden had done.

"It is finished." Jaden's words still rang in her ears. The shock of what he'd done had passed, and now her stomach fluttered with a mix of hope and anxiety about what was to come. She could still see Jaden in her mind, standing on the stage after the Chase. His expression had been resolute. His voice never wavered. Instead of creating a new law that would benefit the Western Alliance, he'd freed the Coalition from the Law itself. Could he do that? Whether or not he could was no longer a question. He had.

A throat cleared beside her. She turned to be certain the man next to her wasn't peering over her shoulder to read her article. His rumpled suit coat and tie that didn't quite traverse the length of his rotund belly gave her some comfort. He could be an overworked businessman returning home from a long overseas trip and likely hadn't the time to view the Chase. His deep sigh confirmed he was asleep. She rumpled her nose at his aftershave and returned to her article.

Chuck, her editor, was going to kill her for not playing it safe this time, but she had a promise to keep. Willis, Perryn, Jaden, and Kane had done their job. Now was her time.

SAFE-GUARDING THE FUTURE?
By Sheila Kemp

The truth. We live in a world where truth is difficult to clearly discern. Every citizen of the World Coalition is familiar with the message we have been told. Things were bad. The Law was created. Things are better. Year after year, the greater population of the World Coalition submits itself to this mantra—with or without questioning whether or not it should—but still we cross our fingers as we watch the Chase, hoping that this will be the year for our alliance. If our alliance is the fortunate home of that year's law-changer, our protest quiets down because we know for a time that things will feel a little easier. Our stomachs might grumble less, but there is no meaningful change in our future. Have we traded our dreams, our hopes, for an extra slice of bread?

The Office of the Chairman continues to silence criticism with the idea that any serious change threatens a return to chaos. They declare that protecting the Law is to safeguard our future.

Did the World Coalition protect our future when they encouraged a system where children are removed from their homes to train for a Chase in which they may never compete?

Did the chairman defend the rights of all alliances when none but the wealthiest could afford the genetic recoding procedures required to consistently produce elite racers?

Did those racers feel sheltered by the goodness of the Coalition as they endured the pain and horror of having their consciousness ripped from their body and placed in a genetic copy?

Did those less privileged, who had to break the Law to survive, feel shielded by the Law when their rights were stripped away and sold into a system of rehabilitation that never releases its members?

The truth. The truth is less than desirable for even the most open-minded to hear. We are slaves. Whether we are part of the literal workforce of servants that makes up the unspoken underbelly of our society or some of the few who live lives of relative comfort, we were each born into a world in which we have no real freedom.

A young man by the name of Jaden changed all that when he declared the Law completed. Rather than use his moment to make our oppression momentarily bearable, he chose to open our eyes. He exposed us to the uncontrolled limitless world of possibility beyond the confines of the Law—ready or not. He ripped away our too-comfortable chains to expose the raw wound hidden beneath. Laid bare it hurts, but it is the good pain like what a patient experiences as they recover from surgeon's wound knowing the deadly tumor has been removed.

We will recover. We will learn. In time, we will thrive. And maybe for the first time in generations, we will have a future to safeguard.

Chapter Two

Six Months Later

Buzz.

The cell door opened with a metallic clang to reveal a uniformed guard on the other side. "Prisoner 513, you have a visitor." He spoke in a monotone, not moving his eyes from his notepad.

Sheila stared at the stone wall across the cell. Let him wait for a response. After all, she'd done nothing but wait. Six months had passed since Chuck had published her article. He'd been so eager to get her words about the riots following the Chase uploaded online that he hadn't even glanced at them. If he had, he never would have sent them to print. It took an hour after her words hit the internet for the Law-keepers to arrive at Sheila's door.

"Prisoner 513, on your feet." The guard struck the bars with his notepad and glared down at her.

Sheila's dirty fingers curled on the floor around her as she turned to glare at the guard. Her dry, cracking lips parted as she sucked in enough air to speak. "I told you I'm not interested in seeing anyone." Her voice creaked from disuse.

He rolled his eyes. "No choice this time, I'm afraid."

"Oh yeah, who's the special guest?"

"The Administrative Liaison to the Coalition Chairman is here to see you."

Sheila's stomach turned at the title. She remembered the greasy-haired man she'd last encountered on the space station. He'd threatened her and her sister if her words did anything but glorify the Western Alliance. Her half-starved existence in this isolation cell remained far preferable to ever laying eyes on the weasel again. She was about to protest when she noticed the two other guards standing outside the door.

"Wow. I've gotten popular, haven't I?" She smiled. Sarcasm wasn't going to win her points with the guards, but she had to admit that it felt good. She turned over on her knees to stand, her arms shaking with weakness. "Don't suppose your friends could offer me a hand."

A nod from the guard brought the other two inside. They roughly grabbed her upper arms, hauling her to her feet. The cell spun as she adjusted to standing again. All at once, she realized she might vomit or pass out. She opted for the latter. The guard's cursing was the last thing she heard before losing consciousness.

———————◆◇◆◇◆———————

"Ms. Kemp?" The tone was soft, almost pleasant. "Ms. Kemp, can you hear me?"

Sheila squinted as light poured into her eyes. The smell of disinfectant and clean sheets roused her from semi-consciousness. She was lying on a bed in what appeared to be a hospital room. Monitors beeped beside her displaying her heartrate and blood pressure, and an intravenous line was delivering fluids into her arm. Otherwise the tiny space was empty of furniture.

"There you are Ms. Kemp," came the voice again.

She turned in the direction of the speaker. A middle-aged woman sat in a chair next to her bed. She was dressed modestly in a gray, professional-looking skirt and jacket. Her perfume, a sickening fruity aroma wafted in Sheila's direction with each movement. Her eyes creased when she smiled at Sheila as she reached out a hand to the side of the bed. Several golden bracelets jingled as she touched Sheila's arm, which Sheila withdrew the second she saw the Alliance insignia on the woman's lapel. It couldn't mean anything good.

"Who are you?" Sheila eyed her suspiciously.

"My friends call me Penny." She smiled again. "You gave us quite a scare when you collapsed, and I insisted that you be brought to the infirmary at once. I have longed to meet you. I serve humbly as the Administrative Liaison to the Coalition Chairman."

Sheila's eyes widened. She bolted upright in bed, finally noticing the guard at the door. She turned to the woman. "I don't want to talk to you. And I'm not your friend."

"Oh, honey. I understand."

"Somehow, I don't think you do."

The woman pursed her lips while glancing down as if embarrassed. "I know you had dealings with my predecessor."

"Dealings would be a polite way of putting it." Sheila's forehead throbbed—with anger or pain from sitting up so quickly, she couldn't be sure. Possibly both. "He sent me to that station. He threatened my sister. And he put me in here."

"After the chairman uncovered the shameful coup attempt of the Western Alliance, many officials were—" She paused before finishing, "—replaced."

Sheila shuddered as she considered the meaning of *replaced.* "You mean, they were—"

"Sweetheart, it doesn't matter." Penny returned to smiling sweetly. "What matters is I'm here to help you."

"Help? How?" Sheila lay down to ease her pulsing temples.

"For starters, a hot meal and a shower. I honestly had no idea how you were being treated here, or I would have come much sooner. You were severely dehydrated. It's fortunate we found you when we did, or things might have been worse."

"I'm sure that was the idea of your—predecessor." Sheila doubted her supposed compassion, and she didn't mind if this woman realized it. "Don't get me wrong, a meal and a shower sound great, but why the sudden change?"

The woman's smile instantly disappeared. "All in good time." Her eyes and tone gave nothing away. She brightened again as if a switch was being thrown on and off in her mind. "But to get started, we need to get you cleaned up. I am afraid you are still at the prison, so you will be under guard. That is, until we can do something about your sentence. You leave that to me." A glance at the guard caused him to step aside and rap on the doorway. Two female nurses, dressed in yellow Alliance uniforms, entered.

Sheila must have shrunk backward because Penny was quick

6

to add, "Oh they are here to assist you. I'm assuming you do not want the guards helping you clean yourself."

Sheila nodded.

"Very well." The liaison held her hands out in front of her acting as though ready to embrace the room. Her bracelets jingled with each movement like they were celebrating the sterile environment. "I am pleased with this. Is there anything else I can do for you?"

"New clothes would be nice, if it's not too much trouble." Sheila continued to take in this woman. She could not make up her mind about whether to trust Penny. "And if I'm going to get out of here, I'd like transportation somewhere."

"I'm sure that can wait. There are things, dear, that we must attend to."

We? Sheila didn't like the sound of that. "I can't wait." She straightened her posture to show the seriousness of her request. "I need to see my sister."

Penny crossed her hands in front of her as her face darkened. "Very well." She frowned. "You can see your sister, and then when you are ready to appreciate those who have helped you, you will get around to seeing me. That is—if it's not too much trouble." Penny spoke the last few words slowly, clarifying that it was not a request. Without another word, she exited along with the guard leaving Sheila alone with the nurses.

The door clicked behind Penny, and Sheila let out a long breath. The hair on her arms still stood at attention, and she couldn't help feeling like an animal after a predator had left her cage.

Chapter Three

A twig scratched along the side of Perryn's face as she sat crouched in the brush. She could hear footsteps on the trail, and she refused to move a muscle to rid herself of the annoyance. She couldn't allow herself to be discovered.

She slowed her breathing as the footsteps drew nearer. Any moment, the approaching feet would come into view. Her body tensed with anticipation, and she silently reminded herself to relax her muscles. A second is all she would get to react. Her timing would have to be perfect.

The steps were close.

Three.

A twig snapped under the weight of the footfalls.

Two.

A pair of boots rounded the corner.

One.

They were right in front of her.

Now! She hurled herself off the ground and out of the bushes in one movement. Her voice roared as she reached out to grab him from behind. Her hands gripped his shoulders, and she could feel the instant tension in them.

"What the—" he shouted, his voice cracking. He pulled away. Turning to locate his attacker, he tripped over his own feet. In a whirl of motion, he spun as he crashed into the bush on the other side of the trail.

Perryn stopped, staring at the tangled form writhing in the branches. Slowly, a chuckle rose in her throat. The more she tried to suppress it, the more it fought to come out. Finally, she could hold it no longer.

"Bwhahahah!" she blurted. "You should have seen yourself."

"Ha…ha…ha." The words leapt off Willis's tongue slowly as he made no effort to hide the rolling of his eyes. He sat up inside the bush a bit scratched, but his frown communicated his pride hurt worse than anything. "I'm not sure it's all that funny."

"Startling you, maybe not." She breathed deeply to slow the laughter. "But seeing the once great Chase runner trip over himself like that—definitely." She resumed her giggling.

Willis glared at her before nodding in resignation, which made her snort as her fit got the best of her. He let out a breathy chuckle. "You can bet that payback is coming." He gave her a smile.

"Uh-huh. Somehow I don't think you'll get me nearly as well as I got you."

He grabbed at the branches to push himself up. "We'll see about that."

She shoved him playfully as she walked by, causing him to fall to his seat in the bush again. She headed down the trail biting her lower lip to contain her laughter as he struggled to regain his feet.

"Can you at least help me carry this equipment?" He bent over to begin grabbing the fishing tackle he'd dropped.

"You were doing fine without me," she called back to him.

"Yeah, but that was before I realized what was lurking in these woods." He ran to catch up to her, the fishing poles becoming tangled in his hands. "Never know when something is going to jump out at you on this trail."

"Good thing you're here. I don't know what I'd do without you." She nearly spit trying to hold her laughter inside while sounding serious. She reached over and grabbed the tackle box out of his hand. Grasping his newly-free hand with hers, she smiled as he squeezed her hand in return.

They walked in silence toward the waterfront. This was the life she'd dreamed of on the station. It had been mere months since she'd resigned herself to dying under the hands of doctors as she was eventually recoded her hundredth and final time, yet Willis's gentle but firm grip on her palm reminded her that so much had changed. She had peace. She had freedom. Fear was no longer her constant companion, and life at their cabin hideout with Willis's parents allowed her to breathe comfortably for the first time in years.

And then there was Willis. A friendship for sure—but it was something more. What that something was, she couldn't be certain. For the moment, she would enjoy what she had. There was time to figure that part out.

Max Thomson handed a cup of coffee to his wife, Brenda, as he sat next to her on the cabin porch. The remote cabin was small, with barely enough space for the two of them along with Willis and Perryn, but it'd been the perfect hideaway since the Chase riots.

"I think it's time we told them," Max remarked, sipping his coffee and staring out at the lake where Willis and Perryn fished from a boat in the distance.

"Look at them, Max." Brenda's eyes fell. "Our boy is finally sleeping through the night after adjusting to the quiet of this place."

"I know. I love seeing him at peace." Max stopped to gaze at the two young adults on the water, who were doing more splashing at each other with their paddles than actual fishing. "But this world isn't at peace, and I can't help but believe that Willis and Perryn still have some important role to play in this."

She slipped her hand into his, lacing their fingers together, and laid her head on his shoulders. She didn't have to respond. She understood. A trembling breath as she relaxed into his side confirmed his belief. They would need to tear back the relative protection their isolation had given Willis and Perryn, but he hated to do it so soon.

He watched Brenda, who stared out at the water. They'd been through a lifetime of pain together as parents without a child, and the past months had allowed them to feel whole again. Despite all that'd happened to them both, she was still beautiful to him. The years hadn't changed that. The few extra lines at the corners of her eyes merely reminded him of her smile. He loved her and ached over the pain she had endured. Part of her had always been missing when the Alliance had taken Willis as a child. She had him back, and Max could tell she was afraid to lose Willis again. So was he.

Max kissed her on the head and turned to Willis and Perryn. "You think they'll catch anything with all the noise they're making?"

A small smile appeared on Brenda's lips. "As long as they're happy, that's all that matters." She released a deep sigh. "At least for today, anyway."

"At least for today."

Chapter Four

Sheila regarded the likeness in the mirror. The image that met her was of another woman, gaunt and pale. She had dark, sunken eyes and a sickly narrowness to her face. She touched her cheek to make sure it was her in the reflection. The nurses couldn't be described as gentle as they'd helped her shower and dress, and the fresh cleanliness couldn't mask the neglect of being forgotten in a prison cell. The simple flower-print dress they'd given her to wear exposed her knees which trembled, still unaccustomed to standing.

Her instincts told her to turn away, to not admit that the person in the reflection was her. *How has it come to this?* She instead steeled herself and put her hair up with a lone clip the nurses had produced. Smoothing the dress with her hands, she straightened her spine and took a deep breath. If this was who she was, then she would at least insist on appearing somewhat presentable.

"Prisoner 5…er…Miss…uh—" The guard stumbled over his words. "Ms. Kimp, is it? The Liaison has arranged for your transportation."

Kemp. My name is Sheila Kemp. She didn't have the strength to correct him, yet her soul winced at the dehumanizing effect caused by his habit of calling her by a number. She was nothing more than Prisoner 513 to the guard—a number in a file somewhere that represented a forgotten human in a cell. She slowly turned to face him, her face showing no emotion.

He fidgeted, his eyes unable to remain in one place and never on her. "Uh…your ride. It's here."

She realized it might be the dress. No longer in a prison uniform, she was suddenly a woman in his eyes, even if the clothes didn't fit her correctly. How many times did he walk by her cell and ignore her as she starved?

"I take it that the Liais—er—Penny has already had my sentence removed? How efficient." Her voice lowered with the last word. Sheila couldn't bring herself to use the woman's title. It was vinegar in her mouth to say it.

"Yes, ma'am."

"Ma'am?" She allowed her voice to show the first signs of interest in speaking with this man. She arched a brow to let him know she invited an answer.

"Yes, ma'am. My mother raised me right."

"Did she? And what would your mother say about you having a part in this?" Sheila gestured to her emaciated figure. She imagined it was a dagger to the guard's soul, but she couldn't stop herself. She instantly regretted the question when she saw his eyes fall to the floor.

"Ma'am, I…um…I'm sorry that I…er—" he stammered.

Sheila stepped over to the guard, gingerly at first, not trusting her legs. She laid her unnaturally bony hand on his shoulder, noticing his nametag. She waited until he met her gaze. *Help him see.*

"Mr. Mallory, slavery comes in many forms. We obey because we're told, nothing more. We're all the same."

It was more than the guard could bear, and he quickly stepped back, breaking their connection. He wiped his face with his free hand, returning his gaze to the floor. "Ma'am, your car is waiting." With that, he turned to lead the way out the door.

They marched in silence down the cold, gray passageway. She observed the cell doors that passed on either side, their clean whiteness sterilizing the horror that lay beyond each one. They passed cell after cell, and she was left to guess how many were occupied by other inmates like herself. The corridor took a right turn that led to the front of the facility, blocked by a double set of doors. An alarm buzzed announcing the first door was unlocked, and Mallory held it as she stepped through. She jumped at the slamming of the door behind her, a sound she'd come to associate with being forgotten for days at a time.

"Prisoner 513, scheduled for release." Mallory spoke toward

a watchful camera in the corner. A second later the second door buzzed, revealing a large area where those entering the facility were screened. Beyond laid the front entrance.

Sunlight blinded her as the front door to the building swung open automatically. She held her thin fingers up to protect her eyes, while still allowing her to soak up the warmth on her face. Her lungs filled with fresh, cool air, exhilarating her after endless days of the stale prison cell. She could sense the tears welling in her eyes, but she wouldn't allow that. Not here.

"Ma'am, your car." Mallory motioned toward a black car with heavily tinted windows that awaited her. The concept of hours in another confined space nauseated her. She was finally outside. The desire to run and breathe overwhelmed her.

Once again, she turned to the guard. "I know you heard me." She paused. "Some slaves are half-starved in a prison cell, and others are uniformed and forced to keep the cell door closed. You don't have to be a slave. Not to them."

Mallory studied his shifting feet.

Sheila opened the door to the car and climbed in. She lowered the window on the door prior to closing it so as not to miss one second of the sunshine and fresh air. A screen between the front and back seats lowered revealing a driver in a black and yellow Alliance uniform.

"Ms. Kemp." The driver's voice was deep and rich. He tipped his cap to her. "Where to?"

"Drive anywhere for the time being. Please take me away from here." She waved a shy hand in the direction of the road before pulling it back to wipe at the tear clinging to her eyelid.

Without another word spoken, the car rolled away from the prison. Sheila kept her face in the open window for miles. The wind on her cheeks was all she needed to begin refilling her soul.

Sheila stared at the grave of her sister. The tombstone indicated she'd passed barely two months after Sheila had been arrested, overtaken by her lifelong illness.

Silent tears streamed down her face, which clung to her jaw

and shook from the quiver of her chin. Slowly she sank to her knees and allowed the sobs to overcome her. Clutching her gut, her soul tore inside her as the guilt spread through her like cancer. The Alliance had made good on its threat, and her sister's care must have ended the hour Sheila was imprisoned.

"I'm sorry, Audrey." She whispered as she placed a hand on her sister's name. She traced the lines of the engraving. "I'm so sorry."

For years, she'd watched over her sister during the worst nights when her sickness brought on feverish fits. Lying in the overgrown grass, she curled next to the grave as she had as a child while sleeping next to her sister.

The sun waned as the hours passed. Sleep arrived in the middle of the night, finally stopping the tearful flow.

Chapter Five

"So how big was the fish?" Perryn joked.

"I swear. It was huge!" Willis held his hands out, trying to show the size of the fish he claimed to have caught—and then promptly lost. It was clear no one was falling for it.

"So where is this monster, and why is it not our dinner tonight?" Max eyed his son, trying to contain his laughter. Perryn snorted as his eyes met hers across the table. It was clear she didn't believe him. This was not the first time she'd teamed with his dad to poke fun at him.

"I'm not kidding." Willis frowned, mildly hurt by their disbelief.

"Really, Max." Brenda's voice softened. "How do you know he didn't catch a fish that big?"

"Because that old fishing line he was using would never have put up with a fight from something that size. The line would have broken the instant it took the bait without ever forcing it to surface." Max bit his lips, unable to prevent the escaping smile.

"Don't laugh at him. You never know. Maybe it held this *one* time." She held up a finger as she defended him. "Or maybe the fish didn't have much fight in it."

"Okay, okay. Maybe it was this big," Willis admitted. He brought his hands closer—but barely an inch. With that, Perryn and Max lost their composure and the laughter burst from their lungs. Even Brenda started to chuckle.

Willis let out a frustrated sigh. He would never hear the end of it if he admitted that the fish had jumped out of the water at a distance breaking the line, and he was apparently overestimating the size. He was too deep in his fish tale at this point. Instead, he let himself smile and join the rest of the table.

They were a family. After years on the space station, he'd finally met his parents during the Chase. They'd made a daring escape through the ensuing riots, and months at the cabin in the woods had allowed for many scenes like this. It was everything he'd imagined a family should be, and he never wanted it to end.

He glanced over at Perryn. Her eyes watered from her laughter, which made her brown eyes sparkle even more. They had yet to honestly discuss their relationship, which started while training on the station. She'd become part of the family so seamlessly that the conversation had never felt urgent. Her eyes caught his, and she flashed him a smile. It was a smile he rarely saw on the station during their training. It never failed to light up his day. They lingered on each other's faces for a moment, and that's when Willis realized how silent his parents sat.

Max stared at Brenda with a knowing look. An unspoken conversation passed between them. It was clear his mother didn't want to bring something up, but then she agreed with a single resigned nod.

"What's up, Dad?" Willis smiled, secretly loving the use of the word dad.

Max sighed heavily dropping his gaze to the table. Slowly he raised his head and took in Willis and Perryn. "There's something I—rather, we need to talk to you about." He hesitated.

"Is something wrong?" Perryn questioned, no longer smiling.

"No. Well, yes. Sort of." Max bit his lower lip.

"What he means to say is that these months have been everything we could have dreamed of." Brenda patted Max's hand as she took over. "Seeing you—both of you—happy has been a joy for us to watch."

"We are happy, Mom." Willis tried to smile but offered a pained expression instead. "I still don't underst—"

"Your mother and I feel it's time to leave here," Max interrupted. Frustration contorted his face. Willis could sense him silently chide himself. It hadn't been what he'd meant to say—at least not first.

"Leave?"

17

"What do you mean?" Perryn's brow furrowed.

Max took a deep breath. "After the Chase—after what Jaden did to free the world from the Law—all we could think of was getting you two to safety. We didn't know what the world was going to do in the wake of it all. We'd prepared this place in advance as a way to reintroduce you slowly to society, but we never expected it to be forever. Given what is happening in the world, that expectation has become even less necessary."

"Happening?" Perryn glanced at Willis, and turned to Max. "What is going on?"

"You see—" Max bit his lip. "Things aren't going well." He eyed Brenda for help.

"When Jaden ended the Law," Brenda whispered, "not all of the world was ready for it. The World Coalition saw their chance to step in and manipulate knowledge of what happened. They've spread organized lies and deceived many around the world. Some people have embraced their new freedom, but many are too afraid."

"Afraid?" Willis's voice cracked as the word came out quickly.

"Afraid because the Coalition has started using any means, even violent ones, to enforce their will. Riots have led to arrests. Those have led to unfair trials and scapegoats. There have even been—executions." Brenda choked on the last word.

"So, you're saying—"

"The Law remains." Max's words hung over the table with a feeling of finality.

A long moment passed. Then, Perryn whispered. "I can't believe it."

"How? I mean—" Willis struggled for the words. "How could this happen? Jaden freed everyone. The riots started. Every time we asked you about it, you said the world was changing—that people were breaking away from the Law. You told us the Coalition was falling—slowly—but falling. And if we hid out here long enough, then change would eventually—"

"Change never came, Willis." Max bowed his head. His

shoulders slumped as he let out a long, slow breath.

"So—you lied?" Willis grimaced, the words coming in a breathy whisper.

"We didn't tell you the whole truth, son. We were afraid to. We so badly hoped you would be able to live a life of peace."

Father and son stared at each other in silence.

"Son, what we told you was true, but it wasn't everything. We didn't want you to worry. The truth is most of the Coalition, and especially the Western Alliance, have taken these months as an opportunity to tighten their grip. It's not safe to be one of the Liberated. That's what they're calling themselves. Anyone who speaks out is hunted down and silenced. Including—" Max paused and glanced at his wife.

"Including who?" Willis's eyes riveted to his father's face.

"Your friend—our friend—Sheila Kemp. She was imprisoned."

Willis's eyes widened at the name. *Sheila, in prison?* He glanced over at Perryn who had her trembling hand over her mouth. Her eyes darted from Willis to Brenda, who reached silently to take Perryn's hand.

"When did this happen?" Willis wouldn't meet their gaze. He stared at the table, dreading the answer.

"Not long after the law-passing. She was one of the first to be caught."

Willis's mind raced as the questions piled like a crowd all vying for the same doorway. Sadness gave way to fear, which morphed into anger. He couldn't believe that months had passed without being told this.

"Willis." His mother reached for his hand across the table. He withdrew at her touch.

"Why didn't you tell us?" His anger made him breathless. "We should have known. We should have done something."

Max shook his head. "Willis, there was nothing we could have done."

"We should have tried!" Willis pounded his fist on the table as the shout escaped his throat. Tears gathered on his eyelids, and he blinked them away in anger. He glanced at Perryn who was clutching her middle with both arms.

Max straightened in his chair. His voice was firmer, but still gentle. "We would have found ourselves in the cell next to her."

Willis fumed. "You don't know that."

"Yes, I do." Max hesitated. Brenda nodded as though to urge him to keep going. "All four of us are hunted by the Alliance. So far, the assumed names we use when we go into town for supplies are working. They haven't stopped searching for us since the Chase."

Willis put his head down, unable to slow his breathing. His hands clenched into fists as his insides felt like they might burst.

"Willis, I'm sorry. We needed to keep you safe here. We wanted you to enjoy your new life, if merely for a time. We didn't intend to hurt you."

Willis suddenly stood. He longed to scream and shame his parents for keeping Sheila's fate a secret. "Well, you did." He spoke through gritted teeth and walked toward his bedroom. He didn't look back, and the door shut behind him.

Chapter Six

Willis lay in the darkness staring at the ceiling. Hours had passed since the blow up at the table, and the rest of the family had long since retired to their own rooms. The silence of the cabin made his thoughts feel painfully loud in his mind.

How could they do this to me? It was the question that kept him up. Sheila hadn't merely been a friend to him on the station, but she was the one who had assisted in reuniting him with his parents. Without her, the last few months may never have happened. The entire Chase might have even ended differently. Chairman DeGraaf had activated the mental suggestion implanted years earlier that, upon winning, Willis would give the Coalition special powers. He'd been ready to win the Chase for that purpose. Meeting his parents had allowed him to break through the mental shackles and defy the Alliance. The family—the world—owed Sheila so much.

To withhold the news that Sheila had been arrested and imprisoned stung like a betrayal. Yet, he couldn't help questioning if he was being fair at the same time. The whole scenario had him confused. His heart ached, swinging from anger to sadness and back.

Maybe they're right. Maybe there was nothing we could do. But they still should have told me. His brain hadn't been this muddled since that night in the Chase sleeping quarters when the voice of his parents and the chairman fought for his allegiance.

He needed to sort this out, and there was one person he could think of to help him. He needed Perryn.

"Perryn?" Willis whispered. He stared at her shape illuminated by the slightest moonlight that filtered through the trees. A few loose locks of her brown hair lay as dark tendrils across her face. He softly brushed them aside with his hand. "Perryn, wake up."

Perryn moaned quietly. She peered at him with half-open eyes. "Willis?" Her voice croaked, laced with sleep.

He offered her a shy smile. "Hey, sorry to wake you."

"It's okay. Couldn't sleep?" She rubbed her eyes and blinked them hard several times. Sitting up, she swung her legs over the edge of the bed as he took a seat next to her.

"I can't believe that happened tonight."

Her brow scrunched together. "Me neither. I mean—Sheila—in prison." She stared at the floor, shaking her head.

"What happened to Sheila is horrible. But the more I think about it, I guess we shouldn't be so surprised the Alliance would do something like that." He paused. "That's not what's bothering me, though."

"You're concerned about what happened with your parents." Raising her head, she studied his face. Perryn always could read Willis like a navigator could read the stars.

He frowned. "I can't believe I yelled at them."

"Willis, people fight with their parents. It happens." The words came out almost as a breathy laugh. She placed her hand on his as though to encourage him.

He shook his head. "Not me. I've never had the chance to fight with them. All my life I've dreamed of being reunited with them, and I don't know what to do with this. I was—so hurt that they didn't tell us."

She squeezed his hand gently. "I don't think they meant to hurt you."

"I know. I don't understand, but I know that much at least. I got so upset. I don't want to feel this way. I've lost too many years with them to be this angry. What should I do?" He waited for her answer with hope. She was familiar with pain from her years in training and the horrors of the constant genetic recoding. It gave her a wisdom he lacked—a wisdom he needed.

Perryn took a deep breath and blew it out like she was snuffing a candle. "I think you need to go to them."

A minute passed. "Probably."

"No, definitely. And right now. You're right. It can't wait. You've waited long enough to have a family. Don't waste another second."

Willis let out his own long slow breath as he nodded in agreement, and he bowed his head to rest it on her shoulder. She wrapped her arms around him and held him tightly. He stared at the moonlight in the window over her shoulder and allowed himself to take in the warmth of her skin and the softness of her hair. In that moment he accepted the truth.

He loved her.

It had never been clearer to him. Here he was, in the midst of pain, and she was the one he sought—not for comfort alone, but for counsel. He trusted her—completely. Even with his limited experience with the world, he understood that was rare. She was rare. As much as he needed his family and longed to be with them for the rest of his life, he needed her.

He would wake his father to make things right tonight, but he resolved that he would reveal to her how he felt in the morning. Before breakfast. On the deck. She always stepped outside to breathe the fresh morning air. That is where he'd approach her. He didn't want to be with anyone else, and he couldn't deny his heart any longer. She was right. The seconds of this life couldn't be wasted.

A flicker in the moonlight caught his attention. He focused on the window, doubting he saw anything. Then, it happened again—a shadow on the sheer curtains, quick and moving. He straightened, his senses on full alert.

"What is it?" Perryn followed his gaze to the window.

Willis held his finger to his lips to let her know to stay silent. Easing off the bed, he crept in a stoop to the window's edge. He peered with one eye through the gap in the curtain, needing a second to adjust to the low light. Slowly, tree branches took shape outside the window, and he waited to find the source of the movement. His eyes widened as he made out the shape of a person, half-crouched in the tree line. The figure suddenly turned, waving an arm to his left.

Even in the shadows, he could see the yellow insignia of the Western Alliance on the uniform.

He opened his mouth to cry out, but fear swallowed his voice. Starting to turn, blinding light from outside suddenly flooded his vision. He covered his eyes and retreated backwards, falling over onto the bed where a startled Perryn still sat. He heard the muted buzz of floodlights turning on one by one around the cabin.

Crack! The door of the house splintered as Alliance Law-keepers broke it down. Glass shattered in the living area. Shouting. Footsteps.

"Willis!?!" Perryn cried. As he reached for her, the door to the bathroom swung open.

"Willis. Perryn. Come with me." Max's face was like stone, no emotion. He waved a hand as he whispered. He'd crossed from his room into hers through the common bathroom. Grabbing both of them, he hauled them to their feet and pulled them inside. Reaching in the shower, he pounded firmly on a grouping of tiles on the wall, which slid in an inch. Pulling the hatch to the side, a small opening could be seen with the top of a ladder visible beyond. Without a word, he pushed Perryn toward the opening, helping her crawl inside. Turning to Willis, he whispered again. "The tunnel lets out beyond the tree line. Close the panel behind you, and don't leave the trees for anything. Do you hear me?" He placed both hands on Willis's shoulder to stare in his eyes.

"You're not coming, Dad?"

"Son, they know that *someone* is here. If they don't find anyone, they'll spread out and surround us. We'll all be trapped. Now, go."

Willis nodded, not fully comprehending in his fear.

With that, Max left the bathroom to return to his bedroom. Willis stood for a moment panting. It wasn't until another crash, this time from the hallway, sounded that he dove into the opening. He shut the panel, which closed seamlessly.

The tunnel appeared endless in the darkness. He'd found Perryn at the bottom of the ladder waiting for him and led the way into the dark. He was met with the unmistakable odor of damp earth. Guiding themselves with their hands dragging the walls, slender roots brushed their hands as if reaching out to warn them of what awaited above ground. They slowly crept through the complete blackness underground.

"Willis, what's happening?" she whispered. Her voice shook slightly.

His own voice shuddered as he spoke. "It's the Alliance. They found us."

"Are your parents coming behind us?"

"I don't think so." The words sent a dagger to his stomach. His parents weren't coming. They were staying to confront the Alliance Law-keepers. He couldn't think of any way that would end well.

They said nothing else as they continued moving forward. Willis let out a grunt as his toe caught the edge of something solid in his way. He guessed they'd gone about fifty yards, but it was hard to tell in the darkness. He reached out. It was a second ladder. He grabbed Perryn's hand, showed her the ladder's location, and then started to climb. The upward slope of the earth on this side of the cabin meant that this ladder had to ascend higher than the first to reach ground level, but he soon found himself pushing on the door above his head. He winced at the slight creak the hinges made, certain it could be heard for miles. Peering into the darkness of the night, he listened. To his relief, the Law-keepers had abandoned stealth, and the house through the trees echoed with the muffled sounds of talking and footfalls.

"Come on up." He spoke softly down the ladder. Perryn didn't answer, but the slight tremble of the ladder let him know she'd started climbing.

He pulled himself out of the hole on his belly, not daring to stand. He crawled on his elbows until he could get a view of the house through a line of bushes. With the floodlights illuminating the house, Willis ensured his position was shrouded in darkness, and he had a complete view of the front and side of the cabin. Leaves rustled next to him as Perryn joined him.

Law-keepers were posted at each corner of the house with most of the group gathered in front of the cabin where several vehicles had parked. The commotion from the cabin was finished. Whatever had happened inside, it was over.

"Bring them out," a voice commanded. An officer emerged from the shattered front door. He appeared upset. "Outside. I want them outside, this instant!"

"Willis, look." Perryn gasped a little too loudly, causing a bolt of anxiety to travel Willis's spine.

To his horror, Max and Brenda emerged handcuffed. Max walked dazed and weak. His shirt was torn, and his head was bleeding. Both of them stumbled into the clearing in front of the cabin. Whatever fight his father had brought to the intruders, it must have ended with the butt of a rifle to his head. Medics were treating three Law-keepers nearby who were injured far worse than Max.

"Place them here on their knees." The officer barked the orders to the Law-keepers holding Max and Brenda. The Law-keepers shoved Willis's parents to their knees in the center of the lighted area.

"I don't like this," Willis whispered uneasily.

"Willis Thomson!" The officer shouted toward the tree line.

Willis's heart leapt, and he had to remind himself that he couldn't be seen.

"I know you're out there and can hear me. You've done a fine job hiding from the Alliance, but it's time for you to come home. It has been determined that you were complicit in the actions of the fugitive, Jaden, and the Alliance Law-keeping Ministry would like to question you.

"Let me assure you that it isn't our desire to harm you or your family, but we simply need information. Surrender willingly, and you'll merely be questioned and genetically recoded. No prison. You and your family can go free."

"Do you actually believe those lies?" Max growled at the officer. A nod to a Law-keeper brought a swift kick to Max's mouth. He fell over, still handcuffed, a cry of pain escaping from his bleeding lips.

"Willis, listen to reason." The officer turned to the tree line. "It doesn't have to be this way. Turn yourself in." The officer's face scanned the forest, and Willis instinctively ducked as his gaze turned toward them. Back and forth, the officer's head turned as he waited for a response.

Willis sat still watching the scene. He started to stand when Perryn grabbed his arm. "Willis, you can't."

He hesitated.

"He's—he's not here." Max was crying out from the ground, his voice garbled from his swelling lip. "He left a week ago. You're wasting your—" A second kick, this time in the stomach, silenced Max.

"I don't have time for this." The officer snapped at his men. "Lieutenant, I hold you responsible for not securing all four fugitives. Because of you, we're going to have to get messy. If the boy doesn't emerge in the next ten seconds, shoot the mother. Let's see if this boy is willing to sacrifice others for his own safety."

A Law-keeper with a pistol stepped behind Brenda, who simply knelt crying. Willis immediately rose to a half-crouch, but Perryn clung to him.

"Don't." Her voice was desperate, and she was crying. "You heard your father." Willis glanced in panic at her and back at his parents. His heart thumped with each passing second. He couldn't decide. His breath came in quick gasps as he stood half-stooped in indecision.

"Fine." The officer shook his head. "Time's up."

"No!" Max shouted through tears willing himself to his knees. He scurried to place himself between the Law-keeper and Brenda. "Please, don't do this. Please. Do whatever you want to me, but leave her alone."

"Very well." The officer nodded at the Law-keeper with the pistol who turned the gun toward Max.

"Brenda, I love—"

The flash of the pistol lit the night, blinding Willis.

Chapter Seven

"I'm Sheila Kemp, and that's all for today's broadcast. Tune in tomorrow for more from *Keeping up with the Kemps!*" Sheila *announced. She smiled shyly at a teenage Audrey awaiting her response, while she bit into the hotdog that'd been a microphone a moment earlier.*

"Sheila, that was great." Audrey beamed at her little sister. Reaching out a hand, she brushed a loose strand of hair out of Sheila's face. "See, you should try reporting more. I think you're a natural."

"Nah. I like to write my words down better." Sheila tried to sound like a modest ten-year-old. "I feel so weird saying them out loud."

"But how are people ever going to know you the way I do unless they can see and hear you?"

"I don't know." She gazed down at her food. Ketchup was dripping from the end of the bun, and she pretended to be interested in it while she waited for her sister to speak again. Audrey crossed her arms on the table and rested her chin on them. She grinned at her sister, almost laughing, to see how long she would pretend to be fascinated by the dripping.

"Hey." Audrey broke the silence.

"What?" Sheila frowned, still not meeting Audrey's eyes.

"You're great at telling the story of the world around you. You have a voice. Use it, Kemp." It was the name Audrey used when she desired to make a serious point with her.

Sheila didn't respond.

"I don't even have a real microphone to practice with." Sheila held out the still dripping hot dog.

Audrey gave her a serious expression. "Let me make you a

promise. You keep practicing, and I'll save for a real microphone."

"You mean it?" Her voice lifted as she asked, finally looking up.

"Absolutely. That is, unless you want to use a hotdog the rest of your life."

They sat in silence. Slowly, a smile appeared on Sheila's lips as she withheld the laughter. Audrey's returning grin widened as she watched her sister's struggle to keep the giggle inside.

"At least then, if being a journalist doesn't work out, I could open a hotdog stand."

That was more than they could take. Audrey was the first to burst into chuckles. She hid her face in her hands as the laughter overtook her. Sheila joined her, unable to resist. For several seconds, they held their stomachs trying to contain the outburst.

Without warning, Audrey sputtered and choked on her laughter. Realizing the terrifying fit that was coming, her smile disappeared into fear. The merriment ceased as she continued to wheeze and cough, unable to stop the spasm for several minutes. Sheila was forced to watch as her sister struggled.

"I'm sorry. I'm sorry. I'm sorry." Sheila apologized through tears as her sister's lungs calmed down. "I shouldn't have told a joke when you're sick."

Audrey's eyes grew sad. Reaching over to grab Sheila's hand, she spoke softly. "And how am I to ever get better unless my little sister helps me be happy?"

Sheila stared at her sister helplessly unable to stop crying. "But Mom says you're sick."

"All the more reason I love it when you make me laugh."

Sheila cracked her eyelids barely enough to see that the sun was up. As consciousness fully returned, she remembered where she was lying. She slammed her eyes shut and breathed deeply to avoid crying again. The memory of Audrey had been so vivid in her dream, and she hated waking to this reality. Somewhere a bird was chirping, ignorant of her sorrow. Her body ached from sleeping on the hard ground in front of Audrey's grave, but she didn't have the strength to care.

Her arms complained as she pushed herself upright. Sitting up, she surveyed the graveyard outside her hometown. The smell of dew-covered grass filled her lungs. At the edge of the lawn, the Alliance car still sat. *Had the driver waited all night for her?* He could have insisted they move on, but he hadn't. She wiped her face, removing a strand of hair that stuck to the saltiness left from the tears she'd shed for much of the night.

The driver stood there silently, his mostly black uniform and sunglasses out of place in this rural setting. The Alliance insignia stood like a yellow inkblot on his lapel from this distance. The two of them had hardly spoken on the long drive from the prison, and she had no idea what kind of person he was. Yet, he was still there, waiting. He wasn't guarding her escape from what his posture communicated. Rather he appeared to be giving her the space she needed to mourn.

Sheila rose to a crouching position, fighting to arrange the ill-fitting dress. Resting her forehead on the cool gravestone, she whispered a goodbye to her sister. She kissed her fingers and placed them on her sister's name. *I love you, Audrey. I won't stop using my voice. I promise.*

Standing up, she smoothed the dress across the front of her body and walked toward the driver. Her legs still stiff from sleeping, she had to focus not to walk like a drunkard. His head turned almost imperceptibly in her direction, and she decided it was time to get to know this man. He'd waited all night for her. She could at least speak to him.

"Ma'am," he said quietly as she approached.

"Thank you"—she paused for what to say— "for waiting."

"You're welcome." He gave a slight nod with no other change in his expression.

She couldn't see his eyes behind the dark shades, but his voice was one of deep kindness. She pushed the conversation a little more. "What is your name?"

"Marcus Raymond. You can call me Raymond, ma'am."

"Mr. Raymond. It's a pleasure to meet you. And please, no more 'ma'am.' Despite my appearance in this ridiculous dress, I'm not old enough for 'ma'am' yet." She stared into the blankness of his sunglasses. "I'd prefer my name. It hasn't been used in months."

She extended her hand and took his in a firm handshake. Her hand's ghostly complexion appeared sickly against his strong, dark hand. The slightest, almost imperceptible smile appeared at the corner of his mouth. Had anyone ever paid him this much attention? His posture and dress were professional and official, but his face wore the expression of a man ignored most of the time. "You got it, Kemp." With that, he turned to grab the car door for her.

The memory of her sister flashed in her mind one more time as she heard the name 'Kemp.' Warmth spread through her chest as her sister's love overwhelmed her. She decided that she liked him using the name. "So where to?" She hadn't thought beyond visiting her sister.

"I'm afraid we're overdue to meet with the Administrative Liaison to the Coalition Chairman."

She frowned. "Overdue. I'm sorry. You won't be in much trouble, will you?" She couldn't place why she cared, but she didn't want him to get in trouble.

"Some things are more important."

"Things?"

"Your sister. You needed time to see her. That's worth a reprimand."

Her heart melted in gratitude. She'd read this man rightly. Beneath his firm exterior, there was compassion. He'd allowed her to mourn all night knowing he would pay for it.

"In that case, Raymond. Let's not keep her waiting."

"As you wish." He opened the car door for her. She eased into the seat, glancing at Raymond, who removed his sunglasses to look her in the eye. "Breakfast is on the seat next to you, Kemp." He smiled and quietly closed the door.

I think I made a new friend. She smiled and breathed in deeply.

The idea of a friend warmed her. The smell of coffee awakened her senses. Sure enough, upon examining her seat she found the promised meal. Her stomach gurgled with an awakened hunger, and she realized how little she'd eaten in the last day. *Thank you, Raymond.*

"Sweetie, welcome!" Penny quickly scurried over to Sheila extending two jingling arms. Sheila let her arms hang limp as the woman embraced her. The pungent smell of her overly floral perfume sickened her, and Sheila worried she might start gagging. "Please come in and sit. I trust your driver…er…Mr. what's-his-name treated you well."

"Raymond." Sheila supplied the answer, sitting down.

"What was that, dearie?" She was examining a piece of paper on her desk uninterested in Sheila's information.

"His name is Mr. Raymond. And, yes, he treated me well." She'd considered screaming it. It was clear Penny was not interested in anyone who she considered beneath her. Penny had likely gotten Raymond's name incorrect hundreds of times as he carted her around town.

"Good—" Penny let out a long breath. "I'm glad for that. Thank you for coming to see me."

"Not sure I had a choice." Sheila bit her lip to rein in the sarcasm.

"Yes, well, we did arrange your release, didn't we?" Penny's tone remained sickeningly sweet, but Sheila swore she could hear a tone underneath the words.

Sheila chose to play this carefully. "Yes, you did."

"Yes, we did." Penny repeated her words smugly. "I trust your visit with your sister was pleasant?"

I hate you. She rarely used the word 'hate,' but Penny's comment had been meant to wound her. She wouldn't dignify it with an answer.

"No? Yes?" She let out a *humph.* "I'll assume it was." Penny filled in the silence while sitting in her yellow, ornate chair behind her desk. "On to more important matters. Your release wasn't accidental or random, Ms. Kemp. We have an opportunity we'd like to discuss with you."

"Excuse me?" Sheila sat backward trying to breathe through her anger. "Who is 'we?'"

"Honey, I represent the Western Alliance and the Coalition Chairman. In fact, the two have almost become synonymous in the months since you were imprisoned. It has been a remarkable privilege to serve such an influential world power."

"And that—power—" Sheila choked on the word.

"Wants you." Penny smiled and leaned forward in her chair eagerly awaiting Sheila's excited reaction. Slowly, the smile faded as Sheila sat unflinching with her arms crossed. "Ms. Kemp, you are to become the voice of the Western Alliance—of the whole Coalition, in fact. Doesn't that excite you, dearie?" One more time she smiled with fluttering eyelids.

Sheila didn't move a muscle.

"And why would I want to do that?" Sheila questioned, forgetting to hide the snark.

"Well—" Penny maintained her determined excitement as she sat straight. She folded her hands as if praying. "The fact that you have been given your freedom again aside, you will be given the freedom to report the truth. Isn't that what you want?"

Sheila frowned. "You mean, I become the propaganda pawn of the WA. I think I'd rather be in prison."

Penny grinned with raised eyebrows, apparently expecting this response. It made Sheila shift in her seat to think this woman was a step ahead of her. "You are mistaken, Ms. Kemp. We do not wish to change your insightful perspective. We want you to report the truth. To tell the world what is happening, in all its gory detail. No sugar-coating. No censorship."

Penny had her attention. Sheila considered her next words carefully. "The chairman has to know how I feel about the Coalition. If I report the truth, it won't paint the Coalition in a positive light."

"Precisely!" Penny almost shouted, unable to contain her enthusiasm. "You're beginning to understand."

I'm completely confused. Sheila eyed Penny warily, not sure if she wished the woman to keep explaining.

"The world is in trouble. The criminal Jaden threw everything into chaos. By abolishing the Law, groups around the world have risen who openly question everything."

"Sounds beautiful to me. Sounds like freedom." The words came to Sheila, and she spoke them wishing she could rein them in.

Penny was suddenly serious. "What you call freedom, we call anarchy. Dangerous chaos. Not since the Great Collapse has there been this level of disorder. We stand on the brink of repeating history, and we cannot allow that to happen."

Sheila arched a brow. "And you think that I can help by telling—the truth?"

"Anarchy feels like freedom when you cannot see the cost." Penny stared at her, the words seemingly still echoing in the room. "You will show the world the cost of chaos. You will show them how close we are to destroying ourselves again. The rebellious of the world trust your voice. They know you've paid the price for speaking out. They will listen to you. And when they do—they'll beg for the safety of the Law."

Sheila straightened in her chair, considering the offer. The woman talked as though she genuinely believed the plan would work. *She believes showing how bad things are will convince people to return to the way things were?* Sheila believed otherwise, but she didn't have to say so. People were smart enough to realize who was truly responsible for the hellish conditions around the world. Someone like Penny would not, could not understand the hope of freedom. Experiencing that hope for a short time after the Chase allowed Sheila to endure the hell of her prison cell, so she could imagine the hope others had around the world. The realization made her pity Penny.

I can't do much from prison. The realization was sobering.

"Your agreement, then?" Penny leaned in again, awaiting an answer.

"I have your word? I can report the truth as I see it?" Sheila held her breath, expecting the offer to be withdrawn as a cruel joke.

"Yes."

Then, that's what I'll do. In front of the camera...and behind it. Sheila promised herself. No, she'd promised Audrey. It was this that allowed her to stomach the idea of becoming the weird truth-telling pawn of the Alliance's propaganda machine.

"Fine. I'll do it."

"Oh, dearie, I am so pleased." Penny was smiling from ear to ear. Her bracelets clattered as she clapped to herself. "We already have your first story for you, and it's a big one!"

"Oh, really?" Sheila hadn't expected to get started so soon.

Penny's eyebrows bounced with an eager playfulness. "You get to report on the capture of a wanted fugitive."

"Who?" Sheila frowned, unsure she wished to hear the answer.

Penny leaned even further in like she was revealing a secret. "Brenda Thomson."

Sheila's insides lurched.

Chapter Eight

From the top of the tunnel ladder, Perryn could see the sunlight peeking through the cracks of the trapdoor they'd exited the prior night. It'd been hours since the Law-keepers had left the area, unable to find the hidden tunnel. It took all her strength to wrestle Willis to the ground when he'd tried to rush the officer who ordered Max's execution. Once she had him, he surrendered and didn't have the strength to put up a fight. She'd been forced to drag him to the tunnel entrance before he climbed down under his own power.

She peered down the ladder into the darkness below. A barely visible fetal shape, Willis still lay in the same place where he'd surrendered to his sorrow last night. They had to leave this place before the Law-keepers sent a better equipped search party to hunt for them.

But what will I find up there?

"Willis, I'm going for a look," she said in a low whisper. He didn't move, but she trusted that he heard her. Slowly, she pushed the trapdoor upward a few inches to allow a view of the surrounding area. Squinting, she scanned in the direction the soldiers had been.

A sudden rustle of leaves sounded to her right.

In her panic, she yelped and let go of the trapdoor. The heavy lid slammed downward, striking the top of her head. Her foot slipped, and she grunted as the top rung of the ladder jammed upward into her armpit. Her head throbbing and her arm numb, she silenced herself to listen. The leaves were still moving, a harsh sound that made her wince. She was certain whatever was out there could hear her heart pounding. Quietly repositioning herself, she peered through the crack at the door's edge.

She cursed to herself. The gray, bushy tail of a squirrel darted in view of the opening, continuing the crunching sound. A black, pea-sized nose sniffed at the door. A second later, the creature scampered away.

"If he feels safe to move around, I guess the coast is clear." She spoke aloud, trying to convince herself. "I guess I should thank you, little guy, even if you did nearly scare the life out of me."

Pushing once again on the door, she eased out of the hole and carefully lowered the hatch to the ground. Kneeling, half-crouched, she listened. The area was silent except for chirping birds and her squirrel friend. She chanced standing. Nothing. Softly, she approached the tree line where they'd hidden from view.

The cabin was a mess. Windows were broken with their curtains caught in the shards of glass. She could see glimpses of furniture over-turned from what must have been a thorough search. No Law-keepers. No vehicles. Tire tracks where they had all been.

Her gaze found him in the middle of the clearing.

The body of Max Thomson lay on the ground. His hands were folded across his chest, no doubt the work of Brenda who had positioned him prior to being hauled away. Perryn took a deep breath, remembering Brenda's cries as she'd embraced her husband's body. She didn't want to, but she needed to inspect closer. She needed to prepare Willis for what he would see. She steeled herself.

Slipping out from the tree line, she skittered to the corner of the house. Glancing around the corner, she gave one last glance for Law-keepers, hesitating to walk out in the open. No signs of anyone or any surveillance could be seen. Steadily, she padded barefoot toward Max while concentrating on breathing deeply.

He appeared peaceful with his eyes closed and could have been mistaken for sleeping except for the entry wound on his forehead. She whispered a 'thank goodness' that the far uglier exit wound was toward the ground and much of the blood soaked into the soil.

"I'm sorry, Max. Thank you for watching out for us." She removed her robe to place it over his face. The morning chill sent a shiver, and all exposed skin burst into goosebumps.

"Don't." Willis's voice came from behind her. She sucked in a breath of surprise and turned toward him.

She held out a hand. "Willis, I don't think you should."

"Yes, I should." His voice was flat, but she could see the tears in his eyes. Cautiously, he walked toward his father and knelt next to him. Silence followed, but Perryn could see the quiver in his shoulders as grief overcame him. "I'm sorry," he whispered. "I never should have argued with you last night. I was going to make it right—to explain to you that I understand you've done everything you can to protect us. And—now I can never tell you."

Perryn knelt next to him and wrapped him from behind with both arms. For several minutes, she cried with him over the body of the father he'd briefly known.

"I—I can't do this." He let out a shuddering breath. His voice croaked with anguish. "He said we need to do something. Help people. I—I can't help the world without him."

The words pierced her heart. They were the same that she'd spoken to him on the station when Jaden had been temporarily removed from the team. Willis had been so strong for her then. He believed she could survive the Chase training. He'd held her and given her hope when he could have left her crying in the hallway outside his quarters.

This time, she was the one embracing him.

It's my turn to be strong. The reminder gave her resolve. The right words eluded her, but she should say something.

"Your father," she said, gently turning his face toward hers, "believed you were the one who could do what was needed. He was right, you know."

He stared at her, lost, but longing for what hope she could

offer. She breathed out slowly, considering her next words. He needed a nudge to move forward, but not a shove. *He's not ready to take on the world yet.* Then, it occurred to her.

"Willis, your father believed in you—and one day soon it will be time to help the world. But—there's something we must do first."

"What is that?" His voice was shaky. His eyes searched her face.

"They have your mother—and Willis, she needs us. She needs you."

An expression of realization washed over his face. His eyes then quickly transformed into rage. As she'd hoped, Willis's protective instincts must have turned on, and some strength returned to his posture.

"You're right." He was whispering still, but the tremor was missing from his voice. "I can't let them have her."

"We won't, but first we need to get out of here. We need to get supplies from inside, but we can't disturb anything in case they return. That would give them a starting place to track us, which means leaving everything as we found it. That includes—" She hesitated to continue. He wasn't going to like what she was thinking.

"Includes what?" He raised his brows, noticing her pause.

"Your father." She sighed. "If we bury him, they'll know we came back."

Willis's brow furrowed with hurt at the idea, but he eventually nodded in agreement. She hugged him again and stood. Leaving him to be alone with his father, she entered the cabin to see what she could salvage. Glass crunched under her feet as she entered the main living space, and she had to be careful where she stepped. Nothing had been left undisturbed.

In the living room, she could see the struggle that took place as Max had challenged the guards. The blood on the carpet and sofa was evidence that the Law-keepers got more than they'd bargained. She whispered a 'thank you' to Max. His fight had let them escape through the tunnel. It was a losing battle meant simply to buy them time.

Entering the master bedroom, she saw that Brenda hadn't gone quietly either. The shattered remains of the nightstand were testimony to her resistance, and the drag marks on the floor told her someone, likely a Law-keeper, hadn't left the area conscious. Perryn wasn't sure the soldier who received the corner of the nightstand could have survived that hit. Brenda must have stayed behind as the last line of defense to slow the Law-keepers from reaching the bathroom where they'd escaped.

Walking through the doorway, she noted the hatch to the tunnel was perfectly hidden in the closed position. Max and Brenda had prepared well. The cabin was meant to hide them, but they'd known what the Alliance was capable of. She changed her clothes and chose some from Willis's drawers. Grabbing a backpack from the closet, she packed what non-perishable food she could find in the kitchen as well as the hunting knife and a wad of Alliance credits she found in a drawer.

The kitchen window faced toward the clearing outside of the house where Willis still knelt next to his father. The broken shards that still clung to the windowpane appeared from her perspective to pierce Willis's form. She dared a long glance at his private moment with his father. *His soul is as shattered as this window.* Symbolically, she grabbed the hanging glass and ripped it from the window. She had to believe he would get through this.

Willis stood slowly, whispering something inaudible to his father and walked toward the cabin. He crunched his way into the open living space and scanned around. His gaze finally resting on her, he pointed at the piece of glass still in her hand. Not wanting to explain the shard, she set it down and handed him the clothes she'd grabbed.

"Here, you should probably get dressed."

"Thank you." Willis took the clothes from her.

"It's some of your clothes. I'm not even sure they are what you'd want."

His chin quivered as his gaze fell. "I meant thank you for last night."

"Last night?"

"If you hadn't stopped me, I'd be dead out there next to him. If you hadn't shoved me down that hole and hid me in the tunnel, they would have found me in the woods. I was angry with you all night. I wished that I had died with him, but then you reminded me of my mother. She'd be on her own if you hadn't stopped me." He walked to her and gazed in her eyes. He softened his voice. "And if you hadn't talked to me last night, I would be left wondering if I wished I had made things right with him simply because he's gone. At least I get to know I planned to, even if I'll never get to. I—I don't know what I'd do without you, Perryn. I promised myself I'd tell you that this morning. I—"

She waited as he stood there seemingly ready to continue, but he closed his mouth and left the sentence unfinished. He sighed as he glanced in the direction of his father's body and then returned his gaze toward her. For several seconds, they stared into each other's eyes in silence. Stepping forward, she wrapped her arms tightly around him and rested her head on his chest. His arms quickly followed her lead, and they embraced each other. A flood of affection for him washed over her, and she almost burst with a confession of how she felt about him, but they needed to get moving.

"I can't think straight. How do we begin?" He breathed deeply and then let go of her.

"After you left the table last night, your parents talked about a train station in a town not far from here. If we follow the road, I think it'll lead us there. I'm not sure how else we'd get out of here."

"We'll have to be careful not to be recognized."

"Here." She handed him a hat. "Keep this low on your head. You've been the hope of the Alliance your whole life. Everyone knows your face."

He put the hat on, pulling the brim low over his eyes. "What about you?"

She pursed her lips. "I have an idea about that."

She returned to the bathroom and slowly braided her hair as best she could, considering the shattered mirror. Wrapping the braid around her head, she placed Max's worn baseball cap over it. She then slipped on a jacket belonging to Willis. It was far too big for her, but hiding her form was the idea. She inspected herself in the mirror again.

I'm not sure whether it's good or bad that I can't fully pass for a man. She allowed herself a small smile. *This will have to do.*

Returning into the kitchen, she looked sheepishly at Willis. It wasn't exactly how she wished for him to see her, but she needed to get his reaction to her disguise out of the way. Willis contorted his lips as if trying not to grin.

"And what shall I call you, Mr.—" he joked.

Something inside her brightened that he'd told a joke, and she allowed herself to hope that his soul may not be beyond repair. She punched him in the shoulder. "Stop. They're not hunting for two men, and I can pass for a man far better than you'd ever pass for a woman."

Willis grimaced as he rubbed his arm where she'd hit him. "The hat suits you. I think he'd be glad you are using it." He disappeared into his room to change.

She scanned through the contents of the bag one more time and found herself doubting her plan. *What if the road doesn't lead to town? What if we're discovered?* She hesitated and considered whether they should stay in the cabin. *We could hide in the tunnel anytime they showed.* Max's pale face flashed through her mind once more, and she was newly convinced they needed to get out of here.

Willis emerged wearing the clothes she'd given him. Walking to the front door, he added a hoodie that further hid his face.

Inspecting the shelf next to him, he grabbed a photo of the family. He plucked it gingerly from the shattered frame and shoved it in his pocket.

Breathing deeply, she motioned to the door. "Shall we?"

He picked up the backpack and put it on. "I think I'm ready. One thing, though—"

"What is it?"

"I'd like to leave out the back door if we can. I've said my goodbyes, and I don't particularly want to see him again like that."

She nodded and took his hand.

Chapter Nine

"How much to Central City?" Perryn tapped on the glass in front of the agent at the ticket window, trying to disguise her voice. Willis had debated with her which of them were more likely to be discovered—Perryn if she attempted a male voice, or him because he was Willis Thomson, hope of the Alliance.

"Four hundred credits." The ticket agent sounded bored as though he'd said it a hundred times that day. With one hand, he punched keys on a keyboard.

Perryn was grateful that he was too focused on his crossword puzzle to glance at her. She counted out the credits and slid them under the window. Head still down, he counted the credits and two slender cards with chips on the end appeared out of a slot in front of her. She grabbed them and turned to leave, not daring another word.

"Hold on." His voice was louder. His eyes must have finally left the crossword.

She froze, unable to move. Needles of fear rose along her spine. Something inside her told her to run, but she steadied herself. She turned partially toward him, not wanting to fully show her face. Her breath had caught, and she couldn't make herself answer him.

"You don't happen to know a seven-letter word that begins with 'w' and means 'moves while lost,' do you?" She almost choked on her relief and shook her head. "Dang, I've been stuck on that one for an hour."

Perryn held her breath all the way to where Willis was sitting in the corner with his head bowed, trying not to be noticed.

"Any luck?" He kept his head down as she approached.

"Train leaves in twenty minutes. We barely made it." She

breathed heavily as though she'd run a mile, her hands still shaking. She held out the two tickets. "Our job at this point is to try to not get noticed for several hours in a confined space with other people all the way to Central City."

"You sound nervous."

"And you aren't?"

"I don't know what I am. I know that I want to get there before something happens to my mother." His voice was angry, and she hoped he was in the right place to think clearly. Anger would give him power, but too much would make for recklessness.

A commotion on the other side of the outdoor waiting area drew her attention. People were gathering around a screen to listen to a broadcast. Perryn's eyes widened as a face appeared, reporting on the incident.

"Willis, look." She whispered with a harshness that made him raise his head. Willis dared to peek, and she could see his jaw clench as he tried to react without a sound. They both stared as Sheila Kemp spoke on the screen. With her much thinner features, she was barely the same woman Perryn remembered.

"A crowd has gathered here in the capital," Sheila said, "to see authorities escort the alleged fugitive, Brenda Thomson, to a holding facility. After months of searching, Alliance Law-keepers were able to track down the secret cabin where Brenda and her husband, Max Thomson, had been hiding since last year's Chase event. Authorities were forced to use deadly force when Max Thomson attacked officers during the raid."

Willis muttered the word 'traitor' under his breath.

The camera cut away to pictures of an obviously bruised Brenda being forced from a truck, while officials commented on the arrest. Perryn placed her hand on Willis's, which was balled into a fist.

"She doesn't know what went down here, Willis. Law-keepers would never admit to executing him." She patted his arm, hoping he'd calm down.

"I know." He clenched his teeth. "It's not right. It's not the truth."

"Shh, she's back up."

"While authorities were not able to apprehend Willis Thomson, the Thomson's son and alleged conspirator to the still-at-large Jaden, there was evidence that he and fellow Chase runner, Perryn Davis, had been in residence at the cabin in recent days." Perryn held her breath as her face appeared next to Willis's on the screen. "Officials speculate that the Thomson's relocated the two prior to the raid. Any persons with information on the two suspects are encouraged not to approach them as they are considered dangerous but are instead urged to contact local Law-keepers. This is Sheila Kemp, watching the world for news."

"How could she work for them?" Willis's nostrils flared as he searched the floor for answers.

"Did you see her?" Perryn pointed to the monitor. "She did not appear good. She may not be in prison, but I'm not sure she volunteered for the job. Besides, she can't possibly know the whole story."

"I guess."

Perryn frowned at his doubt of Sheila's allegiance. "I don't. She was willing to endure prison to speak the truth. Heck, she risked her neck to connect you to your parents, didn't she?"

"And we know how that ended." He gave her a dark look.

"That's not fair, Willis."

He hung his head and put his hands in the pockets of his hoodie. "You're right. I don't know why I said that."

She softened her tone. "You're grieving. No one can blame you."

"I can. I—"

She grabbed his arm to interrupt him. "Willis, hold on."

The few people at the station had resumed their conversations without another thought after the broadcast, except for one. A man, not much older than twenty-five, stood near the ticket window holding a screen in his hand. He was slender and wore an Alliance Transportation uniform, and the screen in his hand must have been the manifest of the train that would arrive soon. He wasn't watching the screen, however. He was staring directly at Perryn and Willis.

Perryn glanced down and pretended not to notice him. "He sees us," she whispered. "Should we run?"

Willis didn't answer, but his quickened breaths told her that he was panicking as much as she. Perryn leaned forward and placed her elbows on her knees, trying hard to sit like a man would. To her horror, the transport official slowly walked their direction.

Whoosh! A rush of air followed the nearly silent, high speed train that'd pulled up to the station. The doors opened, and a few people could be seen exiting.

"Let's board the train." She urged him to stand with a wave, remembering not to grab his hand in the process. Grabbing the backpack, they walked as quickly as they dared to the open train door. The official stopped and watched them enter. "I don't think he's following." They found their seats in the car and tried to appear inconspicuous. She breathed a sigh of relief as the train lurched away from the station.

"That was close," she whispered softly.

"Not as close as this." Willis nodded toward the front of the train car.

She gasped as the same official entered from the next train car. Approaching the first people seated in the car, he held out his hand. "Tickets, please." The couple handed over their cards, which he scanned and returned. Row by row, he moved closer, occasionally glancing their direction. Perryn didn't dare to speak, but her mind raced. The train was moving well over one-hundred miles per hour at this point, so jumping from the car was impossible. Moving would draw attention. He was two rows away when her instincts told her to run, and it was a hand from Willis that stopped her for the moment.

"Tickets, please." The expressionless transport official stood over them.

Perryn produced the two cards from her pocket and watched as he silently scanned them. She prayed that he might move on.

He cleared his throat. "Sirs, it seems you're in the wrong seats."

"Are you certain?" Willis responded before she could speak.

"Yes, you're in the wrong section. Manifest indicates these ticket numbers are in a different car. I'm afraid you'll need to come with me." He fluttered two fingers indicating they should rise.

Willis darted a glance at her that communicated to play along and follow his lead. They stood and exited the row, ignoring the stares from the other curious passengers.

"Next car, please." The man directed them to walk in front of him, which brought Perryn's anxious stomach to her throat. The three marched slowly toward the rear of the car. Crossing into the next car, the official waited until the door behind him closed. "Stop here," he commanded.

Willis turned with a fierce stare. "Where are you taking us?"

Ignoring the question, the official unlocked a private compartment and opened the door. "Inside."

"Why?" Perryn questioned, her artificially masculine tone unable to hide the tremble in her voice.

He glanced over his shoulder. "Inside, please."

"And what if we won't go in there?" Willis spoke slowly, rising to his full height.

"Then, I'll be forced to contact security. Please step inside." He pointed and then pushed his glasses back on his nose as he examined his manifest again.

Willis put his hand on Perryn's shoulder, and the gentle pressure told her to start walking. She stepped inside the private compartment and walked to the opposite wall. Turning to Willis, she sucked in a breath when she saw his expression. His eyes were wide and full of anger. He was going to do something—something rash.

"Thank you. Now about your seats." The official closed the door behind him. "I think you should know—"

Willis didn't wait for him to finish his sentence. In a split second, he whirled around and landed his fist on the transportation official's jaw. The blow forced the man backward into the wall, against which Willis promptly pinned him with a forearm across his throat. The official's glasses clattered to the floor. Unable to combat Willis's superior size, the official relented, and Willis relaxed his pressure to allow him to speak. Perryn simply froze.

"What do you want with us?" Willis growled. "We both know there was nothing wrong with our seats."

"Please. Let me explain." His eyes were saucers as he begged.

Willis shoved him again into the wall. "I'd love to hear it."

"Willis, please." Perryn pled. The cool and collected Willis she was used to had been overcome by grief. He had no control. Placing a hand on his shoulder, she spoke softly. "Let him speak." His muscles relaxed under her touch, and he took a step backward to release his hold.

"What do you want with us?" Willis repeated, his voice mildly softened.

"I'm..." *cough* "...sorry. I'm so sorry. I didn't mean..." *cough cough,* "...to frighten you." The official's voice rasped, and he rubbed at his neck. "You were..." *cough cough* "...too exposed." He squinted at the two of them and cleared his throat several times.

"Too exposed?" Perryn stooped to pick up the glasses. She handed them to him.

"Thank you." He sighed, returning the glasses to his face. "Everyone knows who you are, especially after that broadcast. I mean, I noticed you right away. Once they showed your faces on the screen, I had to do something."

"We don't know what you're talking about." Perryn lowered her tone, realizing she'd forgotten to disguise her voice since entering.

"That's right." Willis was suddenly stiff in his stance.

"Please—" The man snickered, catching Perryn off guard. The lightness of how he said the word struck her as out of place in the tension that filled the private quarters. "Don't bother. Even if you hadn't forgotten to lower your voice, you couldn't pass for a man if you tried, Perryn Davis."

Perryn couldn't help but grin. She wasn't sure she should feel complimented or worried. "Anyway, even without you, the face of

Willis Thomson is far too recognizable."

Perryn felt the muscles in Willis's back tighten as he prepared to attack again. They were discovered, and he wasn't going to allow this man to get far with that information.

"What do you plan to do with us?" She waved a finger at herself and Willis.

"Please, listen." He held his hands up. He was staring down at Willis's balled fists. "I'm trying to help you. Please hear me out."

"Sure you are," Willis seethed through clenched teeth. Perryn could sense he'd spring at any moment. If this guy had a point to make, he'd better make it soon.

"Really, I am. That's why I brought you here. You were far too exposed."

"So you keep saying."

"Please, my name is Bryan." He held one hand to his chest. "This is a private cabin. I've checked the manifest several times to be sure, and no one has booked this cabin all the way to Central City. You were bound to be recognized out in the passenger car. You can hide in here."

"And you're nothing more than a good citizen willing to betray the Western Alliance and World Coalition to hide us." Willis's lip curled as he mocked Bryan.

"Willis, please, hear him out." Perryn gently squeezed Willis's shoulder. He relaxed under her gentle reminder to keep calm.

"I don't know where you've been," Bryan said, "but it's pretty much all the same. Western Alliance. World Coalition. Might as well be the same. The Coalition is simply operating through the Alliance to fund and supply their campaign to hold power across the globe. As for being a good citizen, well, I belong to neither of them." Bryan pulled at the collar of his shirt to reveal a small tattoo above his collarbone of an 'L' in a circle. "I'm one of the Liberated."

Willis's head was ready to explode. It'd taken a few minutes for him to calm down. Bryan had offered several more assurances that he was there to help before excusing himself. He offered details of the Liberated movement of people who chose life free from the Law that was occurring around the world and even showed them the manifest that proved their cabin was, indeed, unreserved. He left in a hurry.

"I have to keep up appearances." Bryan tapped the screen in his hands. "If I'm missing for too long, my supervisor will come searching for me, and that won't end well for any of us. He's as Loyalist as they come."

Bryan gone, Willis sat with his throbbing head in his hands. Perryn sat down across from him with a hand on his knee. He'd been ready to hurt Bryan badly if necessary to protect his chances of saving his mother. *What is wrong with me?* He kept asking himself how far he would have gone. *I'm not like that. I've always been the one who could talk my way through a situation.*

"Are you done?" Perryn tapped his shoulder after several minutes.

He glanced at her. "Done with what?"

"Beating yourself up." She offered him a shy smile.

"I am not." Willis berated himself for letting her see his inner turmoil. He was stronger than this. He needed to be, anyway. For his mother.

"See, there you go again."

"What am I supposed to do?" He said it more curtly than he intended. "Sorry." Standing, he paced the tiny cabin. "You saw me. I was ready to do something—anything—to keep from being discovered. I lost control."

"Yes, you did." Her affirmation stung. He loved and hated that she never lied to him. "I think you're permitted one or two moments with all you've been through."

"I shouldn't—"

"Shouldn't what? Grieve your father?" She stood and grabbed his arms to turn him and meet his face. "Of course you should. He was a great man. He was the father you deserved after all those years on the station, and he was taken from you."

"I—I—" Willis hung his head in grief and allowed a

shuddering breath. The memory of his father from the night of the Chase filled his mind. It was when he'd awoken as if from a nightmare. He'd been the programmed pawn of the Coalition his entire life until his father released him. Jaden's abolishment of the Law had liberated many, including Bryan. It was Max Thomson who had freed Willis's mind, allowing him to choose to let Jaden win. If he hadn't, the world would belong to the Coalition. "I can't believe he's gone."

Perryn said nothing. She stepped into his arms and held him tightly. Willis remembered again how much he loved her. She wasn't running from his grief. She was helping him embrace it. He had to tell her how he felt. He'd missed his chance at the cabin, and there was no knowing if they'd even make it to Central City.

"Perryn, I—"

Knock. Knock.

Willis quickly moved to the door and peered through the peephole. Bryan stood there watching nervously over his shoulder. Opening the door, he let Bryan slip inside and closed it quietly behind him.

Bryan breathed with a sigh of relief. "I've finished my rounds. They won't be expecting me to check in for a while." He sat down and gazed at them, motioning that they should join him. Willis, frustrated that the moment was gone, flopped down next to Perryn who sat across from Bryan.

"So, what do we do?" Willis waved a hand, resigned to the fact that Bryan was running the show. "How do we get off this train without getting noticed?"

"I have an idea about that, but I want to know something first. Why in the world would you travel to Central City? You must know that you'll be found out there. The city is crawling with Law-keepers."

"We have to get there." Willis sat up resolutely.

Bryan arched a brow and glanced back and forth between them. He didn't believe Willis. "But why?"

"My mother. They have her. Remember the broadcast? I have to get her out of there."

"Of course, but she's in custody." Bryan paused and searched them for a reaction. When he got none, he spoke again. "You won't get far by yourself. What's your plan?"

"We don't have one yet, but we have to try." Willis looked down at the floor. *He's right. We won't get far.*

Bryan slumped in the seat. "Well, I think you're fools. It will be a miracle alone getting you off this train without raising an alarm. But—" He hesitated.

"Anything you can do would be helpful." Perryn placed a hand on Willis's knee. Her hope was stronger than his, and he was glad for it.

Bryan leaned forward. "You're going to need help. In Central City, the Liberated who are brave enough to do something have mobilized. They've organized, calling themselves the Underground. Here and there, they've struck to disrupt Coalition activity. If anyone can help you, it's them."

"You sure they'd want someone as recognizable as me around?" Willis frowned despite the intrigue.

"I don't know, but I hear their leader is a former Chase runner. Not sure who, but he might be open to having you link up with them. I would join them if I could. Six months ago, I was the biggest fan of the Chase and would have been asking for your autograph. Today, I hate working for the Alliance, but I fear the Underground would trust me even less than you did if I show up wearing this uniform."

"Without that uniform, we'd still be sitting in the passenger car. Maybe you should give them a chance." Willis tried to be encouraging since any information he had about Central City would be helpful. "Tell us. Where can we find this Underground organization?"

"That's the problem for someone as recognizable as you. From what I hear, they find you. All you have to do is make yourself known."

Chapter Ten

Sheila stared into the blank lens of the camera, which was turned off, and imagined the faces on the other side. Her role must look different to the world than it felt to her. True to Penny's promise, she'd been allowed to report the news as truthfully as she could present it. She hadn't been prepared, however, for what it was like to witness the strong-arm tactics of the Alliance first-hand. Prior to the Chase, the sickness of the World Coalition had been subtle, tucked into the background and well behind the cameras. Care had always been taken to portray the World Coalition as a peaceful, orderly society. This was different. The camera was turned directly on Law-keepers arresting dissidents, speeches from Alliance officials giving their twisted truths, and those living in poverty in areas hit hardest by the governmental persecution.

"Oh, dearie, it's perfect." Penny grinned as she watched the footage from Sheila's last report. Scenes flashed across the viewscreen, hungry children living on the street while others walked by in their Alliance educational uniforms, well-fed and happy. Sheila listened to the video version of herself as she explained how the newly formed Coalition policies denied basic programs to the hungry children. How could Penny be watching the same report as her?

"Perfect?" She lowered her eyebrows, not sure if she wanted an explanation.

"Yes." She smiled widely betraying a sickening enthusiasm. Her bracelets, more numerous than ever, jingled as she motioned with each word. "People will see the true cost of departing from the glorious Law. Life is found in obedience to the Law. Suffering comes to those who wish to live apart from it." Penny continued to observe the footage with fascination all over her face.

I'm not sure the masses will see it that way. She couldn't help but doubt those thoughts as Penny continued her excited frenzy. *Or else they'll become so afraid that they'll fall in line.*

"I'm glad you like it." Sheila tried to hide her sarcasm. Her heart sank as she digested the reality that even her truth-telling was advancing the agenda of the Coalition.

"Sweetheart, it's wonderful. I'm certain the chairman will be so pleased. He simply wants to call these lost souls back to a path of peace and prosperity."

Sheila said nothing.

"So," Penny continued after a silent second, "your next assignment will give you an opportunity to truly highlight the damage caused by these dissidents."

"Next assignment?" Sheila swallowed hard.

"Oh my, you haven't heard? The Chase training center is in a complete upheaval. The rehabilitation candidates serving there are rioting. Can you believe that?" She paused watching for agreement from Sheila.

"Rioting?" It was all she could think to say, trying not to stare too darkly at Penny. Thoughts of her father's experience as a 'rehabilitation candidate' flashed through her mind.

Penny shook her head while holding her hands out in a half-shrug. "Unbelievable, isn't it? The goodness of the Alliance has allowed them to avoid prison for their crimes, and this is how they respond. The shame of it all."

"And you want me to report on…what exactly?"

"That is the one light in all of this sadness, sweetie. The Coalition Chairman is in Central City wishing to resolve the matter, and you have been given the privilege of being one of the official Alliance journalists to report live from his speech later. To think, the chairman will be here on his first official visit of my tenure, and I'll get to stand right next to the podium as he speaks." Penny squeaked in delight.

Sheila stared at her. *Well, I can't deny her enthusiasm.*

"Silenced, I see. It's overwhelming, I know." Penny patted her chest as if to calm herself. "Come with me. There is much to do to prepare."

Like trying not to vomit in my mouth.

⸺⸺•✦•⸺⸺

People scurried everywhere as Sheila found her reserved place near the podium. Penny had chosen the angle best suited to capture herself in the frame. She stood on the stage obviously trying not to turn in Sheila's direction, but she couldn't help herself. Sheila caught her more than once glancing toward the camera.

This is her moment in the sun, I guess.

Next to Penny stood an empty podium emblazoned with the Coalition seal, a scroll wrapped tightly in the fingers of a fist meant to declare the Coalition's absolute commitment to the Law. This time, it was yellow instead of red, one of the first tangible signs that the Western Alliance and the Coalition were merging.

"Ladies and gentlemen, the humble servant of the World Coalition, Chairman DeGraaf," came the booming announcement.

Without hesitation, the bustling crowd quieted and turned to the stage. Slowly, Chairman DeGraaf made his way to the podium. His black robes were, this time, trimmed in yellow, matching the new seal. Taking a second to adjust his glasses, he appeared somber as he took in the crowd gathered to hear his words. Sheila caught Penny breathing deeply and smoothing the lapel of her suit jacket. She laughed to herself, imagining the woman might swoon before the event was over.

"Proud inhabitants of the Western Alliance, loyal citizens of the World Coalition," said DeGraaf, "and to all who remember and uphold the glory of the Law, I greet you today with a grieving heart. Recent months have seen one of the darkest seasons in our memory, perhaps the darkest since the Great Collapse. The shameful endeavor to undo the Law and the violent attempt on my life have created a world on the brink of coming apart at the seams. While the wise majority still sees the great value and grace of the Law, it is no secret that there are pockets of confused outlaws around the globe who have been misled by a few dissidents bent on perpetuating the lies created at the Chase."

Penny huffed in agreement.

Sheila could see many nodding in the crowd.

"Today"—he pointed to the sky—"the most grievous example of discord is threatening the very system that has allowed this great Alliance to experience unprecedented prosperity. The station orbiting the earth, on which the best and brightest of the Western Alliance train to run the Chase, has been overrun by rioting workers. Efforts to suppress these violent actions have failed, and it is the belief of the highest security advisors that these graceless dissidents have taken control of the entire station, holding hostage the staff and trainees."

Gasps spread throughout the crowd at the news. *Where was he going with this announcement?* Anyone could have shared these words. This kind of news was usually beneath the chairman.

DeGraaf paused, adding drama to his next words. "There can be little doubt that these actions were the direct result of the presence of the fugitive known simply as Jaden. Intelligence has confirmed that he returned to the station after the Chase events, posing as a rehabilitation candidate, and he stands as the likely organizer of this heinous crime."

If he's there, he went to save his mother! Sheila internally shouted these words. She couldn't believe the chairman's accusation. Some in the crowd became restless, angered by the information.

"I cannot regret more the decision I must make to demonstrate how we must respond to those around the world who would threaten to undo our way of life in the name of a misguided philosophy." DeGraaf frowned, an expression of regret passing over his face. "As of today, I am moving the headquarters of the World Coalition to Central City and adopting the resources of this great alliance to personally oversee the reestablishment of order in this part of the world. As my first action, I intend to send a message that the greatness of the Law will not allow the Coalition to negotiate with terrorists, whether they mask their supposed cause in the name of freedom or not. Anyone who cannot see the grace of the Law clearly cannot think morally, so it is my belief that those who have taken control of the station have no intention of releasing their captives. What I do today, I do to protect that which has benefited us all and to personally stand in the way of anarchy."

With those words, DeGraaf exited the stage, followed by a bewildered group of officials who appeared puzzled at the chairman's final words. Sheila lifted her microphone to begin her follow up on the speech when a faint rumbling filled the air. Onlookers whispered and scanned about, searching for the source. Sheila tried to stay calm as the crowd behind her became increasingly restless.

Addressing the camera, she tried to ignore the sound. "World Coalition Chairman DeGraaf has delivered a strong ultimatum to the population around the world who have chosen to remain free of the Law. Reactions from the crowd following his announcement have—"

Sheila's gaze followed hands lifting from the crowd to point at the sky to the right of the platform. In stunned silence, Sheila stood forgetting the camera as the obvious shape of a missile rose above the city skyline. Higher it rose, leaving a streak of smoke that glowed red in the dimming light.

Taking his cue from Sheila, the cameraman turned to follow the trajectory of the missile. Sheila's lip quivered as a single tear escaped down her cheek. All she could think was of the millions of people worldwide who observed silently as the missile found its mark and the Western Alliance training station became a distant fireball in the sky.

Sheila sat in the darkness of her Alliance-issued apartment staring at the screen of her computer. The television glowed red in the background for what felt like the hundredth time as the Alliance-controlled news repeated images of the station breaking up and burning in the atmosphere. She'd cried for hours, unable to fully swallow the world in which she lived. The chairman had grasped for power and exercised it without mercy, and the world was praising him for it. When she voiced her distaste of the event in her report afterward, Penny had demanded that she be mindful that the watching world was on the side of the chairman.

Are they? Are they truly watching? Is anyone watching what is happening?

She breathed deeply. *Penny may be able to twist my words in front of the camera, but she could do nothing to prevent what happens when the camera turns off.* Placing her hands on the keyboard, she tried to remember her confidence right after the Chase. Inside her, the overwhelming desire to help others see the truth rose to the surface. She tried to remember what it was like to be certain—and to speak from that certainty.

Chapter Eleven

To all who would listen,

Peace. Comfort. Solidarity. Perfection. These promises are familiar to the generations of people who have lived following the establishment of the Law. We have all hoped for these ideals. While the original intentions of the Lawmakers were noble and just, today proved their hopes to be empty or at least antiquated. When peace is sought through violence and unity through the silencing of alternative voices, the supposed utopia becomes a lie.

The promises of the Law are a lie.

Peace will come when the power to oppress others is held in check by those who refuse to lie down and accept it. Today's act of violence in the sky was meant to fill the world with fear. Peace cannot be birthed from terror.

Comfort will be found when mothers and fathers can kiss their children at night, knowing that no one will burst through the door to take them away. When people can voice their heart without trepidation, then will they be content.

Solidarity is unachievable through uniformity. The chairman wishes to create all of us in his twisted image, but that pursuit will do no more than further the divide between the misinformed and the liberated. Do not be deceived. Unity will not come until we learn that our differences are what make us beautiful.

Perfection is impossible. The pursuit of perfection requires a denial of ourselves. We are flawed. Humanity is gloriously flawed. How can we ever become more than we are if we cannot accept this basic truth?

The promises of the Law are a lie.

Learn to see the world as it is. It will take time, but as one who has had their eyes opened, I believe that true freedom begins when we admit the truth. We must not rest until all learn to see reality.

Until then, I will be watching the world for you.

Your friend in truth,

The Watcher

Chapter Twelve

Three weeks had passed since they'd exited the train and found it easier than expected. With all the confusion after the missile strike on the station, Willis and Perryn were able to make their way across the city to a section rumored as being sympathetic to the cause of the Liberated. They'd even secured a small apartment to hide in while they planned their next move. What had been far more difficult was locating the underground movement Bryan had mentioned. Hints. Speculation. These were the most they could get from anyone. Willis tried hard not to blame the Liberated. After the chairman was willing to destroy the space station, even the most dissenting person would hesitate to speak openly to a stranger.

"I don't understand." Willis sat down hard at the table. "We've been quietly asking around for weeks about the Underground, and no one will talk—not even those bearing the same tattoo as Bryan."

Perryn emerged from her bedroom in the apartment. She was dressed in jeans and a t-shirt, but her hair was still in a towel. The apartment they'd rented with some of the money from the cabin was a small, dusty dwelling that smelled of mildew. Willis had given a false name and simply asked for a place with separate quarters for he and Perryn. The apartment was little more. Outside of their quarters, it sported a tiny restroom with a shower that ran cold and a combination living area and kitchen space barely big enough for a couple of chairs. Still, it was all they needed until they found the Underground.

"Be patient." She sighed. "I'm frustrated too, but we have to keep trying."

Willis ran his fingers through his hair, which was getting

longer than he was accustomed to. "I believed we were on to something last night after the explosion around the corner."

"Whoever the Underground are, they are good."

"No kidding. By the time we ran over there, they were gone."

Knock. Knock.

They fell silent at the sound. Perryn's eyes grew wide as she stood frozen. Slowly, so as not to cause the floorboards to creak, Willis made his way to the door. Peering through the glass, he breathed a sigh of relief. He opened the door to reveal the short, middle-aged landlady standing outside wearing a worn dress with flower print.

"*Buenos dias*, Mr. Smith." She gave him a smile that could make any stranger feel right at home.

"*Buenos dias*, Mrs. Sanchez." Willis returned her smile. "How are you this morning?"

"Bright and free as always. Our table may not have much on it, but we are thankful people." Unlike most, Mrs. Sanchez was not afraid to speak about freedom, which had cost them access to some of their food rations.

"Us too. How can we help you today?"

"I came to bring you these." She handed him a basket of fresh fruit. "Your kitchen is so bare, and you need to keep your strength."

Willis's face flushed. The gift was too much. "Thank you. Really, Mrs. Sanchez, you shouldn't have. There's so little food to go around anyway. Your family should eat these."

"Mr. Smith, please accept them. We are no longer under the Law which tells us where to get what we need. If we are free, then we are free to share what we have. We must care for each other." As she spoke, she swiped her hair off her left ear to reveal the encircled 'L' tattoo on her neck. "I think you will find the best ones down at the bottom."

"*Gracias*, Mrs. Sanchez. Please thank your family for us."

"You're welcome." She beamed at him. Glancing over his shoulder, she waved to Perryn. "*Buenos dias, señorita!*"

"*Buenos dias*, Mrs. Sanchez." Perryn returned the gesture.

Willis waved and shut the door.

"Man, did we luck out with her," Willis said. "I can't believe they'd share with us after charging us so little for this place."

"She's everything right about the Liberated." Perryn nodded joyfully. "She makes me happy every time she stops by."

"Best ones at the bottom, huh?" He grabbed an apple and bit into it quickly. It was watery and flavorless, but it was the freshest thing he'd eaten in a while. That's when he noticed the piece of paper hidden beneath the fruit. This had been more than an act of kindness. She'd brought them information. He ripped the paper out of the bowl, dumping the rest of the apples in the process. "It zam nudder leddur fum da witcher."

"Say again? I couldn't hear you through the mouthful of apple." Perryn laughed and gave a curious look at the strewn apples. Willis chewed quickly to clear his mouth. Juice from the apple dripped down his chin, which he swiped at with his sleeve. Perryn pointed at her chin still chuckling. "Sophisticated, aren't we? You've got a little something right there."

Willis wiped the apple juice from his mouth, feeling his face turn hot as he did so. He waved the paper excitedly. "Sorry, I suppose I should have waited. I said, 'It's another letter from the Watcher.'"

Letters from this unknown voice had been circulating almost daily since the missile strike. The Watcher was becoming a name among the Liberated, as the anonymous source revealed openly the corruption of the chairman and the Coalition. Yesterday, they'd watched as Sheila announced the chairman's condemnation of the Watcher as a voice of anarchy and his declaration that possession of any Watcher publications would be cause for arrest. Even so, someone had recently spray painted 'Listen to the Watcher' with the 'L' symbol underneath on the wall outside their window.

Perryn's eyes grew wide when he mentioned the Watcher, and she stepped closer. She bounced on her feet and appeared ready to rip it from his hands and read it herself. "What does it say? Mrs. Sanchez has never brought us stuff like that."

Willis scanned the letter and gasped. He took a second to take in the information.

"Seriously, you're killing me." She tapped her foot in impatience.

"Sorry. I think I know how we can find the Underground."

He handed her the letter. She stared at Willis a long time before speaking. "We have to be there."

To all who would listen,

Chairman DeGraaf has issued orders to raid and possess the Central City Mission on 8th Street. The staff of the mission is charged with aiding fugitives from the Law. Hear me clearly that this mission was simply feeding homeless children. Because some of these children are among the Liberated, the mission has been deemed in violation of the Law. Per my sources, this raid will take place tomorrow morning at 8 a.m. We, the Liberated with the means to do so, cannot under any circumstances allow this heinous act to remain unchallenged. Speak and let your voice be heard.

Always watching,
The Watcher

Chapter Thirteen

"This is our best chance to find them, Willis." Perryn hugged him.

"We can't blow it, then. Whatever it takes, we have to make ourselves known."

Perryn stepped away, retreating to her hiding place. "Promise you'll be careful. It's not worth getting hurt or captured."

"Whatever it takes, Perr. I have to free my mother."

The statement came out more abrupt than he'd meant it, and she appeared hurt as he turned and walked away toward the alley. They had to find the Underground quickly. They'd wasted weeks trying to find the hidden organization, weeks that his mother had to endure God-knows-what.

Willis crouched behind the dumpster in the alley. Across the street, the gray stone of the Central City Mission stood lifeless as if deliberately hiding the goodwill that was taking place inside. He watched two volunteers ascend the steps while discussing preparations for the meal that would be served at lunchtime. They smiled and laughed in conversation, their faces appearing as though they looked forward to the work that awaited them. They appeared completely unaware of what was coming. A few children could be seen hovering on the sidewalk near the stairs giving Willis the impression they had nowhere else to be. *Perhaps they don't. They have nothing outside this mission.*

He leaned farther out of his hiding place to peek down the sidewalk on his side of the street. Perryn couldn't be seen as she was hidden behind a set of bushes about a block away. They'd elected to split up and increase the chance they might be able to get the attention of the Underground. If the Watcher's information from the note Mrs. Sanchez had given them was correct, they guessed the Underground would be unable to resist taking action.

He didn't like walking away from Perryn like he did and considered running over to her spot and making things right, apologizing for his tone. The low rumble in the distance stopped him—the coming Alliance troops?

Stay low, Perryn. Don't let them see you. He willed the thoughts in her direction.

Around the corner, two blocks away, an armored car turned onto their street. A machine gun nest pivoted on top of the car as the Law-keeper behind it scanned the buildings on either side. Behind the car came several rows of trotting troops, each armed with semi-automatic firearms. Lastly came a truck, obviously meant for hauling prisoners, flanked on both sides by motorcycles.

They expect a fight.

The armored car rolled with cautious authority as it approached the mission, and that's when Willis saw her. An elderly woman, who had been walking on the sidewalk, turned and began crossing the street. Each step and movement of her cane was painfully labored. She moved slowly, seemingly unaware of the coming danger. In horror, Willis watched as the car neared the woman. Her pace was far too slow.

Move! He shouted the words at her in his mind. *They'll run you over!*

Willis stood, the urge to rescue her almost irresistible, but indecision won out and froze him to the spot. Part of him desired to run to the woman's aid, and part of him realized that would blow his cover and possibly his chance to contact the Underground. He waved silently trying to get her attention, but she didn't show any sign she'd noticed. Without warning, she stopped and balanced herself on her cane, turning to face the armored car. She stared down the car, her glare daring it to run her over.

He flinched at the metallic squeal as the armored car hit the brakes at the last second. It rolled to a halt not a foot away from the woman, who hadn't budged an inch.

"Move it, old woman," the soldier in the nest shouted. "Make way for the chairman's authority."

The woman put her hand to her heart as if to calm herself, but her words were ones of composure. "Young man, the chairman has no authority here." She spoke with a surprising strength to her voice. "We are a liberated people." Without warning, her chest-clutching hand revealed a pistol that'd been hidden in her coat. *Phoot!* The pistol produced a quiet rush of air. A tranquilizer dart found the neck of the soldier. Instantly, he collapsed over the edge of the machine gun nest.

Phoot! Phoot! Phoot!

Darts shot from all directions, scattering the Law-keepers who were on foot. Several ducked for cover behind the armored car, merely to be hit from behind. A couple of soldiers fired aimlessly in the direction the projectiles were coming from. The elderly woman had disappeared. The Underground was here.

Willis stared at the chaos as soldiers shouted orders and attempted to find protective positions in the crossfire. Panicked, he scanned the windows of the adjacent buildings, but he couldn't see where the near-silent darts were coming from. Glancing over, he could see Perryn peering from behind the bushes up the street. She was too far out of position to do anything. Their eyes met, and she shrugged her shoulders in confusion.

The armored car attempted a hasty retreat, incurring shouts of disapproval from soldiers forced to dive out of its way as it reversed course. Willis saw a window open on a building above the car, and a smoking canister flew from the opening. It missed the car and clattered to the side, the fumes causing soldiers to cover their faces. A second canister found its mark as it fell directly into the machine gun nest, disappearing into the cavity of the car. Seconds later, smoke poured from inside the car. The doors opened, and soldiers fell to the ground, coughing on the fumes. Out of the haze of smoke, a motorcycle engine revved as the driver attempted an escape. Willis held his breath as he realized it was headed right for his position.

Bracing his feet on the wall of the building, he readied his hands on the dumpster and prayed it was empty. Listening to the engine, he tried to guess at the position of the motorcycle.

He pushed as hard as he could.

The dumpster rolled with surprising ease out into the street, and his timing couldn't have been more perfect. The motorcycle appeared from the mist of gas exactly as the dumpster rolled into the lane. Willis winced at the smack of the cycle hitting the dumpster followed by the thud of the soldier landing on the other side. He ran from the alley as the Law-keeper rolled over to get on all fours. The first wisps of the ever-expanding mist of smoke surrounded him, but his focus was on the Law-keeper.

Seeing him coming, the soldier pulled a pistol to fire at Willis. Launching himself at the Law-keeper, the stinging bite of the bullet grazing his forearm made him wince. His body crashed into the dazed soldier, who attempted to redirect his aim. Willis's skin singed as his hand brushed the barrel of the pistol. Finding the grip with both hands, Willis strained to match the strength of his attacker, forcing the pistol straight upward in a momentary stalemate. He could see the adrenaline-filled fear enter his own eyes in the reflection of the soldier's black helmet visor. With a final burst of effort, Willis believed he might overpower the man until the soldier's knee connected with his ribs. Falling backward, Willis grunted as his head smacked the ground.

Stunned, he squinted through blurry eyes that burned from the smoke cloud at the shape of the soldier standing above him. Slowly, the pistol rose to point at Willis.

"Willis!" Perryn shrieked as she ran from her hiding spot.

The soldier glanced in her direction, and it was all the time that was needed. *Phoot!* A dart suddenly appeared in the Law-keeper's shoulder. He fell to his knees, the pistol clattering to the ground. With a thud, his helmeted head hit the ground as he fell forward.

"Willis!" A breathless, coughing Perryn appeared at his side. "Are you..." *cough* "...okay? What were you—?"

Her voice cut off.

"Perryn?" Willis watched as her face glazed over. Her body went limp and slumped over his chest. A dart protruded from her back. "Perryn!"

A dark shape appeared from the smoke, lit on one side from

the yellow glow of the flames engulfing the empty armored car. The crackling of the flames filled his ears. The Law-keepers had all been subdued by darts or run away. Willis's eyes watered from the gas, but he could make out a masked person holding a dart pistol like the one the old woman had produced. Without warning, the pistol raised toward his chest.

Phoot!

His vision went black.

Chapter Fourteen

"I don't care if the files are encrypted," Penny snapped. "You need to un-crypt them or whatever it is you do."

Sheila stood outside the door to Penny's office. Despite the solid oak barrier, she could hear most of the conversation inside. The voice wasn't the composed Penny to which she was accustomed. Something had caused her to come unglued, and the other person on the line was paying the price for it. She leaned in to hear better, trying not to let it appear to any passerby like she was eavesdropping.

"No. That is unacceptable. I am the Administrative Liaison to the Coalition Chairman, and I will not accept excuses. Do you hear me? No excuses."

Sheila snapped upright at the sound of the phone being slammed to the table. Apparently, the call was finished. The faint clip-clop of Penny's heeled shoes could be heard as she paced in her anger. As Sheila tapped on the door, the sound abruptly stopped.

"One moment." Penny's pleasant tone sounded forced. Some shuffling around could be heard, and then she called again, "You may enter!"

Sheila pushed open the door to reveal a completely put-together Penny. Her hair was perfect, and she sat calmly behind her desk like she'd been there the entire time. Sheila noticed the flush on the skin of her neck slowly receding, betraying Penny's emotional state a minute earlier. *She certainly knows how to put on a face when she needs to.*

"Dearie!" Penny exclaimed, standing from her chair. She shuffled around the desk with her bracelet-jingling arms extended. She pulled Sheila into an uninvited embrace that Sheila didn't return, allowing her arms to hang limp. "Come in. Come in. I am so pleased you came to see me."

"Your assistant called saying I needed to see you for a mandatory meeting," Sheila said.

"I love that we can visit as friends." Penny picked up some paperwork from her desk to examine, ignoring Sheila's comment. "In a position like mine, so many are intimidated by my title that there are precious few that are as comfortable and candid as you, sweetheart."

Sheila paused to consider the words as she sat down in the chair next to the desk. She'd never thought of Penny as lonely. The veiled admission was surprising. Pity rose in her heart. Penny was self-important and obsessed with garnering the chairman's attention, but she was human somewhere underneath the plastic smile and clattering jewelry.

"I'm glad you came because I have something very important to speak to you about." Penny rounded the desk and perched on the front edge with her hands folded in front of her. The position was intentional, approachable yet still condescending to the seated Sheila. She leaned in. "What I am about to tell you is top-secret at the highest levels."

If it is so secret, then why are you telling me? Sheila's face gave a blank stare.

"I'm sure you have heard of 'The Watcher'." Penny could barely hide her distaste for the name. "It's that so-called 'truth-teller' who writes blasphemous things about the chairman and the Coalition."

"Yes, I've heard." Sheila kept her voice calm. Meanwhile, her heart began to pump faster.

"I mean, today, a word from this 'Watcher' spread lies that prevented the delivery of needed supplies to a local shelter. Several Law-keepers were killed." Penny shook her head in disbelief.

Sheila forced the words. "No kidding. That's awful."

Penny leaned in again. "That's not all. Our sources say the blatant lies are being delivered from someone *inside* the Coalition." She paused letting the information hang in the air and studied Sheila's response. Sheila tried desperately to act surprised.

"That seems hard to believe." Sheila gave her best skeptical smirk.

"I know. To think that someone would receive the goodness of working so closely with the glorious chairman to return that grace with words so—so—incredulous!"

Penny's expression gave the impression she'd tried to find the most complicated word she could remember. Fear was the one thing that kept Sheila from chuckling.

"How do they know it came from inside?"

"Dear, Coalition intelligence employs top experts from around the world. I'm sure they know what they are doing with their—their code-breaky stuff."

Sheila smiled at the foolish description. *How incredulous of me to question the 'code-breaky' methods of Coalition intelligence.* For all her desire to act the expert, Penny clearly didn't understand certain procedures.

As if listening to Sheila's mind, Penny stood and circled the desk. Placing her hands on either side of the edge of the desk, she glared down at Sheila. "I don't suppose your digging as a journalist has uncovered any information as to the identity of this imposter. Has it?" Her voice almost squeaked the last two words out.

Sheila's smile disappeared.

"No. It hasn't."

Penny sighed dramatically. "That's unfortunate. Well, feel free to pass the word that *when* the Intelligence office discovers the pretender, they will be dealt with most severely. We cannot have the chairman's reputation and the glory of the Law openly mocked."

Sheila swallowed hard. "I hope you find them."

"Oh, we will, dearie. I am the Administrative Liaison to the Coalition Chairman. Since the Alliance and Coalition are essentially one, that means I have a world's worth of resources to call upon. I will not disappoint his grace, the chairman. I will find the hypocrite—whoever they are." She stared at Sheila.

Sheila nodded feeling very exposed.

"That will be all, darling." Penny turned to the window behind her, announcing the end of the meeting.

Sheila stood. She could feel a lone bead of sweat slip between her shoulder blades. The warning had been clear. *The Watcher had better be careful.* Not wanting to break the fragile tension in the room, she held her breath until she reached the hallway.

———————————◆∷●∷◆———————————

"Where to, Kemp?" Raymond greeted her in what had become his usual way. It still made her smile when he said it. It left her feeling like she had a secret ally in this mess.

"Raymond, I need to get to Central City Mission. Do you know it?" Sheila patted his shoulder.

"I do."

Not fifteen minutes later, they turned onto 8th Street. Barricades kept them from pulling all the way to the Mission, so Raymond pulled the car over two blocks away.

"I won't be five minutes." Sheila started to get out of the car.

"If it's all the same to you, Kemp, I'd like to walk with you."

She paused and shook her head. "Raymond, I can take care of myself."

"It's not that." He went quiet. It couldn't hurt to have him come along and wasn't like him to ask.

"All right, I can get you in with my press pass. Stay with me."

Walking toward the mission, she made out the smoldering wreckage of what used to be an armored car. Flashing her Alliance-issued pass at the barricade, she and Raymond walked to the stairs in front of the mission. She didn't know what she was searching for among the clean-up crews and investigators.

"Father Anthony." Raymond's deep voice caught her by surprise. He was a man of few words, and he almost never spoke when they were in public. He pointed at a gray-haired man in robes walking down the steps of the mission. His hands were folded in front of him. The black pants, black shirt, and priest's collar gave him away as the one likely in charge of the mission. His complexion was a shade lighter than Raymond's, and his face wore the creases of one carrying years of burdens.

"Raymond, my son!" The priest waved as he approached. He embraced the huge driver, his hands barely able to wrap around Raymond's frame like those of a small child hugging a parent. Still holding his shoulders, he smiled broadly. "What brings you back to this neighborhood?"

Raymond pointed a silent hand at Sheila, who was still putting together what was going on.

"Sheila Kemp." She extended her hand.

"Ah, yes. The reporter who tells the truth without telling the truth." Father Anthony frowned at her without taking her hand. "Explain to me, where are your cameras as they clean their attempt to shut down humanitarian aid?"

"Father, please." Raymond raised a hand. "Kemp is a friend."

"Are you sure?" Father Anthony eyed Sheila one more time. "I've seen enough of the Alliance today to know we have few friends out there."

"If you'd seen what this woman has been through, Father, you would agree. She's a friend."

"I'm sorry, Ms. Kemp." Father Anthony, this time, offered an apologetic handshake. "I'm still shaken by this morning's events."

"I understand," she replied, taking his hand and giving it a single firm shake. "Father, what did you mean when you said Raymond was 'back' in the neighborhood?"

"Oh, that's simple." He smiled, shooting a quick glance at her driver. "Raymond here grew up visiting my mission. I've known him since he was this tall, if he ever was that tall." He motioned with his hand to the height of a small child, chuckling.

"You grew up here?" She cocked her head toward Raymond, unable to hide her curiosity.

"On the streets. My parents were arrested by the Alliance when I was young, but I ran away when they tried to take me to an Alliance home. Had it not been for Father Anthony, I may have starved that first year." Raymond paused, staring off in the distance. Sheila imagined him remembering his days on the streets.

"Oh, don't let him make it sound so dramatic. I caught him stealing food from the kitchen." Father Anthony laughed and gave

Raymond a jab. "You should have seen his face when he realized we were giving that food away in the next room. He was always getting into ridiculous trouble—like the time he got that huge head of his stuck in between the bars of the fence. I tell you, it took an hour for us to—"

"Father, I don't think Kemp is here to hear those stories." Raymond flushed.

"Actually, I'm quite amused." Sheila chuckled, smiling at him. "Sounds like there's more to my driver that I need to learn about." She elbowed Raymond playfully.

"Okay, okay. Suffice it to say," Father Anthony continued, "he did eventually grow into the fine man before you. I wish I could say all of our young men did so well. We've seen far too many leave this mission simply to find themselves in the rehabilitation camps."

"Father, what happened here?" Raymond pointed around the scene. While the stories were fun, Sheila appreciated him getting on subject. "They're saying a shipment of humanitarian supplies was intercepted and stolen. They say Law-keepers were killed by the Liberated."

Father Anthony glanced around warily. With two fingers, he waved toward the door. "Come inside."

They entered through the mission doorway into a hall brightly painted in sharp contrast to the gray buildings outside. The wood floors were worn in the center from the feet of thousands that'd walked through the door over the years. Father Anthony took them into the first entry on the left. The office was empty except for a small metal desk and a set of bookshelves with various worn books and pictures.

Closing the door behind him, Father Anthony spoke again. "I'm sorry, but I can't say this outside. Whatever happened here today, I wouldn't expect a shipment of supplies to involve armed Law-keepers and armored trucks."

"I believe they were coming to arrest you," Sheila said. The statement got the immediate attention of both men.

Father Anthony placed a hand on his chest. "Arrest me? Why? What have I done? I seek to help those who can't help themselves as I have for years. Why now?"

"Because among those you help are the children of the Liberated."

"And that makes me a criminal?" Father Anthony sighed and sat down on his desk. The question was more of a statement of fact than an actual question. They all knew the answer.

"If there's anything you can tell us that would help us prove otherwise—"

"Tell you? I can do better than that. One of the boys here filmed everything on my phone." He handed the mobile device to Sheila.

Sheila played the last recorded video. Sure enough, she could see the armored car surrounded by soldiers. Suddenly, the Law-keepers cried out and ducked for cover. Rifles in the hands of the soldiers fired aimlessly. An object was thrown, and the armored truck coughed smoke, forcing the occupants out. The shaky video became almost imperceptible until a motorcycle emerged from the cloud. The camera followed as the dumpster took out the cycle, followed by someone from the alley. She watched the figure wrestle with the Law-keeper until he was shot by something. A masked person stepped out and also shot a woman running across the street before coming to stand above the man from the alley. Whoever had operated the camera chose that moment to zoom in on the two figures. Sheila's eyes grew wide.

"Willis?" She almost shouted the name.

"You know that young man?" Father Anthony motioned to the screen.

"Who is he?" Raymond stepped forward to get a better view of the video.

"A friend. They shot him." Sheila covered her mouth with one hand, still in shock.

"No, they didn't." Father Anthony held one finger up.

"They didn't?"

"No. I found several of these lying around prior to the officials arriving to clean up." He reached into his pocket to reveal a tranquilizer dart. "Whoever attacked the Law-keepers, they weren't wanting to kill anyone—including your friend."

Chapter Fifteen

"What should we do with him?" It was a woman's voice.

"Not sure." An older male voice came from nearby, a little friendlier than the woman's voice.

"I say we get rid of him." The third voice, also male, sounded younger.

Someone stood. "And why's that?" It was the woman.

"He's a liability. You saw what he did—reckless. Besides, there's no way he could go unrecognized."

"And the girl? You suppose we should get rid of both of them?" The older male appeared to be pleading with the others.

"That's not our way," the woman said matter-of-factly.

"He's too much of a risk. You both saw it." The younger male wouldn't let the issue rest.

Willis could hear the argument as he slowly awoke to consciousness. The blackness in his vision faded to a bright blur as his eyes cracked open. Appearing as moving blobs of color, Willis could tell three figures stood above him. He tried to rub his eyes, but his arms wouldn't respond.

"Look! He's coming to." The woman pointed a fuzzy hand at him.

"Send word to the Chief that he's awake," the older man said.

"I still think we shouldn't have brought him here," the younger male said as he exited. A door clicked out of Willis's sightline.

Willis's vision cleared to reveal the faces of the two remaining voices. One was an elderly man, his gray stringy hair slightly unkept. Smiling down at Willis, his eyes creased in the corners giving off the air of kindness. He was dressed in jeans and an untucked shirt. The woman, likely in her late twenties, stood with her arms crossed. Her blonde hair was pulled tightly into a bun, and she wore the same gray uniform as those who had attacked the Law-keepers. Willis tried to speak.

"Where—?" His voice creaked.

"Slowly." The man held up a sympathetic hand. "The tranquilizer will leave your mouth dry, and it'll be hard to speak for a while."

"And you'll have a wicked headache when you sit up." The woman still spoke with no emotion. The man frowned at her, annoyed. She shrugged. "Never hurts to know what's coming."

"My name is Barney." He pointed to himself. "This here is Lydia." Lydia nodded at the mention of her name. "You've been out for hours."

"Another–?" Willis groaned as he sat up. Lydia hadn't been kidding about the headache. He gripped both sides of his forehead trying to equalize the pressure. "Girl—with me?"

"Ah, her. She's fine. She's been awake for a while and is meeting with the Chief now. And you—well, you'd be Willis Thomson. Wouldn't you?"

"Yes." There was no denying this. His face was too well known.

"What you did today was pretty brave, young man."

"Brave, yes." Lydia scoffed and crossed her arms. "Brave and stupid. You're lucky not to be dead."

"Are you—the Underground?" Willis still rubbed at his temples.

"Ha!" Lydia laughed sarcastically. "I sure hope so. If helping people find freedom from the Law is up to people like you, we're all lost."

Barney put a gentle hand on Lydia's shoulder, which she shrugged off. "Lydia, that's enough. This young man's been through a lot already."

A teenage boy, also in uniform, ran through the door. He stopped short when he saw Willis sitting and alert. He turned to Lydia. "Chief's on his way." Willis recognized his voice as the third he'd heard earlier.

"This here," Barney pointed, "is Chris. He's one of the newest of our number and the fellow responsible for that headache you have."

"Newest and best." Chris pointed at himself with both thumbs. "Coalition's got nothing on me. I wish we could use real bullets in these things." He pulled his tranquilizer gun and held it for Willis to see.

"You know we don't aim to kill anyone, Chris. And stop pointing that thing aimlessly." Barney's voice sounded parental, and Willis imagined he had some level of respect from the others.

"I know. Feels like it would be easier if there were fewer Law-keepers. Why did the Chief insist on tranks anyway?"

"Because I won't take another life as long as the choice is mine." The voice was deep and filled the space. The other three immediately straightened. Willis turned in the direction of the doorway to see its source. In front of him stood the biggest, strongest human being Willis had ever known. Nothing could have filled Willis with more hope.

It was Kane.

"You've got to be kidding me. It's you? They said a former Chase runner was in charge of the Underground, but I never imagined—" Willis cut himself off and smiled.

"Long time, boss." Kane smiled and gave a single upward nod. His bright white teeth gleamed behind his dark lips. He roared in laughter as he stepped forward to embrace Willis in a giant bear hug. For a moment, Willis forgot his headache as he held his friend.

"I'm so glad you made it out of that mess after the Chase. We talked about coming for you, but—"

Kane cut him off, shaking his head. "But that would have been the dumbest thing you could have done. I'm no stranger to running from arrest. You were the real target and needed to get out of there. Once I saw you were gone, I got lost in the crowd. Law-keepers had their hands too full to worry about me."

"Guess that answers your question about getting rid of him." Lydia punched Chris in the arm.

"Chief, what are we going to do with him?" Barney patted Willis's knee.

"All in good time. I'll explain later, but right now, come with me." Kane grabbed Willis's upper arm with his huge hand and pulled him to his feet. "Someone wants to see you."

"Willis!" Perryn shouted and almost stumbled over herself as he walked through the door. She threw her arms around him. Willis relaxed in her tight embrace. They were safe.

"Boss," Kane walked into the room and closed the door. "There's much to discuss."

"I can't tell you how glad I am to see you." Willis let out a long sigh. Kane held out a hand to quiet him before he could continue.

"Please." Kane pointed toward a seating area. "Sit down." Willis and Perryn took a seat on the old, tattered couch in the corner of the office. Kane sat down behind the metal desk, which was covered in maps and drawings. The wall behind him was littered with messages from the Watcher, bright red check marks and 'x' marks on them. Willis noticed there were far more check marks on the more recent messages. "You're lucky we figured out who you are. Our normal policy is to tranquilize anyone who gets in the way and leave them."

Willis nodded. "Makes sense."

"You'd be in Alliance custody if we hadn't taken you. What you did was foolish."

Willis sat quietly absorbing the scolding. Kane was right. Their action had been too brash. He was angry at himself, less for getting in the way and more for putting Perryn in danger.

"I'm sorry, to you and to Perr. We—I was getting desperate. We had to find you. We need your help to—" Willis's voice caught. He realized he hadn't mentioned his mother by name in weeks. His breaths shuddered. A rush of emotion overtook him.

"To find his mother." Perryn reached over and grabbed his hand. He stared at her, tears momentarily welling in his eyes. She was incredibly strong—stronger than him.

"Boss, I know you've lost much." Kane's tone was somber. "Pretty much everyone here in the Underground has lost someone. So many of the Liberated out there live in secret and are so frightened to do anything that it often takes loss to move them to action." Kane paused and folded his hands in front of him. "But— we can't allow our anger to make our decisions for us. We exist here for one purpose, to help those who aren't free, namely slaves, workers, and anyone who hasn't been allowed the choice to be free of the Law. Jaden's law-passing freed everyone, yet the Coalition still maintains its control on most of the population. People are too afraid to stand up to the might and power of the Chairman."

"Are you saying you won't help us?" Perryn raised her brow in concern.

"No, I'm not saying that. I'm saying that *when* we help you, we'll do it *my* way. Training. Discipline. Caution. The Underground isn't the shoddy, unorganized mess the Coalition makes us out to be."

"Do you know where my mother is?" Willis glanced at him, afraid what the answer might be.

"Not yet, but I've had our intelligence operatives working on it since the announcement of her arrest." He smiled sympathetically when Willis sucked in a breath. "Don't worry, Boss. We'll find her."

"So, what do we do?"

"You'll take a bath. You stink, my friend. Then you'll rest. Tomorrow, you train to become one of us. Many out there," Kane motioned with his head to the doorway, "think you're too much of a liability. You'll have to prove that we can't operate without you. I may be Chief, but my authority barely kept them from disposing of both of you. I can't have my people questioning my motives or doubting themselves. You'll have to win them over tomorrow if you wish to join us on the mission to get your mother."

Willis cocked his head. "Shouldn't be a problem."

"We shall see." Kane wouldn't meet his eyes, and Willis's confidence waned.

"All I can think," Perryn squeezed his hand, "is that I can't believe almost the whole team is together."

Perryn had a point. "Has the Underground found out about Jaden?" Willis hadn't heard a word about what had happened to him save for what the Coalition said about the space station.

"Sadly, no." Kane stroked the well-trimmed beard on his chin. "As far as we know, Jaden was on the station when the chairman destroyed it."

It was like a punch in the gut to Willis. He could hear Perryn shudder at the thought. Jaden had been the first to see that Willis was meant for more than simply bending to the Law. He'd been a friend to Willis and Perryn. *How could he be gone?* No goodbye. Gone in a blink. Willis hated to think of it. He breathed deeply to calm himself.

"Tomorrow, then." Willis slapped his palms on his knees.

"Tomorrow," Kane repeated.

Chapter Sixteen

Willis awoke with a sour stomach. The pressure to perform in front of the Underground kept him up much of the night, and the weariness was not going to help him. He rubbed his eyes to wake himself. He had one day to prove himself. One moment—that's all he had to make a good first impression. Sitting on the edge of his cot, he took in the scene around him. Other male members of the Underground were already out of their cots and half-way prepared for the day. Next to his cot he found a neatly pressed gray uniform that someone had laid out for him. He quickly changed and followed the crowd out of the room.

Kane had explained last night that the 'Underground' name was more literal than the Coalition expected. Their entire base of operation took place in the tunnels and corridors of an underground railway system that'd been used prior to the Great Collapse. Without the means to maintain infrastructure, the tunnels had been sealed off by the Alliance and largely forgotten. While many routes were dangerous, several were still open, giving the Underground unseen access to large portions of Central City.

The dimly lit corridor led the group to an open area. Tables had been set with provisions. *Breakfast time*. His stomach growled, and he considered how long it'd been since he'd eaten. The smell of food and coffee filled the area with a welcome aroma.

"Hey, famous boy." Chris smirked at him from across the space. "Rookies to the back of the line." Several other young men in uniform laughed, bumping into him as they passed. Willis bit his tongue. Respect wouldn't be earned through witty banter. On the station, his presence had brought awe from the rookie trainees and mutual admiration from the veterans. Here, he had neither at his disposal and needed to take a careful approach. He nodded at

Chris and allowed those behind him to move ahead.

"Don't worry, young man." The voice belonged to Barney who came behind him and patted his shoulder. "You'll get your chance to show that boy you belong here."

"Thanks." Willis tried unsuccessfully to smile. "Guess I shouldn't be surprised. It was the same on the station for new trainees."

"Respect must be earned, Willis, not demanded. Chris is a talented soldier, but I fear his arrogance is going to catch him one day."

"Overconfident, huh? I'll have to keep that in mind."

Barney winked at him and moved forward to get his meal. Willis scanned the area to locate where Perryn might be seated. Lydia was busy introducing her to several young women at a table. He sighed in relief to see her engaged in discussion. He'd dragged her into this quest to free his mother. She'd never complained or asked for anything the entire time. She was smiling again, and he was grateful to see it. He'd forgotten how much he loved her smile.

<hr />

Perryn could see Willis watching her from the other side of the mess hall. Lydia had warned her that the guys wouldn't be kind to Willis on his first day. He was too famous, and many didn't want him there. While Perryn had run the Chase with Willis, she was "nowhere near as well-known" Lydia had explained.

"You did well, talking to the other girls last night." Lydia whispered in Perryn's ear during the meal.

"Thanks," Perryn said. "Not what I expected."

"What did you expect, an interrogation?" Lydia laughed at her own comment.

"Maybe. People are so disciplined here. I didn't expect anyone would want to know me. On the station—"

"This isn't the station, Perryn. Chief has seen to that." She nodded in the direction of Kane's office. "While we may wear uniforms and act like soldiers, we're more of a family than you might think. You shared your story last night with the other women in the barracks, and it showed strength. You didn't hide your flaws, and believe me, that took courage. Want to be respected here? Be yourself. That's what you did last night. You're going to fit right in."

"So, Perryn—" The voice belonged to a girl in her late teens who had introduced herself as Maria. "They giving your boy a hard time over there, or what?"

"He can take it." She offered a confident grin, but something twisted in her stomach. Willis was not accustomed to being the odd man out.

"So, you and he like—a thing or something?"

"A thing?"

Maria rolled her eyes. "Yeah. You know. You together?"

"Oh, that." She could feel her face blush.

"Ha ha, I told you." Maria laughed pleasantly as did many of the other girls. "She got the hots for famous boy over there."

"I guess we're a *thing*."

"You guess?" Maria stopped laughing and raised her eyebrows. "Girl, what do you mean you 'guess'?"

"Why? You interested?" Perryn smirked. The verbal dodge worked, and the group turned on Maria with playful shoves and 'she got you, girl' remarks.

Maria grinned, enjoying the banter. "Nah. I mean—he's cute and all. Not my type." The laughter surged again. "But seriously, what do you mean you *guess*?"

Perryn remembered Lydia's comment about being herself. Honesty is what worked best in this world. "We haven't ever talked about it. Every time I think we will, something happens." The others nodded and recounted their stories of guys who couldn't work up the courage to say how they felt.

Lydia leaned closer and whispered, "See? You're going to fit right in. Excuse me, I need to get to a meeting."

"What, Captain?" Maria redirected the teasing as Lydia stood. "This conversation to juvenile for you?"

"No, Maria. It's better that I should leave before I reveal to everyone at the table that I caught Stevie quoting poetry to you in the tunnels last night. Did he write that *precious* little bit of poetry for you?"

Maria buried her face in her arms to hide her embarrassment. The girls at the table cackled with delight to see the tables turned on Maria. Perryn liked this group. Age didn't matter. Background didn't matter. What mattered was people.

This is my new home. A pang of guilt struck her heart at the notion. They were there to save Willis's mother. She was Perryn's family, too. She couldn't be distracted from that goal. *But certainly, we won't abandon the Underground once she's rescued. In fact, I bet she'll want to join too. These could be our people if we want them to be.* The idea calmed her. Joining this family would help save what remained of Willis's.

She glanced over at the table where Willis sat with Barney. He appeared concerned, and she could see the wheels in his head turning, trying to figure out how to become one of the group. *Be yourself, Willis. You'll win them over.*

"Your friend over there appears to be getting along well." Barney's entire face creased as he chuckled.

"Yeah, seems so." Willis frowned. He couldn't help but feel slightly jealous. Here he was sitting at a mostly empty table with the oldest guy in the Underground, who probably pitied him more than liked him. She had a whole table laughing. He was happy for her, but it made the bitterness in his stomach rise.

"I know what you're thinking, young man. Trust me. Don't try to impress anyone here. Do your best. People will respect your ability. You were a leader on the station, right? Do what you know how to do. If you try to impress them, they'll see right through it."

He shrugged. "Yeah. I guess."

"Come on, everything begins in a few minutes. I'll show you to the training room."

The training space was a large underground station where several railcars had once been able to park. Between each of the tracks was a raised platform upon which members of the underground practiced different training regimens. One platform was for target practice with the tranquilizer guns. The constant *phoot* sounds could be heard throughout the space. Another contained soldiers training in hand-to-hand combat skills with instructors at their sides. Even another had what appeared like field medical training taking place. Willis stared longingly at the track upon which an obstacle course had been set and wished that was where he was to prove himself. He'd have no problem dominating the competition there.

"Okay, pretty boy. You ready?" Chris appeared from the group with his entourage. "That's right. Chief said anyone who wished to witness your workout today was free to do so, and I'm not going to miss this."

Willis turned around to see that most of the younger members had gathered on his platform. Most frowned or crossed their arms. They didn't trust him. Far off on another platform, Kane stood at the top of a perch that gave him a view of the entire room. Willis wished he were here to support him, but he understood why Kane had to keep his distance. Willis would have to win this group over on his own

"All right, Willis. We begin here." Lydia's voice commanded the attention of the platform. "Do you have much melee training?"

"Not really. That wasn't exactly our focus on the station," he said. Snickers could be heard from the group of Underground members.

"Captain, let me have first shot at him." Chris spoke to the murmured agreement of a few other boys.

"Quiet, Chris. I make the calls here." Lydia shot him a glare, and Chris responded, immediately straightening. Whatever role Lydia had among the group, Willis could tell she was highly respected. "What we test here on this platform, Willis, reflects what we face out there. We have an impossible task before us. Compared to the Coalition, we're nothing. The balance is always against us unless we're willing to stare into the face of impossible odds and remain completely calm and steadfast. That's the goal here today. Understand?"

Willis nodded. He didn't understand what she meant at all, but he didn't dare admit it. Appearing weak in front of this group was not going to win points. He stepped toward the middle of the platform, and the gathered crowd quickly formed a ring around him. Lydia stepped forward with a pair of handcuffs. With a twirl of her finger, she motioned him to turn around. His stomach leapt as she clamped the cuffs onto his wrists behind his back.

"Your job, Willis, is to protect this box for thirty seconds." Lydia held out a cube about nine inches on all sides in the flat of her left hand. "Your opponents will try to hit the box with a shock stick like this one." In her right hand was a metal baton about two feet in length. She touched the baton to the box, which glowed and let off a loud tone. "Get it? You'll reset after each tone. Three tones, and you lose."

"Doesn't sound so bad." Willis tried not to sound too confident. *What's the catch?*

"Willis, they're not called shock sticks without reason." Without warning, Lydia jabbed the baton into his ribs. The resulting shock sent a bolt of pain up his spine that took his breath away and made his head feel like it was about to explode. Falling to his knees, he gasped for air. "They're not lethal, and they cause no permanent injury. But—they've earned their name."

"What a wimp!" Chris jeered to the approval of his posse. "He won't make it thirty seconds without crying."

Get up, Willis. Everyone is watching. He forced one foot underneath him and pushed down on his knee, willing himself to his feet. Staring at Chris, he tried not to grimace from the pain.

"Not bad, rookie." Lydia had a smirk on her face. "Got on your feet at least ten seconds faster than Chris did." Laughter and elbow jabs followed, but all Willis could focus on was Chris's fuming expression.

"Captain, please let me participate in this exercise." Chris stepped forward, his pride clearly hurt.

Lydia sighed and rubbed the bridge of her nose. She waved a hand at Chris. "Fine, Chris. Pick your team, but you'd better remember the rules of the exercise."

Turning to the group around him, Chris handed shock sticks

to a team he'd obviously preselected. A huge twenty-something male, nearly rivaling Kane's size, took his place to Willis's left. A teenage girl who appeared like she'd seen plenty of battle experience and a tall lanky boy took the positions to his right and behind. Chris stepped in front of Willis tapping the bottom of the baton in his hand. Willis straddled the cube on the floor, trying hard to fight the instinct to pull at the handcuffs that were cutting into his wrists.

"Three hits, that's all you get, Willis. Defend the cube however you're able. Got it?" Lydia cocked her head, waiting for his response.

Willis nodded.

Lydia blew a whistle. Willis tensed, waiting for the first move.

Chris grinned, his mouth pulling to one side. Suddenly baring his teeth, he lunged at Willis who reacted with instincts honed on the space station. As quickly as he'd moved, Chris retreated. *It's a fake!* His mind roared at him. Willis spun barely in time to kick the hand of the lanky boy who was reaching his baton for the cube. The move worked, but it left his other side exposed. The huge male and the girl both hit Willis with their shock sticks. A scream escaped involuntarily as Willis's back arched almost to the point of injury.

Falling to his face, he could hear Chris's laughter.

"So predictable. You Chase runners only know how to think in a straight line." Chris grinned as he calmly stepped forward. He paused to eye Willis before casually tapping the cube.

Tone. The cube glowed green for a second before beginning to slowly fade.

"One hit! Reset!" Lydia held out both hands, ordering the four attackers back into their positions.

Willis gathered himself to his feet and took his place over the cube. Sweat beaded on his forehead, and his lungs heaved. The melee couldn't have taken more than a few seconds. How he would survive thirty of them, he couldn't begin to imagine. He had no time to think about it.

The whistle blew.

This time, Willis went on the offensive. He kicked at Chris's hand, and Chris nearly dodged the hit. His foot connected enough to stun the loudmouth. Feeling the huge male step forward, he threw his weight to the left into the giant's chest. The audible grunt let Willis know he'd struck hard enough to expel the air from the man's lungs.

Pain suddenly radiated from the back of his knee upward. The girl had reached for the cube and grazed his leg in the process. Willis's leg buckled underneath him right as the lanky boy's baton found his neck. Light flashed in his vision, and he fell awkwardly backward striking his head on the floor. The cube lay to his side, totally exposed.

Chris stepped forward.

"Nice moves, but not good enough." His eyes squinted, and his jaw flexed. He raised his baton but brought it down on Willis's leg instead of the cube. Willis screamed as the pain caused his whole body to become rigid.

"Chris!" Lydia shouted. Grabbing his shoulder, she yanked him backward. "The subject is down. Touch the cube or be removed from the exercise."

"Yes, ma'am." Chris never took his eyes off Willis. He tapped the cube with his baton.

Tone.

"Two hits. Reset." Lydia's face glowed green from the cube. Her eyes never left Chris.

Willis gritted his teeth as he tried to stand. His knees shook as he stood, and his legs could barely hold his weight. He scanned around at the crowd, and he could see several shaking their heads. He was losing the exercise. He was losing his chance to win their trust.

He shook his head to clear it. There was no way to defend the cube against four attackers. How could he cover four directions while they each attacked one?

His mind raced for a solution. He had seconds to decipher the challenge or lose his chance to join the Underground. He stared down at the cube. Then, it occurred to him.

Remain calm. Those were Lydia's words. *Steadfast in the face of the impossible. Steadfast—immovable. Don't defend against four attackers. Simply defend one cube.*

The whistle blew.

Chris bit his lip as he swung his baton at Willis's head. He acted eager to finish Willis off. Willis ducked and fell to his knees. He curled his body over the cube so that none of it was exposed. He waited, knowing what was coming.

Four batons came down on his back.

He had never in his life experienced that level of pain. His eyes throbbed like they might burst from his skull. He focused all his willpower on the cube and silently counted the seconds. *Protect the cube. Don't let them get to it. Whatever happens, keep it covered. Focus, Willis.*

Another blow from the batons.

His whole body shook as the shock subsided. Still, he willed himself not to move.

A third blow came.

This one knocked him to his side, but he remained curled around the cube, his legs protecting it from view. Sweat ran in streams down his temples. His breath came in short gasps. He couldn't take another.

Whistle.

A few gleeful 'whoops' came from the crowd. A baton clattered to the floor in front of him as Chris squatted to look him in the face. His scowl was replaced with a small smile.

"I may not like it, but welcome to the Underground, Willis," he whispered. He punched Willis playfully in the shoulder and turned to the others. "Get the cuffs off him!"

Retrieving the keys from Lydia, the girl in the ring unlocked the cuffs. The huge male lifted Willis to his feet and supported him from behind. Willis rubbed his wrists, which were raw from pulling at the cuffs.

Grabbing Willis's arm and raising it, Lydia addressed the crowd. "Having passed the trial and proven his willingness to sacrifice his safety in the face of overwhelming odds, I stand first to officially welcome a new brother to the Underground. Let all who agree sound off."

"Aye!" The crowd shouted, pumping their fists in the air.

"Aye." Chris spoke quietly, extending his hand. Willis took it in a feeble, exhausted handshake. Chris's anger had disappeared and was replaced with respect. "No hard feelings, I hope. We had to know you were more than the reckless idiot we saw on the street."

"And?" Willis hesitated, trying to smile. He was keenly aware that he was soaked in sweat and must have appeared feeble.

"You're still reckless, but not a complete idiot."

The two chuckled.

"Tell me one thing." Willis paused to glance off in the distance. "Will Perryn have to do this?"

Chris let out a belly laugh. "That's the funniest part. She woke a lot sooner than you did yesterday. Went through the trial while you were still passed out from the dart. Figured it out *a lot* faster than you, too."

Willis rolled his eyes and smiled. "Well, I make no claim to be the smart one of the two of us."

"Yeah, don't. She's definitely got you beat. Tough as nails when she needs to be, as well." Chris slapped Willis's shoulder. "Get this guy a shower and a change of uniform. He's sweat this one out already, and it's not even midday." Laughter rose from the crowd.

Willis's smile broadened. He'd done it. He was one of them.

Chapter Seventeen

"Sheila, wake up." A voice startled Sheila to consciousness. "Wake up." Her mother shook Sheila gently. "The doctors said Audrey is awake."

She opened her eyes more fully to see the sterile hospital waiting area come into focus. Barely a teenager, she lay with her head in her mother's lap. Behind the desk sat an overweight receptionist in an Alliance health care uniform shuffling papers into files and singing to herself. Sheila decided her song was too cheerful for this place. She sat up, running her fingers through her hair in an attempt to straighten the matted mess on the left side of her head.

The two of them stood and marched down the hallway to Audrey's recovery room. Sheila hung on her mother's arm, unsure what they would see. Her hands trembled, and she gripped her mother tighter. Finally, the door neared, and a nurse exited. Noticing Sheila and her mother, she stopped.

"You can see her." She stared at her duty roster, her mind clearly on her next patient.

"Is she going to be all right?" Sheila glanced at the door.

The nurse didn't even look up. "We won't know much for the next couple days."

"Thank you." Sheila's mother didn't wait for more information, instead nodding toward the door.

Sheila grabbed the handle of the door and turned it slowly, fearful that disturbing the quiet of the room would injure her sister further. Pushing the door, she entered uneasily as her mother followed.

"There's my little reporter," came Audrey's weak voice.

Sheila tried to return her sister's smile, but choked, unable to *contain the tear leaking from her eye. Her sister lay in the hospital bed surrounded by machines, each beeping their indications of Audrey's pitiful state. Tubes connected to her arms injecting countless medications to fight infection from the surgery. Bandages, newly changed, could be seen peeking out from under the sheets.*

She approached the bedside, scared to touch her sister. Audrey seemed so fragile. Her mother stood in the corner quietly wiping at the tears and taking deep, shuddering breaths. Slowly, Audrey reached out her hand and took Sheila's.

"Tell me what you see," she whispered. She gave the gentlest of squeezes on Sheila's fingers.

Sheila shook her head. "No, Audrey. I don't want to be a reporter today."

"Sister, you have a gift for seeing the world. Tell me what you see. Be honest. What do you see beyond the obvious?"

Sheila's lips trembled. She bit her lip and paused. "I see injustice."

The corners of Audrey's mouth curled into a slight smile. "That's a funny thing to see in a place like this. Why injustice?"

"Because my sister loves better than anyone I know, and she doesn't deserve this. Because the doctors don't even know if this surgery will help, and yet you have to feel this much pain. Because—"

She could barely continue. Tears salted her mouth as they found the corners of her lips. She swallowed hard to finish her words.

"Because you're the sick one, and you take better care of me than I of you."

Audrey reached her hand to wipe a tear from Sheila's cheek and brush the wet strands of hair from her face. Her fingers felt slight and dry on Sheila's skin. "Sister, you're wrong."

Sheila sniffed. Wrong?

"Yes, you are," Audrey said, sensing Sheila's thoughts. "This isn't injustice. This is a miracle in the making. Things are always at their worst before they get better. Miracles aren't miracles

unless all feels lost."

"But how do you know?" She sniffed again, wiping at the tears that continued to escape her eyes.

Audrey winced as though something hurt inside. Regaining her composure, she smiled again. "Because, my precious sister, some people deserve a miracle or two in their lives. At some point, the light has to enter the darkness."

"Isn't it exciting?" Penny exclaimed. She bounced around the conference table, double-checking that the materials at each chair were set perfectly. "The chairman has called a special session of the deputy chairmen and chairwomen, and I have been invited." She paused to breathe deeply as she scanned the room. "Everything must be perfect."

Sheila stood in the corner watching Penny's display. It was amusing to watch and somehow saddening at the same time. Penny barked orders to two assistants who were preparing several folders. Bracelets jingled as she directed the flurry of activity like an orchestra conductor. The assistants hurriedly finished their task and made a hasty retreat.

"Excuse me, Penny." Sheila raised a questioning finger at herself. "Why exactly am I here?"

Penny grew serious. "Because, dearie, history is going to be made in this room today. I can feel it. You need to be here to witness the events and tell the world." Penny nodded slowly as if to make her point.

"Are you certain the chairman wants me here?"

"He gave me special permission to have one member of the press here. What is it you always say in your broadcasts? 'Sheila Kemp, watching the world for news?' Well, sweetheart, today the world will be at this table. So, *watch* carefully." Penny sighed deeply, inspecting the space one last time.

Without warning, the doors to the conference room opened and several security Law-keepers in black suits entered. They searched throughout the space, moving chairs and jostling papers, producing a *humph* more than once from Penny. She scurried behind them to straighten anything they moved. Sheila held up her credentials to the lead officer, who scrutinized them carefully.

The lead officer lifted his radio. "Security sweep is clear. Send in the chairman and deputies."

The deputy chairmen and chairwomen filed into the room taking their places around the table. The Western Alliance deputy chair was the last to enter, a small man dressed in a black suit with yellow trim. His expression smug, he ignored Penny as he brushed past to take a seat directly next to the chairman's spot. With the near fusion of the Western Alliance and World Coalition, Sheila guessed this deputy chairman held a significant amount of power at the table.

Once everyone was seated, the doors again opened. The chairman, in his usual robe entered with his hands folded in front of him. Penny pulled her seat from the table to allow him to sit, but he stopped her with a raised hand. Holding his arms wide, he addressed the table.

"The greatness of the Law proceeds us into these important discussions. Its wisdom shall guide us. Its glory shall lead us. It is the Law that protects us all."

"The Law is good." The deputies parroted the familiar phrases. Sheila noticed Penny edged the rest of the group in volume and enthusiasm.

"It is the Law that preserves us all."

"The Law remains."

"It is the Law that saves us all."

"The Law is good."

The chairman accepted the seat Penny offered and placed his elbows on the edge of the table. Adjusting his glasses with one hand, he scanned the table silently. Penny took a spot in the corner right behind the chairman. Despite her efforts to remain composed, she bounced in place. Sheila smiled at her eagerness.

She certainly is loving every minute of this.

DeGraaf folded his hands in front of him. "Honored deputies, it is truly the Law that saves us in these unsettled times. It was the Law that allowed for emergency powers to be invoked, merging the Coalition with the strongest of the Alliances."

The Western Alliance deputy smiled arrogantly at the other deputies. Some nodded in agreement, while others appeared less sure. Sheila noted that the deputy from the United African Cooperative stared coldly at the table.

DeGraaf continued. "It is the Law that allows us to maintain a force of Law-keepers to keep the peace despite those who would seek to ruin it. Indeed, it is the Law that allows me to make my first announcement today."

Several of the deputies turned to each other with questioning glances. A few stared at the papers in front of them, shuffling through them for information.

"No, you will not find this on the agenda you received from Penny, who has been more than gracious to arrange these proceedings." Sheila could see Penny sigh in relief, worried that she'd forgotten something. "No, I came to the following decision as I reflected this morning on the splendor of the Law. It is time we recognized true leadership and unquestioned loyalty. It is time we combined those who truly seek to right the wrongs in this world with the authority needed to do so. Deputy Redstone—"

The Western Alliance deputy straightened at the mention of his name. His smugness disappeared. "Y-yes, sir, Mr. Chairman?"

"Since the blasphemy that took place in the last Chase, these so called Liberated have confused the world and sent it hurtling into chaos. While some of our weaker alliances might have excuse for their inability to contain the threat—" The chairman paused to gaze at the deputies at the far end of the table who shifted nervously in their seats. "You, Mr. Redstone have been afforded every resource to snuff out this rebellion, and yet it is in your borders that these rebels are the most organized and zealous. The recent incursion at the mission sits as a stunning failure on your part."

"Mr. Chairman, please let me explain," Redstone stammered. The chairman held up his hand to silence him.

DeGraaf didn't look at Redstone. Instead, he addressed the rest of the table. "No explanation required, Mr. Deputy. It is clear to me you are not fit for the position you hold, while another under your authority has been making the boldest moves toward a brighter future. You are hereby relieved of your position as deputy chairman."

Gasps could be heard around the table as the words were understood. Redstone's eyes widened in sudden realization. "B-but Mr. Chairman—"

"Security, would you please assist Mr. Redstone from the building." Chairman DeGraaf waved a finger at the lead Law-keeper. "And please see to it his family is afforded all the effects that come from failing to fully support the Coalition."

Two Law-keepers immediately bracketed the flustered former-deputy, who continued to protest. Without command, the officers grabbed him under each arm and began dragging him from the space.

"Please, Mr. Chairman! My wife. My children. We love the Coalition! The Law is good! The Law is good! The Law is—" The door to the conference room shut.

The chairman simply stared at his folded hands as the voice faded down the hallway.

"I take no pleasure," DeGraaf said, "in removing one of you from your post. My reading of the Law allows me this authority. While this may appear a blemish on our glorious Coalition, I believe it is more than mended by my next decision." He stood and turned to Penny who placed her hand across her chest as if unable to breathe. "Among the sorrow of disloyalty, it is you, Penny, who have shown the most ingenuity and passion for ridding the Coalition of these dissidents. Please, take your place as the new Western Alliance deputy chairwoman."

Several deputy chairmen and chairwomen could be heard inhaling sharply. Penny herself was among them and appeared ready to cry tears of joy. Her face flushed with supposed embarrassment. Sliding gracefully into the empty seat next to the chairman, she let out a long breath as she smoothed her skirt. She placed her hands calmly on the table to take in the moment and then proceeded to unhurriedly stare down each of the other deputies.

Did she know this was going to happen?

"My gracious deputies, let me assure you of the wisdom of my choice for this appointment. Would you, Madam Deputy, please share Project Rebirth with the group."

"Certainly, Mr. Chairman, and thank you for this splendid opportunity." Penny stood gracefully and took a stack of folders from the corner. One by one, she placed them in front of the other deputies, who still sat shocked at what had happened. "My fellow deputies, what I am giving you is my proposed solution to the problem we have within our borders. Yours are the first eyes, beyond that of the chairman, to have seen the interesting results of our experimentation. Dearie?"

Sheila started, realizing that Penny was addressing her. She stepped forward toward the table.

Penny cocked her head slightly to the side. "Dearie, your presence is no longer required. I believe you have more than enough good news to tell the world. You may move along." She extended a hand toward the exit.

Sheila slowly made her way to the door, which was held open by the guards. As she passed the chairs, one of the deputies reached for his drink and knocked the folder Penny had given him off the table. It fluttered to the ground in front of Sheila and landed open. She glanced at it without slowing her movement as the deputy snatched it from the floor. Exiting the hallway with the officers, she stopped to catch her breath.

What was Project Rebirth? What did Penny have up her sleeve? And what did Brenda Thomson have to do with it?

She'd barely gathered two bits of information in her glance. One had been a picture of Brenda. The other had been a name: Solution Systems. It wasn't much to go on, but it was finally a lead.

Hang on, Willis. Light is about to enter the darkness, and you, my friend, deserve a miracle or two.

Chapter Eighteen

Willis's body ached more than he could remember in recent days, and the simple cot on which he slept wasn't helping. His muscles complained as he stretched, and he remembered the trial he'd undergone as well as the following days of training. Sitting up, his feet found the cold floor, and the sensation startled his senses. Much of the room was still asleep, and he wished that he could join them. Had it not been for the messenger telling him Kane was summoning him immediately, he would.

He slipped on his uniform and boots, more than once grunting as his body held on to sleep. Joining the Underground was a process oddly familiar to him. He was mentally transported back to the space station with its spartan accommodations and uniforms. As much as he'd longed to leave the space station prior to the Chase, some part of him had grown used to the routine. That kind of routine was comfortable to him, but he didn't see how being with the Underground would work after he saved his mother. He would want her far away from the conflict, not in the middle of it. He couldn't risk her safety again. He'd said nothing to anyone, of course, as he was certain they wouldn't understand.

The hallways were completely empty except for an occasional sentry. Kane had security running around the clock, but most rested safely in the forgotten tunnels. What had once been a maintenance area had been converted into offices for Kane and his officers. He knocked on the plain green door marked 'Chief.'

"Enter." Kane's deep voice came from the other side of the door.

Willis opened the door. Kane's huge presence behind the desk was expected. Lydia stood to Kane's right, also expected, as Willis had learned the 'Captain' title wasn't a nickname. It was the third person in the office that caught Willis off guard.

"*Buenos dias*, Willis." Mrs. Sanchez whispered as she leaned forward with a bright smile.

"Mrs. Sanchez? Why? How?" Willis couldn't form the right question.

"Sit down, Willis." Kane spoke with authority, clearly in charge. Willis sat in the chair next to Mrs. Sanchez. "Willis, I've made mention to you of our intelligence network in past conversation. What few know is exactly who makes up this network. The truth is we've hidden agents all over the city, and the Captain and I are the lone individuals privileged to know who they are—until this meeting.

"Mrs. Sanchez and her husband,"—Kane nodded in her direction—"have been an invaluable part of our communication network among our agents. It was they who first identified you and Perryn to us. We learned of your location long before you showed up at the mission. You have them to thank because we wouldn't have confirmed your identity if we didn't know you were in the city.

"Chief among her responsibilities is disseminating intel from The Watcher as it arrives. She's under orders to deliver messages from The Watcher to all intelligence agents unless she deems it of a special sensitivity. We've asked you here because the latest message involves you."

"Me?" Willis wasn't fully following.

"More specifically, your mother." Lydia crossed her arms.

"My mother?"

Mrs. Sanchez clarified, "The Watcher spoke of your mama in the latest message, Willis. I brought this to the attention of the Chief right away." She nodded eagerly and smiled again. Willis blinked, still getting used to the idea of Mrs. Sanchez being an intelligence agent.

"The Watcher has discovered a link between your mother and the Solutions Systems building here in Central City." Kane pointed to a map. "Our intelligence has long suspected the building housed something important to the Coalition, but this information allows us to guess at its purpose."

"And what's that?" Willis was on edge. The next thing Kane said wouldn't be good news.

"At a minimum, the imprisonment of persons of interest, and at the worst—" Kane paused and glanced down.

"At the worst?" Willis leaned forward impatiently. The slow reveal of the information was killing him.

"The experimentation on genetically recoded individuals." Lydia spoke quickly like she was trying to get the information in the open before she decided against it.

"Namely former Chase runners and trainees," Kane said. "I'm sorry, Boss. Your mother may be in her own personal hell."

They were missing the point. "But we know she's there, right? We can rescue her, can't we?" Willis sat straight in his chair.

"Willis, we're here for the liberation of *all* the Coalition has under its thumb. Yes, we'll save your mother as promised, but an operation like this takes planning."

He nodded, wanting them to see his point. "Whatever it takes, but we need to get her out of there."

"Agreed." Kane turned his attention. "Mrs. Sanchez, thank you."

"You're welcome, Chief." She reached and patted Kane's hand. "Willis, Señor Sanchez will be most pleased to hear you are well and with these good people. Take care of yourself." She grabbed Willis's hand tenderly as she stood.

"*Gracias*, Mrs. Sanchez." Willis gently squeezed her hand in return.

Chapter Nineteen

Solution Systems was a plain-looking, cube-shaped building near the edge of Central City. Security was relatively light, at least from what it appeared from the outside. A simple fence topped with razor wire and a security station checking the identification of everyone who entered were the lone visible protective measures. Other than that, there was little to indicate that anything important was going on inside.

"That's it?" Willis glanced from his binoculars. They were perched atop a building several blocks away with orders from Kane to gather intel and not to engage.

"I don't get it." Chris shook his head.

"It's a genius move by the Alliance." Lydia pointed at the various security measures. "They're hiding in plain sight. A lot of outward security would draw our attention. Lock down the building and surround it with an army, and we'd know its importance. Instead, they disguised it as any other company simply trying to cover its bases with all the unrest in the city."

"You're saying this should be easy?" Chris squinted, his doubt obvious.

"Not at all. If the Watcher was right, I guarantee the security inside is top of the line."

Willis let out a long sigh. In the distance, his mother was enduring God-knows-what. She was so close, and yet she would have to wait. "So how do we get in?" He watched Lydia for an answer.

"That's what we're here to find out. Check out the west entrance." She pointed to a convoy on the road.

Willis raised his binoculars again. A short row of Alliance government trucks approached the gate. The guard scanned the driver's ID card, while two others checked the bottom of the truck with mirrors. A wave from the first guard allowed the truck's entrance, and they pulled into the garage on the first floor of the building.

"Happens every day at 2 p.m.," Lydia said. "Intelligence tracks the movement of Alliance vehicles throughout the city. If we can intercept those trucks on their route, we might have a chance to get in."

"What are they transporting?" Chris pointed. "Why don't they check the rear of the truck?"

Lydia frowned. "We don't know. Those doors do not get opened until inside. Ever."

"Why? What's inside?"

"Not what. Who."

"You mean—" Willis started, then cut himself off.

"People. Recoded individuals for experimentation." Lydia turned away, not meeting Willis's eyes. "That's my guess anyway."

Willis wanted to retch. A government that claimed to protect its people was transporting human cargo under the nose of everyone in the city. This was beyond the exploitation of people of the slave workforce. This was rounding up people like cattle for slaughter. It was mechanized murder in the name of science. Bile soured the back of his throat.

"I can't wait to level that building." Chris spat on the ground. "After we see everyone inside freed, that is."

"Yeah, well—for that, we'll need to talk to the Chief." Lydia said solemnly.

"What do you mean we aren't saving everyone?" Chris shouted the question as he scanned the group for anyone who would reply. Kane sat quietly without answering. "I mean, I signed up to free as many as possible, and you're telling me that we're going in simply to free one person?"

"Soldier, hold your tongue." Lydia stepped forward toward Chris.

Kane raised a hand toward her. "No, Captain. Let him speak. We are not a dictatorship, and people are free to express their opinions." He'd finished sharing with the three of them that the plan was to free Brenda Thomson, and Brenda Thomson *alone*.

Having been given his opening, Chris went on. "It's too risky. All the resources. The lives in danger—for one person? Why don't we storm in and empty the place?"

Willis sat quietly listening. Perryn held his hand. She and several others selected for the operation had been called to the briefing. He couldn't help but feel guilt. How could they walk by all the others inside and merely bring out one? Kane appeared confident his decision would make sense, but Willis couldn't help feeling a little sick to his stomach. While he longed to save his mother, Chris was right. *Why risk so much for one person?*

"And what do you think will happen if we do?" Kane spoke quietly.

"I'll sleep better, for one." Chris pointed to himself.

"What will happen, soldier, is they'll set up shop somewhere else." Lydia gestured to the side with her thumb.

"What you need to realize, Chris..." Kane turned to the whole room. "What we all need to realize is that we know very little about the purpose of Solution Systems or 'Project Rebirth.' As much as freeing everyone would feel good, I'm afraid it'll serve to alert the Coalition and drive their efforts further out of our reach. If that happens, ten or a hundred times more lives may be lost."

"So why risk it at all, Chief?" Maria spoke for the first time in the meeting. She was sitting next to Perryn and smacking on a piece of gum, as usual.

Kane stood from his desk and placed his hands behind his back. Stepping to the side, he scanned solemnly around the team. "Until today, we were forced to guess at what the Coalition was up to. We need to know. We can't fight for long without knowing what the Coalition is planning. The presence of Brenda Thomson is the perfect cover. Invading the facility to extract her is simply a distraction."

Willis's head shot up. He gave Kane a concerned stare.

"No worries, Boss. We'll extract her to complete the diversion."

Willis sighed in relief.

Kane nodded. "But our real purpose will be to gather intel on Project Rebirth. Any plan that involves the chairman himself is of the highest priority. With luck, we'll enter, get what we need, and lead the Coalition to believe this was simply an effort to save a high-profile prisoner without exposing our acquired knowledge of Project Rebirth."

Several heads nodded in understanding. It was a hard plan, but it made sense. Chris sat down hard, apparently resigned to the logic of Kane's words.

Kane sighed and placed a hand on Chris's shoulder. "I don't like the idea of leaving people behind either, but I must weigh the cost against the many more we may save in the end. Remember why we're here."

"We don't fight for today!" Lydia shouted.

"We fight for tomorrow!" The voices came in unison, including Chris's who couldn't keep from sounding half-hearted.

Kane gently squeezed Chris's shoulder. "My friend, the day is coming when we'll be able to free everyone. Count on it."

Chris nodded.

Willis marveled at Kane's leadership. The silent behemoth he'd known on the station had been hiding a depth Willis had not imagined possible. Everything—the tranquilizer darts, the compassion for his soldiers, and the fatherly attention to younger ones like Chris—all added up to a story that Willis would one day have to ask Kane about.

Kane tapped his watch. "Operation sets out tomorrow at o' eight hundred. Dismissed."

Chapter Twenty

Perryn sat crouched on a stone floor, the irregular shapes of the old brick wall digging into her back. She adjusted her position, and the scraping of her feet echoed loudly off the empty walls. The building had once been a shop of some kind, and she tried to imagine a life where people frequented this place. All the buildings on this street were empty, and Lydia had told her it was an important historic area of the city prior to the Great Collapse. Today, it stood as an abandoned area, unnecessary with the population so drastically reduced by anarchy before the Law brought order.

To her right sat Chris, who tapped his foot nervously. He lived for action like this, and she couldn't help but admire his passion for the Underground. Even without knowing his story, she had no doubt he believed in the cause. Perryn was certain he would willingly give his life for it.

Maria was snapping her gum in the corner and pouring over a map. Since the day of Willis's trials, Perryn and Maria had been almost inseparable. She was younger than Perryn, but she'd seen more than her share of Alliance abuse.

"They shot my father right in front of me," she'd once blurted out. Not knowing what to say at the time, Perryn had simply stared. "Thought you ought to know," Maria had said. It was Maria's way of letting her in at the time. Perryn studied her now and realized their relationship would never be the same. Secretly, she'd hoped they would become good friends.

Perryn examined the tranquilizer gun in her hands. She'd shown a natural proficiency with the weapon the first time she'd held it, which was one of the reasons she was selected for the mission. At least, that's what Kane had told her. She suspected it was also to be there in case Willis wigged out again. He was determined to be a part of the mission, and Kane had to be certain someone was there that could talk Willis down if necessary. Either way, she didn't need to worry about it this second as he was posted in the building across the street with Kane, Lydia, and two other soldiers.

"Do you hear that?" Chris broke the silence, startling Perryn.

Maria cocked her head to turn an ear upward. She stopped the gum snapping and closed her eyes. "That's not our truck. Too small."

As the noise approached, it was the unmistakable high-pitched engine of a motorcycle. Staying in the shadows, Perryn tilted her head to peer out of the window next to her. A lone motorcycle approached.

"Everyone, stand down." Kane's voice squawked over the radio into Perryn's earpiece. "It's a patrol. Do not engage. Do not give away your position."

She exhaled, realizing she'd been holding her breath. That's when she heard it. Distant at first, she could make out the low, unmistakable growl of a much larger vehicle. *Here it comes. Remember the plan.* She rehearsed the briefing in her head. Kane's team would approach the front of the vehicle. Hers would approach the rear. She checked one last time to make sure a dart was fully engaged in the pistol.

"Survey team, confirm transport." Kane's voice whispered into the radio.

"Transport confirmed, Chief," the radio squawked.

A third voice spoke. "Roadblock team is a go."

Perryn watched from her window as two Underground men, one she recognized as the large man from Willis's trials, pushed a vehicle from the alley into the roadway. The older roadway allowed one vehicle to block enough of the street to prevent the truck from passing. The men retreated down the alley as the truck turned the corner.

The air brakes hissed as the truck suddenly slowed to a stop. From her vantage point in the building, Perryn observed the two soldiers in the truck cabin in the large side mirrors. She could hear the driver curse loudly as he leaned forward to shift into reverse. The soldier in the passenger seat reached for the radio.

"Engage target!" Kane shouted into everyone's ears.

A dart struck the neck of the passenger soldier through the open window. He slumped over the dashboard a second before he raised the radio to his lips. The driver cursed again, still grinding at the gears.

Perryn slipped down the wall and spun through the open doorway. Pistol raised, she made her way to the rear of the truck. Chris and Maria followed closely behind. Wheeling around the vehicle, she took her position at the far corner in time to see Kane hauling the newly unconscious driver from his seat. Willis quickly grabbed the keys and turned off the engine. Both visible soldiers were removed, but they had little intel on what would be waiting for them inside the truck.

"Get the doors." Chris centered himself behind the truck. He aimed his pistol at the rear of the truck, his finger twitching near the trigger.

Maria grabbed the right door and glanced at Perryn who had taken hold of the left. A nod from her, and both pulled on the handles. Chris extended his pistol arm.

Silence.

Perryn had expected more soldiers to burst out of the truck, guns firing. There were none. An eerie silence remained, broken by the occasional sniffing of someone crying. Stepping toward Chris, Perryn peered inside the truck.

Two families stared at them, squinting into the sunlight that poured into the dark trailer. A mother sat to the left, holding an infant. On the right, two children sat clutching their knees. One, a small girl, had tears streaking the dirt covering her face. Her sniffles were the lone noise that came from the truck.

The father of the infant rose to his knees and held his hand up to shade his eyes. "Please. We've done nothing wrong. What do you want with us?" He eyed Chris. More accurately, he eyed his dart pistol.

Perryn reached over and gently placed her hand on Chris's wrist, motioning him to lower his weapon. He did so, an expression of shock on his face. Maria stood frozen, her gum chewing noticeably stilled.

"Please. Don't harm my family." The man held his hand out in surrender as he pled again.

"Sir, it's okay," Perryn spoke softly. "You're safe now."

"What? What do you mean? Why are we stopped?" His eyes darted from her to Chris and back.

Perryn extended her free hand. "Really, you're fine."

"Team B, what's the status of the trailer?" Kane's voice sounded concerned.

"All clear, Chief. We have it under control." Perryn bit her lip at the lie. The situation wasn't out of control, but it wasn't exactly settled yet. She stepped toward the truck.

"Don't," the man said abruptly. "D-Don't come any closer."

She realized she was still holding her pistol, so she slowly knelt to place it on the ground. "Please, sir, we mean you no harm. We're here to help you." She stood, this time with both empty hands extended.

"Who are you?"

"We are the Liberated—the Underground."

"The rebels? What do you want with us? Don't hurt us."

It occurred to her that these people weren't Liberated. They simply had the unfortunate experience of having been recoded at some point. It wasn't unusual for wealthier families to use recoding to deal with more serious health issues. To them, they would see the Underground as the media portrayed them, ruthless rebels who killed people without warning. His concern suddenly made sense to her.

She held her hands wide to show him she was unarmed. "May I come closer?"

He glanced at her and back at Chris. "Just you. They need to stay there." He pointed to Chris and Maria.

She nodded at the two of them, and they holstered their weapons. Both retreated a single step. Slowly, she inched forward and tried to smile. She needed to convince them that she was not a threat.

"Sir, we mean you no harm. You and your family are free."

"How can I trust you? And who is the person on the radio? I can tell you're listening to someone in your earpiece." His voice rose, so she stopped moving forward scarcely a meter away.

"You have to trust me."

"Why? How can we? They're after recoded people, you know. Maybe you're after us too."

Perryn softened her tone to almost a whisper. "We're not. I promise."

"How can we know?"

"By this." She turned her head and pulled her hair to the side. Pulling at the lobe of her ear, she made sure the number ninety-six behind her ear was clearly visible to everyone on the truck.

"You—you were recoded?" he stammered.

"Ninety-six times." Her gut twisted at the reminder of how close she came to a recoding death. "Merely four away from not waking up."

The man sat down and rested his head on his knees. The woman with the infant reached a hand and placed it on his shoulder. The other family hadn't moved an inch.

"How long have you been on this truck?"

He searched their faces. "Since this morning, but we were held for days before that."

"Why?"

"Our daughter had a genetic defect when she was born," he confessed. "We had her recoded to correct it. Someone claiming to be our doctor called us in the middle of the night and said he had evidence that the genetic code would degrade and to come to the hospital immediately. We were arrested as soon as we stepped outside our home."

"Our story was similar." The woman from the other family finally spoke. "For us, it was our son. He'd been burned as a small child leaving him scarred. We had him recoded, as well."

"We made the connection as we were both held in a facility on the other side of the city," said the first man. "I've no idea where they are taking us."

Perryn let out a long breath. "To a place you can be glad you avoided."

The man slipped off the truck and helped his wife down, who was still clutching her baby. The other family followed. Standing in the street, they stared at the Underground soldiers who had begun to gather.

"Where do we go?" His eyes searched Perryn's face. "We can't return home." Perryn turned at Kane who had arrived to stand by her side.

"These men," Kane pointed to the two who had moved the vehicle earlier, "will get you to a safe house. There, you'll be greeted by some of our people who can help you."

"This way," one of the two spoke, waving his hand.

"Take them to Safehouse B."

"Yes, Chief."

The families gazed nervously at Perryn. "It's all right. You can trust them."

The two families followed, obviously stunned at the events. The mother with the baby suddenly turned toward Perryn and embraced her. "Thank you," she whispered. Perryn's lip trembled as she returned the embrace.

A minute later, they were gone.

"Well done, Perryn." Kane placed a hand on her shoulder. "Let's get this truck moving on to Solution Systems. We've spent too long here already."

Willis approached her as Kane stepped away. "You okay?" He touched her shoulder gently.

She threw her arms around his neck and allowed the tears to come. The intentions of the Coalition were becoming clear, and Solution Systems was far more than a prison for former Chase runners. "Children, Willis! They were going to experiment on children!" She sobbed without shame, and he held her. She could see Chris and Maria both had tear stains on their cheeks. Even Lydia was misty-eyed.

None of them had expected to find children.

She couldn't imagine what else they would find there.

Chapter Twenty-One

Willis steadied himself in the rear of the truck. Kane had urged them to get their minds on the mission, handing out backpacks to him and Perryn. Sitting to Willis's right, he gave instructions to everyone over the radio. Perryn sat across from him in the truck. As Chase runners, all three of them were too recognizable to sit in the cab of the truck. That job had been left to Lydia and Chris.

"Approaching Solution Systems building," Lydia said quietly in everyone's earpiece.

"Acknowledged." Kane held a finger to his ear to hear better. "Remember, the longest stop at the gate has been clocked at thirty-two seconds. Any longer than that means they are on to us." Willis could see Maria tense at Kane's instructions, perhaps realizing for the first time the plan might not work.

Finding the two families in the truck had shaken everyone. Perryn's tears had stopped barely a few minutes earlier. Willis tried to give her a smile, which she returned weakly.

He admired how she'd managed to gain the trust of the families they'd helped. They could have forced them from the vehicle, but that would have reinforced the image the media had portrayed. Because of Perryn, there was a chance those families might become part of the Liberated.

He valued her compassion. It was why Perryn was Perryn.

His thoughts were interrupted as the truck slowed with a hiss. The engine cut off. He could hear the muffled sounds of Lydia and a guard speaking, and then the expected silence arrived while the guard scanned her identification.

One…two…three… Willis counted in his head.

Everyone sat rigid, not wanting to make any sounds that might alert the other guard who was sweeping the underside of the vehicle. Kane was communicating through hand motions what they should do if the doors suddenly opened.

Fifteen...sixteen...seventeen...

The scenario had been planned out. If they were discovered, they were to avoid a firefight and make a break for the alley half a block away. Lydia and Chris would have little chance, but the four in the back might make it. He tightened his grip on this pistol.

Twenty-eight...twenty-nine...thirty...

Still no sound came from the truck cab. Perryn's eyes grew wide as she pointed to her wrist as if to say "too long" to the rest of them. No doubt, she'd been counting too. Kane slowly drew his pistol and pointed it toward the door. He crouched and raised the weapon.

Thirty-five...thirty-six...thirty-seven...

Willis was breathing heavily. Slipping from his spot against the wall, he silently moved to the center of the floor in a kneeling position facing the rear of the truck. He imagined the sound of the latch being thrown. Guessing where the torso of the first soldier would appear, he aimed his pistol.

Forty...forty-one...forty-two...

Maria chomped on her gum with fury and made a slashing sign at her throat. Kane waved off the request to abandon the mission and pointed at the door. Acknowledging the command, she aimed her pistol. Perryn did the same.

Fifty-two...fifty-three...fifty-four...

The truck roared to life and lurched as Lydia shifted the gears into drive. Willis reached out to the wall to steady himself. His eyes darted to everyone else to confirm they were standing down. Perryn sighed, expressing the relief they all felt.

"Report," Kane said calmly.

"Had to run the scan twice. We'll need to talk to Barney about the quality of his fake identification cards." Lydia sounded annoyed. Willis could almost hear her eyes roll as she spoke. "Approaching the building."

The truck tilted as they descended the ramp that led underneath the building. Willis felt it turn twice and pull to a stop, parking inside the building. The engine shuddered to a stop.

"Two guards approaching. Armed. Another one by the door leading inside. Stand by." Lydia whispered over the radio. The truck cab doors opened, and the bed moved slightly as Lydia and Chris hopped out.

"No need to get out. We got—" a muffled voice came, suddenly cut off. The familiar *phoot* sound of Lydia's dart pistol sounded as she took out the approaching guards. A second later, an almost imperceptible *phoot* could be heard as Chris took out the guard by the door.

"All clear," Lydia said. Willis couldn't believe how all-business she sounded. His insides lurched like they might leap out of him.

"Thank God," Maria said. "I want out of this cage."

Willis agreed.

A second later the door opened, revealing Lydia and Chris. Kane jumped out to assess the situation, while Willis allowed Perryn and Maria to exit first. Before leaping out, Perryn turned to him.

"Let's get your mother." She smiled. He could stare at the smile all day, and somehow, he believed everything would be all right. They were together, and they would soon be reunited with his mother.

"Three guards?" Maria questioned. "That's it?"

"You saw how fearful those families were," Lydia said. "Probably doesn't take more than a couple guns to herd them into the building. Besides, intelligence said Alliance offices are on rotation to loan out their Law-keepers to sustain policing the streets. We chose today because it's Solution Systems' day in the rotation."

"Still feels a little easy."

Sure does. Willis bit the inside of his cheek.

"We're in," Chris announced from the doorway. He dropped the arm of the unconscious guard whose fingerprint he'd used to open the door.

The five of them joined Chris and darted into the building.

Intel had informed them that the fourth floor was pulling a large amount of power indicating the presence of quite a bit of technology. It was a dead giveaway.

Kane ascended the stairs silently, pistol drawn. Stopping at the landing, he kept his eyes trained upward as Lydia moved ahead of them, mimicking his maneuver. Back and forth, they crisscrossed as they cleared each level. The team followed for three floors until Kane froze at the fourth. Motioning to Lydia with two fingers, he indicated the presence of two guards. Both of them crept up the stairs, keeping their backs to the wall to stay out of sight.

A nod from Kane signaled Lydia to step out to the other side of the landing. She tranquilized the first guard who dropped immediately. The second raised his weapon and stepped forward, right into the sights of Kane's pistol. He fell a moment later.

Chris darted up the steps and began working on the door lock, which required a key card he found on one of the fallen guards. The team gathered at the top of the steps, Willis and Kane moving the guards out of the way.

Click! The lock gave way, and Chris opened the door. Kane nodded, and Lydia burst through the door and to the right. Willis followed, fanning to the left. Perryn took a position beside him. Kane, Chris, and Maria took positions in both directions.

Nothing.

They'd expected soldiers. Or maybe scientists. Or a mix of both. All that greeted them was the echo of a vacant hallway. Fluorescent lights cast a pale glow that reflected off the white linoleum. The dull mechanical roar of ventilation and the soft buzz of the lighting were the lone sounds. Metal doors with electronic locks lined either side, each with light emerging from a small square window.

"I don't get it." Chris straightened.

"Maybe we caught them totally off guard?" Maria raised an eyebrow and lowered her weapon.

"Not exactly." Kane sounded unnerved. He raised a finger to the wall in front of them. The faint mechanical sound of the lens could be heard as the security camera focused on them.

Click! As if on command, the door from which they'd entered into the hallway locked behind them.

"I don't think we should have—" Lydia started to speak. Her voice was cut off by the alarm.

Sheila stood in the corner of Penny's massive new office. Penny had traded her desk for one even larger and placed it diagonally in front of the corner office view she was enjoying. Sheila imagined that Penny saw herself as peering out over her appointed kingdom and being pleased with herself. Disgusted at the visual, Sheila had to remind herself why she chose to be here.

The operation to invade Solution Systems and rescue Brenda was underway, and Sheila hoped to keep an eye on what was happening. If the Underground members were discovered, Penny would be the first to know. Even so, Sheila couldn't stand to stay in her office wondering what was happening. She longed to be where the action was. She took a deep breath, relieved the phone had hardly rung all morning except for a few late congratulatory calls from dignitaries around the world.

"Sweetheart, you need not stand here all day." Despite her words, Penny didn't appear to mind the attention.

"I wished to witness your first days in office as Deputy Chairwoman to be able to accurately inform the public of your hard work on their behalf." Sheila swallowed hard on the lie. She'd come up with a reason for her presence, but upon hearing it aloud, she worried that it was too over-the-top. She wouldn't buy it if she were in Penny's position.

Penny sat straighter and made a mousey squeak of approval. She obviously liked the extra publicity. "Very well. I love my people. I love my Coalition. It's good for them to know." Sheila half expected her to add, "I love the chairman," as her infatuation was getting increasingly obvious. Pulling out a file of papers, Penny started reading them intently. Sheila laughed inside at the obvious show put on for her benefit.

It was going to be a boring day in the office of the Deputy Chairwoman. At least, she hoped it would be boring.

Sheila started at the sound of Penny's phone ringing. Penny glanced up from her laptop, which she'd pulled out after running out of other ways to appear busy. Reaching for the phone, she smiled. "I wonder who's calling to congratulate me this time? The list keeps growing."

Sheila watched as Penny picked up the phone, using her free hand to fix her hair as if the other person could see her.

"Western Alliance Deputy Chair, how may I serve you today?" Penny's voice was as exaggerated as her perfume was pungent.

Something about the tone of the voice on the line held Sheila's attention. Far too intense, she realized instantly it wasn't another congratulatory call. Her fears were confirmed as she watched Penny's face dissolve from enthusiasm to shock to anger.

"Infiltrated?" she blurted. "How many?"

More hurried sentences from the intense voice.

"I don't want to hear the word 'understaffed' from you. All departments have soldiers patrolling the streets!" she screamed into the receiver. "No excuses. You find the necessary Law-keepers."

The voice on the phone sounded apologetic.

"Yes, shoot-to-kill! We need one for questioning, but the rest are expendable." Penny slammed the phone on the desk, red-faced. One of her bracelets, broken in the outburst, clattered across the surface and fell to the floor. Veins popped out of her neck, and she stood panting. Giving Sheila a wild-eyed glare, she spat her words. "You want to see how I operate from this office? Take notes. You're about to see what real authority looks like."

Spending the morning with Penny was starting to look like a grave mistake.

"She's not here either." Chris shouted over the alarm, stepping out of one of the many doors in the hallway.

"Keep searching." Kane barked his orders, sounding desperate to get the mission moving so they could escape. With a single hand, he ripped the code panel by the stairway door off the wall. Sparks flew, followed by a puff of smoke. "That should slow them down. You can bet they're already recalling Law-keepers to this building."

Frantically, Willis ran from window to window to identify who was inside each room along the hallway. The occupants in each one were all sedated. While some could be ruled out in seconds, the faces of others were sometimes obscured by equipment blocking the view. These doors had to be broken into by Chris, which required maddening seconds while he overcame the electronic lock. He ran to the next door to find Perryn frozen. He peeked over her shoulder. Inside, a small girl lay unconscious in the hospital-type bed. Several machines were connected to her, showing her vital signs. The singular tone from one indicated her heart had stopped. She was dead.

"Willis, what have they done to her?" Her chin quivered. "How can they experiment on children?"

"Because they have no soul, that's why." He sighed deeply to avoid breaking down.

"Keep moving." Kane passed them. "There's nothing we can do for her."

Perryn nodded and blinked back the flood of emotion as she moved on. Willis took one more glance at the girl. How could Kane stay so focused in the face of the grotesque reality of this place? They were nearing the end of the hallway, and so far there was no sign of his mother.

"Not here." Lydia stepped back from a window.

"Not here either," Maria echoed.

That left the double doors at the end of the hallway. Chris had already started working on the lock. The rest gathered behind him, shifting nervously as they waited.

"Doesn't get any faster if you watch." Chris sounded annoyed, but Willis grasped he must be as stressed as the rest of them.

Click! Whirr! The lock gave way, and the doors parted in either direction.

Willis had to choke back the vomit as he viewed the gruesome sight inside. Perryn covered her mouth. Three individuals stood over a table. They were dressed like doctors, but the space made Willis question whether they were. A young, fit female lay on the table, her face behind one of the doctors. To the right, their previous work lay on two other tables. The two corpses were laid out and covered partially with a sheet, an adult male and a teenage female. They were stitched crudely, having apparently undergone an autopsy. Blood and tissue in containers could be seen nearby. The doctors were ready to undertake the same procedure given the tools Willis could see on a tray next to one of them.

"You can't be in here," one of them said indignantly. "This is important scientific research, and time is of the essence."

"What's the rush?" Chris didn't hide his disgust. "They're dead, aren't they?"

That's when Willis noticed the difference between this table and the other two. The others were simply open tables on which one might expect an autopsy. This one, however, was surrounded by machines like those in the hallway rooms. Staring at the screen on one, Willis's breath caught at what he saw—the familiar blip of a heartbeat.

"Willis?" Perryn gasped. "She's still—"

"Alive." He confirmed her unfinished sentence. Glancing over at the others, it was clear they saw it too.

One of the doctors stepped forward with his hands up, a scalpel in one of them. "Please, we understand how this appears, but an important scientific breakthrough has been made, and we must understand it better. Countless lives could be—" His voice cut off as a dart suddenly appeared in his neck. Kane had shut him up with his pistol. Lydia and Maria took the cue and dropped the other two doctors a second later.

Kane spat on the floor. "Disgusting filth," he muttered. He motioned to the three doors on each of the walls, directing the group to check them out in pairs. Willis stood, his muscles feeling like they were made of stone. He stared at the table previously surrounded by doctors.

"Oh dear God." Perryn's breath shuddered.

The girl's jet-black hair had been cropped short, but her fierce features were unmistakable. The muscular tone of her body betrayed the strength and speed of which they were capable. Willis could almost imagine her dark eyes opening and glaring at him with their penetrating stare. Last time he'd peered into those eyes, they'd meant to kill him.

It was Jez.

Chapter Twenty-Two

"This isn't possible." Perryn grabbed the side of the operating table as she, Willis, and Kane stood over Jez's unconscious form, mesmerized. Chris, Lydia, and Maria furiously worked on breaking into the other three doors. The alarms blared in the hallway still, but there had been no sign of Law-keepers yet. Jez lay serene in this state, and her face showed neither the calculated hatred she showed on the station nor the terror she expressed as she'd been hauled off to her one-hundredth genetic recoding. "She's supposed to be dead. No one survives after their ninety-ninth."

"What did the doctor say—a scientific breakthrough?" Willis said. "I guess they finally broke the one-hundred barrier."

Then why cut her open?

"Guess they weren't quite sure how they did it." Willis spoke as if reading her thoughts. He folded Jez's ear over, revealing the number 103. "She survived past 100, and they needed to compare her to those two over there."

Kane walked to the table to peek behind the ears of the other two. He nodded, indicating they both had a one-hundred tattooed on their skin. Chris cursed in the corner as his door revealed a storage closet.

Perryn studied Willis's face, and she could tell he was caught. His eyes shifted back and forth, and his mouth moved. He was speaking to himself. It was an expression she'd seen many times on the station when he sat in the recreation area to work out a training obstacle that was baffling him. She sucked in a breath when it occurred to her what he was thinking.

"Willis. She tried to kill you." She whispered the words, not wanting the others to hear. To her dismay, he raised his hand waving her off—or shutting her up. "You can't be seriously thinking—"

"She was desperate," he said. "She tried to kill me because she was afraid of losing, not because she hated me."

Perryn stood quiet. He was probably right, but this was a distraction. *This isn't why we came. Then again, how could we have expected to find anyone familiar other than his mother here?* Glancing over at Kane, he responded with a nod that said, "If you can't talk him down, none of us can." She placed her hands on the table and leaned in toward Willis.

"You're thinking of taking her with us, aren't you?" She spoke slowly, knowing the answer.

He looked up at her, ending his discussion with himself. "Yes," he said matter-of-factly.

"She's here!" Lydia's shout interrupted their conversation. She was standing in the newly open third door.

Willis and Perryn ran over. Inside they found another hospital bed on which Brenda Thomson lay. The bruises on her face they had seen on television had healed, but her sunken, malnourished cheeks told them all they needed to know about her treatment here. A dozen machines were connected to her, and Perryn could hear Willis's sigh of relief when he noticed the active heartbeat. Lydia pushed forward and proceeded to unhook the various IVs and tubes.

"Thank God she's alive," Perryn whispered. She reached over to grab Willis's hand. He responded with a loose, absent-minded grip. She could read the distraction all over him. Here he was, in the throes of saving his mother, and he was undoubtedly thinking about Jez.

"We came for your mother, Willis." Perryn leaned in close to him. "There she is."

"I know." He nodded. "But Jez was my teammate. We were friends. I can't—" His voice trailed off.

Compassion rose in her throat, and she had to swallow to compose herself. She'd grown to hate the memory of Jez, who had tried to kill the one she loved, but she could see it from his viewpoint. Even in her state of losing on the Blue Team, she appreciated the bonds that were created on the station. Jez had been a big part of Red Team's success, and she was part of the reason Willis had never experienced recoding on the station.

"Captain, when will she be ready to move?" Kane's voice boomed as he entered.

"I'll have her unhooked in ten seconds, Chief." Lydia's hands flew over the various tubes. "You'll need to carry her, though, she won't be conscious for hours."

"They're here!" Maria cried out. "They're cutting the lock on the hallway door."

Perryn rushed out to see with Willis on her heels, and she could see the sparks of the torch cutting through the door lock in the hallway. The Law-keepers had arrived.

"Willis, I don't know the right thing to do." Perryn's voice caught in a cry.

"I—I—" He stammered. He clutched his hair with both hands. There was no time to argue with him. There was no time to embrace him. She was lost as to what to say.

Kane emerged from the doorway, Brenda over one shoulder. He stopped at the table and stared at Willis.

"So?" Maria's eyes searched theirs. "Are we leaving or what?"

"Your choice, Boss." Kane gestured at Willis with his chin. "I may be Chief, but you're still Red Team Leader."

Willis made his choice. "She's coming."

Did I truly decide that? Willis immediately questioned the decision. He glanced at Perryn in time to see her jaw clench and her eyes drop. *Oh, God, what is the right choice?*

"Are you sure, Willis?" Perryn touched his arm.

"We all saw what they were about to do to her. No matter what she tried to do to me, we can't leave her to that." The words sounded right, but they were more to convince himself than them.

"Better hurry, then." Lydia began to rip IVs from Jez.

"You get what we came for?" Kane pointed at Chris.

He wiggled a disc in his hands. "Managed to download a ton of encrypted files from the computer in this lab, but this smash-and-grab mission has gone on way too long. Any idea how we're going to get out of here?" Chris sounded desperate.

"Is there another way besides the stairs?" Maria's voice shook as she glanced at the increasing sparks at the end of the hallway.

"Finished!" Lydia announced she'd completed her work on Jez. In a surprising show of strength, she picked up Jez in both arms. "It can't be more than a few soldiers out there with most of them off-site. If we can get behind them—"

Kane perked up at Lydia's words and interrupted. "Follow me." Brenda still draped over his shoulder, he dragged the unconscious form of one of the doctors and laid him down in the way of the lab door. Leading the team, he ran back down the hallway and opened the cell closest to the stairs. They gathered inside around the seemingly lifeless occupant and out of sight of the window.

Willis let out an anxious sigh. It was a risky move. If the soldiers took the bait of the unconscious doctor lying down the hall, they might be able to sneak out behind them. If they decided to search every space first, they would be cornered.

Clang!

The stairway locking mechanism fell to the floor, cut out by the torch. The door burst open, and several pairs of feet hurriedly slapped the floor as they filled the hallway.

"Over there! End of the hallway!" shouted one Law-keeper.

To their relief, most of the feet moved in that direction. Kane slowly put Brenda down. He motioned to Maria to open the door and for Chris to dash for the stairway door. A three-count on his fingers gave the signal.

Maria threw open the door, and Kane and Chris dashed out in the hallway. The single guard left at the stairwell had no time to react before Kane's massive form was upon him. His huge hand covered the guard's mouth, while his free hand shot a tranquilizer point-blank into his neck. The Law-keeper slumped, and Kane dragged him into the stairwell that Chris had opened.

The kicking open of doors could be heard in the autopsy room, and the team rushed into the stairwell. Retrieving Brenda from where he'd set her down, Kane appeared like a charging bull ready to crush anyone in his way, his nostrils flaring with near rage as he led his team out of the building.

Four flights of stairs later, they burst into the garage, dart guns pointing in all directions. No one.

"Come on," Lydia shouted as she ran. They dashed for the truck, and Lydia threw Jez into the truck bed on her way to the drivers' seat. Firing the engine, she didn't wait to begin moving as the team helped each other climb aboard.

"We're in!" Kane yelled, pounding on the inside wall of the truck. He aimed his dart pistol out the open rear of the trailer.

Lydia floored the pedal, and the truck accelerated, the powerful throttle sounding ferociously loud in the garage. Lydia aimed for the garage door.

Rattattatt! The sound of semi-automatic weapons' fire pierced the air amid the otherwise deafening roar of the truck engine. Holes from the bullets appeared in the side of the truck.

"Get down!" Kane bellowed, and threw himself over Brenda. Willis joined Chris to cover Jez.

"Brace yourselves!" Lydia screamed over the radio.

The truck struck the garage door with a crunch of scraping metal, and the momentary drop in speed threw the seven in the bed of the truck forward. Willis's head smacked the wall as they crashed into a heap at the front of the trailer. The truck jolted upward throwing them about the trailer until the remnants of the garage door flew out behind the truck. Again, they accelerated and had to grab what they could of the wall to prevent sliding out the back.

Lydia's barely audible voice called again. "One more."

The truck lurched again as this time it struck the much flimsier entry gate. Glancing out the open trailer, Willis saw the two guards fall to the ground as they dove to get out of the way. Immediately, both were on their feet and firing their pistols. One bullet sparked off the metal of the trailer opening, but otherwise none found their mark.

Once able to maintain a consistent speed, the team sat up. Willis reached to feel the bump forming on his scalp and shook his head to clear his vision. The five of them sat, backs to the truck walls, sweating and panting. Kane instructed Lydia over the radio, but Willis ignored it. With both arms, he cradled Jez's shoulders. Her body lay limp in front of him.

Looking across the truck, he noticed Perryn watching him. She was supporting his mother's body. He tried to interpret her expression. Her eyes were turned downward and bathed with an expression of mixed fear and sorrow.

He guessed what she must be thinking. This was not the plan. His mother was supposed to be the one rescued. Yet, he couldn't imagine choosing to leave Jez to the horrors of that butcher shop. Here he sat, holding the one who had tried to kill him, while the woman he loved cared for his rescued mother. He increasingly saw how backward it all played out.

We had to make this choice. It was all Willis could think as they sped away.

Chapter Twenty-Three

Sheila scanned around her office and rehearsed the list to herself. *Laptop, phone, bag. Laptop, phone, bag.* They were the essential items she couldn't abandon if she needed to leave in a hurry. She gathered them in her hands. Pausing, she stared at her office door, nervous to face what was on the other side.

Penny had thundered orders in her office, barking into her phone. Updates came every few minutes, and a handful of Law-keepers had been gathered to invade the fourth floor of Solution Systems. Penny hissed at the news that a keycard couldn't be found for the stairway door, and she'd screamed while the soldiers pursued the Underground down the stairs. It was when the news came that they escaped with two 'patients,' however, that her transformation from artificial optimist to full rage-monster was complete. She'd thrown the phone with a force strong enough that it shattered on the wall right next to Sheila. Sheila had left quickly after she'd overturned her desk.

Picking up her phone, Sheila dialed.

"Raymond, I think I'm going to need the car." Her hands shook as she spoke, and she tried not to sound panicked.

"Everything okay, Kemp?" Raymond breathed hard into the phone, seeing right through her words. His voice was one of genuine concern mixed with anger over whatever or whomever had upset her.

She choked with emotion, unable to hide her fear. "Not exactly."

"Returning now. Front door. Two minutes." He sounded serious.

She placed the phone in her pocket and peered around one more time. She had to get out of here. The more time she wasted, the more likely Penny would insist she return. Opening the office door, she glanced around. People moved about at a normal pace, oblivious to what was secretly happening across town. She slipped into the hallway and walked toward the elevator.

Slow down, Kemp. Don't appear upset. Her pulse was racing, and she would much rather have been running. Reaching the elevator, she waited an excruciating minute before the doors opened. She stepped in and pushed the lobby button repeatedly, willing the doors to close, preventing anyone else stepping aboard. She allowed herself a long sigh when the doors finally closed.

Ding. Ding. Ding. The floors chimed as she descended to the lobby level. Stepping out, she hurriedly walked toward the door longing to get in the car and be safely away from here. She stopped in her tracks when she saw the entrance.

Penny stood there.

She was once again composed, standing with her hands gracefully folded in front of her. She didn't move as Sheila approached.

"Dearie, where are you off to in such a hurry?" Penny's sickeningly sweet tone nauseated Sheila. How Penny could be smiling so convincingly after her display upstairs, Sheila was left to wonder.

"I—I—planned to interview the Law-keepers involved in the incident to get their perspective for the report I'm writing about this morning." Sheila's voice shook. She stood less than a meter from Penny and tried to appear natural. Inside, her heart pounded against her rib cage.

Penny's smile disappeared. "Report? Oh, there will be no report of this morning. None except the one you will give the chairman, who wants to see you—promptly."

"The chairman?" Sheila gulped.

"Yes, sweetheart. You see, only a few people were present at the meeting where I presented Operation Rebirth, and—" Penny laughed mockingly. "Somehow the rebels learned exactly where to strike this morning. Tragically, they made off with one of the greatest resources in the Coalition's possession." Penny paused and tilted her head as if to watch the effect of her words.

"Oh." Sheila scrambled for something to say. "Can I give this file to my driver and ask him to deliver it for me?" She pulled a meaningless file from her bag.

Penny raised an eyebrow. "You said you were going to interview Law-keepers."

"I was—am—I was going to deliver this on the way."

"I'll take that." Penny snatched the file, her jaw flexing. She opened it and searched through its contents. "The chairman asks that you grace him with your perspective on who might be the vile traitor. After all, we all know how good you are at—*watching.*" Penny stared at her.

Sheila's eyes widened at the last word. An eternal few seconds passed as both of them stood frozen in place. Penny's eyes briefly glanced away to something behind Sheila, and Sheila could feel the quiet approach of Law-keepers behind her. She reminded herself that they would want her alive. They'd want to question her. And that—gave her the upper hand. Confident they would hesitate before drawing their weapons, she tensed at the ready.

"Honestly, I think—" Sheila began. She never intended to finish. Balling her fist, she brought it upward, knocking the file from Penny's hands and connecting squarely with her chin. The stunned Penny fell backward in a heap of rumpled pink blazer and chattering bracelets. For a split second, she marveled at how much of a thrill it was to give Penny what she deserved.

"Freeze!" a Law-keeper shouted behind her, but Sheila was already at the door. She bolted through the door and whispered a prayer of thanks for the bullet-proof glass standard on all Alliance structures as they closed behind her.

"Drive, Raymond! Drive!" she screamed, running for the waiting car. He was already behind the wheel, the back door sitting open. She dove for the seat, headfirst. The second she landed on the leather seat, the tires squealed as the car lurched forward. The movement of the car slammed the door shut.

Glass shattered everywhere, and she realized the guards had emerged and opened fire. She covered her head with her hands and prayed. Seconds later, the vehicle turned a corner, and the gunfire stopped.

Slowly, she sat up, the beads of safety glass crunching under her feet. Raymond zigzagged through the streets, putting as much distance between them and the Coalition headquarters as possible.

She breathed deeply, trying to slow her heartbeat. She allowed a single uncontrolled sob and choked back any further tears. Lifting one leg, she crawled over the front headrest and flopped down in the passenger seat next to Raymond.

"Where are you taking us? We can't stay in this car. Any idea where we can hide?" Sheila's hands were still shaking. She tried to figure out which road they were on.

When he didn't answer, she turned to him. His eyes were wide and fixed on the road in front of him. Beads of sweat covered his forehead and dripped off his jaw. He drove the car expertly through traffic, but she could see a tremble in his chin. That's when she noticed the blood soaking into his shirt.

"Raymond! You're hurt."

She reached for his jacket to examine the wound, but he pushed her hand away. She tried again, but he shook his head. Sitting back, she stared at him fearfully. He coughed twice, momentarily taking his eyes off the road. Catching himself, he sucked in and straightened. His face grimaced with each bump and jolt of the car.

A minute and a couple of turns later, they turned quickly into an alley and barreled down the tight passage. Suddenly, Raymond slammed the brakes, and the car screeched to a halt. It was then that Raymond released the wheel and started to shake.

"Raymond! We need to get you to a hospital," she cried. Her breaths quickened, and her head grew fuzzy from the panic rising in her chest.

Outside the car, a plain metal door opened into the alley. Father Anthony stepped into the alley, a worried expression on his face. Seeing the car, he rushed to the driver's side door and opened it carefully. Terror filled his eyes as he realized what had happened.

"Oh, my precious son," he whispered. Then he nodded at Sheila. "Please assist me."

Jumping from the car, she ran around the rear of the car. She and Father Anthony each took a shoulder and pulled Raymond from the car as gently as they could. They dragged his huge form inside.

"Sister Josephine. Quickly!" Father Anthony called out.

A young woman in a white nurse's uniform appeared from a doorway and ran toward them. Seeing Raymond's injury, she didn't speak. She joined in helping move him into the room she'd emerged from. Laying him on the bed, she stared at Sheila and Father Anthony.

"Father, I need you to assist. Ma'am, are you injured?"

"N—no." Sheila stammered and scanned around confused.

Sister Josephine placed a hand on her shoulder and urged her toward the doorway. "Then, I need you outside, so I can focus on him. Got it? I'll do what I can."

Sheila slowly stepped backward through the door. Her back hitting the wall across the hall, she slid down to a seated position. Father Anthony gave her a worried frown as he slowly closed the door.

The tears came in a flood. She shook violently. Sliding sideways, she didn't care when her face hit the gritty floor. Her legs curled into a fetal ball. Her gut wrenched, and she cried like a lost child.

Chapter Twenty-Four

"I told you I would not lose," Jez said. Willis could see her standing in front of him in the passage, brandishing the dinner knife. The expression of pure hatred mixed with cool calculation terrified him.

She was going to kill him. He would die in the passageway of the station track. Jaden would be accused. Jez would travel to the Chase. Perryn would be lost to recoding.

The hand with the knife jabbed forward, and he threw his hands out to defend himself.

Willis jolted awake, nearly falling from his cot in the barracks. One hand covered his face in defense of Jez's blow as his instincts blurred the line between dream and consciousness. The other hand gripped the edge of the cot preventing him from face-planting into the concrete below him. The memory of Jez on the station still played in his mind, and his stomach churned when he considered how close he'd come to being murdered by someone he once considered a teammate—perhaps even a friend.

Returning to the Underground hideout, Kane had suggested they rest for the night before discussing the mission. Tired and emotionally spent, none of them had argued. Lydia saw to keeping Jez sedated, so they could sleep before deciding how to awaken her. His mother had been taken to the women's barracks to be placed on a cot near Perryn in case she awoke. Waking to a familiar face, they believed, would ease the surprise of her changed surroundings.

Willis replayed the events of the mission over and over in his head. *Had he done the right thing?* He wasn't sure. A hurried choice had to be made, and they were fortunate to have escaped mostly unscathed despite the change in plans.

I endangered the entire group—for Jez. He shook his head unable to process what he'd done. He placed his head in his hands and tried to sort it out.

"Psst. Hey, Willis. You up?" Chris whispered from nearby. Willis grabbed his shoes and snuck across the room, trying not to awaken others still sleeping, to Chris who was propped up on one elbow in his cot.

"Yeah. Trying to make sense of it all," he said.

"Yeah." Chris spoke louder this time. "You made it interesting. Can't say it helped the mission, but I won't argue about getting another person out of that butcher shop alive."

If he knew that person and what she'd done, he might think differently. He slipped on his shoes. He motioned to see if Chris would join him.

"I need five more minutes." Chris rubbed his eyes. "I'm exhausted."

Willis nodded and found he was relieved. There was one person he needed to see, and it would be far more comfortable without Chris. He picked up the pace once he made it to the hallway, finally turning into the mess hall where they'd agreed to meet that morning. The area was empty except for a single table on the far side. A huddle of women sat at a table talking to his mother. She'd been provided an Underground uniform, but her blonde hair and features were unmistakable.

"So, what *we* want to know, Mrs. Thomson, is whether you are aware that your Willie-boy has the hots for my girl, Perryn, here?" Maria joked loudly. Her comment was met with a roar of laughter, and Willis could feel his face blush. He halted his approach when he heard the conversation.

"Maria, shush!" Perryn scolded her while laughing. "Give her a break. She woke a half hour ago."

"Speak of the devil," said another girl. The entire table stared at Willis. He was transported back to being a preteen boy entering the Lake Placid Training Center cafeteria for the first time after everyone was seated, socially awkward and wanting to make a quick exit.

Maria scanned the faces around the table and was first to speak. "Hey, ladies. Let's chill somewhere else. Let the pretty boy say hello to his mama."

The table emptied—their laughter echoed as they entered the passage to the women's barracks. Perryn and Brenda, who were left standing by the table, remained. Willis took a couple of slow steps before abandoning appearance and running across the space. Brenda opened her arms to him, and the two embraced. Perryn stood a respectful distance, unable to hide the smile that started slowly at the corners of her mouth and spread into a full grin.

Stepping backward, a flood of emotion rose in Willis's throat. "Mom, I'm so sorry about the way I spoke to you that night." He blurted the words quickly. "I never should have said what I did. It was wrong. I needed to make it right. I was on my way to talk to you and Dad, when—when—" His voice caught, and his eyes found the floor.

Brenda stepped forward and gently lifted his chin with her hands. "Oh, my son. Don't do that to yourself."

"But I—I'll never get to—Dad." His incomplete thoughts came between choked sobs. His mom stepped forward and wrapped her arms around him. The two cried together, mourning Max's death as a family for the first time. Several long minutes passed. Finally, they separated and wiped their eyes.

Willis glanced over at Perryn who had been crying herself, and she smiled compassionately. He exhaled as though something gnawing at his insides had finally been released.

"Willis, I can't imagine what you've endured." As his mom followed his gaze to Perryn, she continued. "And I'm so thankful you weren't alone. Perryn, dear, you're a gift to my son." She extended her arms toward Perryn, and the two hugged through tears and smiles.

His mother laughed a little, still hugging Perryn, and gazed at Willis. "So please tell me that nothing official has taken place with this one in my absence. I missed enough of your milestones, and I refuse to miss that one."

"Mom." Willis's face warmed again.

"In truth," Perryn pulled away from her, "every time we start to talk about it, something happens to keep us from getting to that conversation."

The three stood awkwardly in silence, staring.

"Oh my word, you two," his mom said, exasperation tinging her tone. She shook her head while rolling her eyes at the ceiling. "Seriously, Willis. You're so much like your father. Even after the Alliance forced us into a public relationship, it took him a long time to work up the nerve to inform me he'd developed actual feelings for me."

Willis couldn't imagine his father being afraid to do anything, and he let out an embarrassed laugh. His heart fluttered with sadness at the mention of his dad.

"Maybe, we should talk." He gazed at Perryn shyly.

"Yeah, maybe we should," Perryn said, unsuccessfully trying to contain a smile.

"You should talk." Lydia's voice came from behind, startling the three of them. "For all our sakes, you guys need to get it out in the open, but not until later. Chief wants the team and Brenda to meet since we're all up. I'll brief you on the way."

His mother sighed. She pointed a finger at Willis. "But when something is finally decided, I'm first to know. Promise?"

"Promise." He nodded.

"Perryn?"

"Promise." She echoed his response, no longer containing her smile.

"All right, Captain— er—Lydia—er—whatever I should call you." Brenda turned to Lydia laughing. "Please lead the way." She wrapped one arm each around Willis and Perryn, and the three followed Lydia toward Kane's office.

Perryn breathed deeply as they approached the door to Kane's office. The open door revealed a somber Maria sitting next to Chris. Kane leaned forward, his elbows resting on the desk with his hands folded up under his chin. He glanced down as if lost in thought. He'd called all the mission team members together to discuss what they should do about Jez and how they should handle speaking to the rest of the Underground. Rumors were already circulating about the 'extra' person they'd brought home, and Kane planned to make an official announcement before the gossip got out of hand.

Perryn sat next to Willis and held his hand. Brenda, who had been invited since she was the most valuable source of information about life at Solution Systems, sat on Willis's other side. Lydia joined Maria and Chris.

There would be a lot of criticism about the choice Willis had made, and Perryn swore that he would not stand alone in the group. It didn't matter how she felt about it. She'd defend Willis's choice.

The seven sat in silence for a moment. Maria was the first to break the silence.

"Fine. I'll ask it." She sounded annoyed. "Who's the tagalong? And why did the whole mission change for her?"

"Watch your tone, soldier." Lydia placed a firm hand on Maria's shoulder.

"Captain," Kane said, "it's okay. We're all a little raw after yesterday."

"I don't understand." Maria spoke again, throwing her arms out in frustration. "All that, 'Brenda Thomson will be the one extracted,' goes out the window when we find this girl on the table. It's obvious you all know her, but what if we'd found someone I recognized—or Chris—or—?"

"Maria, chill. We saved another life, and I think we should be happy about that." Chris may not have had the same reasons for doing so, but Perryn appreciated his support.

"I *am* happy." Maria pounded her fists on her legs. "But I still don't get it. Chief, you're always telling us that focus on the mission matters."

Chris waved a hand at Kane. "The Chief can make that call if he wants to."

"But that's my point." Maria's voice raised. She leaned

forward and appeared ready to rise from her chair. "He *didn't* make the call. Willie-boy did." She pointed at Willis, who hung his head. Perryn could tell he was still conflicted about what his choice had done to the Underground. "Why?" Maria said. "That's all I want to know. The whole thing bothers me. And it bothers my girl over there too." This time, she extended a finger toward Perryn.

Perryn's mouth went dry as every eye in the circle studied her, including Willis who turned his head to watch her response. Heat rushed to her face. She didn't expect her feelings to be spoken so openly—so soon, and she felt exposed.

"I—I don't know how I—" Perryn stuttered, unable to come up with an adequate explanation.

Maria huffed. "Oh, come on, girl. You telling me all that talk in that butcher shop wasn't you worried about taking mystery girl with us?"

Perryn opened her mouth to speak, but a hand squeezed her knee.

Brenda leaned forward and opened her mouth to speak. "Maria, your question makes sense," Brenda said. Her voice was soft and motherly. The tension in the room quieted as everyone collectively deferred to Brenda. After all, she'd endured the horrors of Solution Systems. "If I were you, I would feel the same way. The girl you saved is a fellow Chase trainee from the station. She and Willis spent many seasons together training, and that creates a bond."

"A bond?" Maria raised a questioning eyebrow and glanced over at Perryn. Perryn stared, feeling caught between Willis and her new friend.

"Yes." Brenda nodded. "Life on the station is incredibly lonely. Every day is the same and focused on one goal—win the Chase. Like soldiers in battle, you bond with those you know are fighting beside you toward that goal. It's not that much different from how you feel about those amazing girls at the table out there." Brenda tilted her head in the direction of the cafeteria.

Maria shrugged, conceding the point. Perryn admired that Brenda had a way of being motherly without talking down to someone, and Maria's edge was softening. For a minute, the group sat in silence, unsure where to take the conversation. Perryn needed to say something—anything. She was about to explain more about Jez's role on Willis's training team, when she heard Willis breathe in suddenly. Turning to him, she saw his hands shaking as he spoke.

"I need to say something." His voice was raspy, and his lips trembled. "Before we decide what to do or say, you all need to know the truth."

You don't have to tell them, Willis. Her heart broke for him.

"My mother is right that there's an incredible bond between teammates on the station. Sometimes that bond is the one thing that keeps you sane under the pressure of the Chase. For a long time, Jez was my friend and teammate. We were going to win the Chase together, but our version of the world was what the Alliance led us to believe. Jaden, who you saw win the Chase, challenged that. He changed it. He changed me."

Willis paused and took a breath. Perryn squeezed his hand, and he returned the gesture, glancing at her.

"Jez hated that change. It scared her. She believed I had gone soft and lost focus. I was starting to see a bigger purpose for our Chase run, and she wished to survive and get off the station. So, she—she—" Willis's voice choked as he recounted the memory.

"So, she tried to kill you." Perryn whispered softly. She winced as she told his secret, but he'd been struggling to get it out. Willis nodded in resigned agreement. She could see Chris and Maria's widening eyes. Lydia crossed her arms and tightened her gaze. Willis breathed deeply to compose himself and nodded at Kane.

"Kane, I owe you my life. I still have nightmares of those moments on the track, but I get to wake every day and leave them as nightmares because of you. I'm not sure I ever properly said 'thank you.'" Kane kept his response to a single nod, respecting Willis's vulnerability. Willis turned to the others. "I guess I want all of you to know that we didn't save a friend of mine. We saved someone who betrayed me."

"Then why—?" Chris's voice cracked, and he leaned forward, resting his elbows on his knees.

"Why did I save her?" Willis's forehead creased as he raised both eyebrows. Chris nodded. "I don't know. All I know is that they were about to kill her. This time her life was in my hands, and I couldn't justify leaving her to that fate. She might have deserved it. Who knows? But the choice is made, and you deserve to know who it is we're talking about."

Chris sat back in his chair, stunned.

Resting her head in one hand, Maria sighed as if exhausted by the story.

Kane and Lydia remained unmoved.

Perryn scanned the circle. *Say something, Perryn.* They all appeared to be deciding what to think of Willis in this moment, and she needed to speak up for him.

"Listen," she said, "I'm not a fan of Jez." She nodded an affirmation to Maria, who returned the gesture. "That's no secret to Willis. But—he believes she acted out of fear and not hatred. No one in here knows what it's like to face your hundredth recoding as much as I do." She pointed to her ear. "Desperate people do desperate things."

"But would you *kill* to avoid your hundredth recoding?" Lydia asked the question slowly.

The question caught Perryn off-guard. Would she? She was not sure she would have. She considered all the ideas she'd had on the station, which included several plans of escape. No, she *wouldn't* have killed someone. Not daring to speak the words aloud because of what it might do to their view of Willis, her doubts about Willis's choice fought to surface. She must have hidden them poorly because Lydia answered her own question.

"Didn't think so." She pursed her lips.

Her gut wrenched. Here she was trying to support Willis, and she'd instead confirmed what the others were thinking. She squeezed Willis's hand again to affirm he wasn't alone, but he didn't return it this time.

"That's it. I've heard enough." Maria frowned, raising her hands. "I say we dump her somewhere topside and let her wake there."

"You can't do that," Chris said. "You might as well give her to the Coalition."

"No, she can't be allowed to leave," Lydia said. "She's an asset. Whatever purpose she served, it was important enough for them to study her. Until we know what Project Rebirth is about, we can't let her out of our sight. Chris, any luck with the disc you brought back with you?"

The group eyed Chris for an answer.

He shook his head. "I haven't been able to break the encryption on the files I took. I'll keep working on it."

"So how about keeping her sedated?" Maria suggested.

"No," Kane said. Perryn's insides jumped when he broke his silence.

"Why not, Chief?"

"Because we don't take life here. I won't allow the taking of a life if we have a choice. Keeping someone asleep might as well be killing them. People have a right to live free from the Law."

"And we'll never know what kind of person she is until she wakes," Brenda said. "If Willis is right, and she was simply afraid for her life, then she deserves the chance to show us who she is when she's no longer afraid."

Nods could be seen around the room, but Perryn could also see the conflict on their faces. They all believed the ideals Kane and Brenda spoke of, but those ideals were pushed to the limit by this decision.

"So, we're agreed?" Lydia eyed the others. "We let the girl

wake and see who she is?"

"Agreed," Chris said.

"I guess so." Maria shrugged.

Kane and Brenda nodded.

"I think it's right." Willis glanced up. He watched Perryn for her answer, as did the rest.

"Yeah. Let her wake up," she said after a long pause. She'd meant it to sound bold and convincing, but her voice cracked with emotion.

So help me, if she does anything to my new family... She allowed her thoughts to trail off as the rest discussed what to tell the Underground.

Chapter Twenty-Five

"Sister?" Audrey whispered hoarsely.

"I'm here, Audrey." Sheila reached out and gently took her sister's hand which lay limply on the edge of the hospital bed. Audrey had been asleep when she arrived, so Sheila had refused to leave the hospital room. Her back ached from the long night in the uncomfortable chair.

"I had the best dream."

"Really?"

"I opened my eyes to see my sister at my bedside, but she lives across the Alliance, so I know it's a dream." The corners of Audrey's mouth turned upward.

Sheila smiled weakly at her sister's shrunken face. Audrey's skin was pale, and her form was small. Her hand felt slight in Sheila's grip.

"You're not dreaming. I'm here, Audrey. The doctors called me and said you weren't doing well."

Audrey smiled with dry, cracked lips and let out a weak, breathy chuckle. "What do doctors know? I plan on living forever." She closed her eyes and took a long breath, gathering her strength to speak again. "You're not in trouble with your boss for being out here, are you?"

"No. Chuck likes everyone to think he's hard-headed, but I know better. I told him I'd strike right before the Chase if he didn't let me come. He gave me the week off." Sheila smirked.

"I have you for a week?"

"Sure do. I leave straight from here to cover the Chase in the United African Cooperative."

"I guess I'll have to clear my calendar to accommodate my famous sister."

"You'd better."

The two exchanged grins for a few moments in silence. Sheila changed the subject before she chickened out.

"Sis, have the doctors spoken to you?" Sheila held Audrey's hand gently.

"Let me guess." Audrey's face lost its light. Her jaw flexed, and she labored a breath. "The outlook isn't good. The options are running out. Prepare for the worst."

"That sums it up, I guess." Sheila studied the floor.

Audrey grunted as she turned her body slightly toward her sister. The movement left her out of breath, and Sheila wished she'd lain still.

"Kemp, I want you to listen to me," Audrey said. "I'm not afraid to die. Not at all. And I don't want you to be afraid, either."

Sheila's eyes watered, and she sniffed to hold in her sobs.

"I've not had the opportunity to do much in this life, but I have you. I've watched you grow from that little girl with an eye for the world around her to the amazingly talented woman who sits in front of me. I'd like to think I gave you a helpful nudge or two over the years. If that's what my life was meant to be about, then it was worth it."

Sheila leaned forward and rested her head on her sister's hand. Despite its skeletal feel against her skin, it still smelled of Audrey's favorite hand cream. She breathed deeply, and her body trembled with heartbreak.

Sheila lay awake on the tiny cot Father Anthony had directed her to after he'd spent a long time with Raymond and Sister Josephine. The car had been disposed of across the city by Father Anthony's assistant, and time would tell as to Raymond's condition. The Underground safehouse, which Father Anthony had explained was for any unfortunate person who was misplaced, was mostly empty except for two small families that'd been saved off a truck headed for Solution Systems the day prior. They mostly kept to themselves other than the quiet 'thank you' they offered each time Father Anthony provided them with a meal.

She'd peeked in on Raymond, who was unconscious, once or twice, but Sister Josephine had assured her she would get her if anything changed. Still, the cot brought little comfort, much less sleep. Her thoughts dwelt on her sister most of the night. More than once, she could hear the worried whispers of Father Anthony and Sister Josephine in the hallway.

"Ms. Kemp?" Sister Josephine whispered with a gentle knock on the door.

"I'm awake." She sat up. The sleeplessness of the night made her head feel heavy.

Sister Josephine slipped in the door and stood with her hands folded in front of her. "I'm afraid I have some bad news."

Sheila covered her mouth to control the trembling.

"Your friend isn't recovering from his wounds. The Underground keeps us well supplied with medical equipment here, but I'm afraid I'm not a surgeon. I'm not even certain a surgeon could have repaired the damage, which was extensive. I'm so very sorry."

Sheila shook, the lump in her throat growing with her emotion. "Can I see him?"

Sister Josephine offered a sympathetic smile. "That's why I've come. He's awake and wants to see you."

Sheila gathered herself and stood immediately to make her way to the door, Sister Josephine at her side. They approached the door in time to see Father Anthony exiting, his eyes red with tears. He sighed when he noticed them.

"My son wished to offer a final confession," he said, noticing their approach. "That included a confession of who you are, my daughter. You've risked much for the Liberated as the Watcher. You're welcome to stay here as long as you need to. The Coalition has yet to find this safehouse."

"Thank you, Father, but my presence endangers what you're doing here," She placed a hand on his shoulder. "I'll need to leave soon for your sake."

"Very well. Do what you feel is right, but our friend is eager to see you."

Both of them stood back to allow Sheila to enter alone. She grasped the handle and turned it. The metal door was surprisingly quiet when she opened it, but she still used one hand to close it gently behind her.

Raymond lay on the bed in front of her. Fresh bandages covered his shirtless torso, and a monitor beeped nearby. Fluids were being delivered intravenously. He peered up at her and smiled.

"Kemp, thank you for coming to see me." He offered a rare smile.

"I'm so sorry this happened, Raymond." She approached the bed. "I shouldn't have involved you—"

He raised a hand slowly to stop her.

"I asked them to get you, so I could tell you something." He coughed, grimacing as he did so. Sheila took a seat in the chair next to the bed. "Most of my life hasn't amounted to much. Living on the streets, I took whatever I could to survive. Father Anthony changed that. He was the first to show me kindness, even when I kept him up at night pacing wondering what had happened to me. Since then, I've been on the receiving end of far more kindness than I deserved, and never have I had the chance to give back— truly give back."

He paused to deal with another coughing fit. Sheila couldn't help but be reminded of Audrey.

Raymond took a cautious breath, his hands gripping the bed as he did so. "Then, I met you. You'd given so much. You said what you did after the Chase, and it cost you everything. I watched you weep at your sister's grave. I watched you keep your mouth shut in front of Penny. I watched you *watch* over this city." Sheila cocked her head and gave him a questioning glance. "Yeah, I figured you out pretty quickly. Remember, I got to see your movement around Central City, and it wasn't hard to see how that lined up with the Watcher's notices."

She smiled at him. Raymond was invisible to most people, but he was not stupid.

"Anyway, my point is this. You were saving lives. And I was helping you. So, as I see it, I helped you save lives. In the end, I got to save your life."

"But at the cost of *your* life?" The dampness returned to her eyelids.

"That's the point, Kemp. I can be at peace because I finally got to give back after taking so much. My life is an even trade. In the end, it *cost* this world nothing."

"But, Raymond."

"No." He held his hand up again. Then he took her hand in his with a surprising gentleness for his huge form. "No regrets. If that's what my life was meant to be about, then it was worth it."

Hearing Audrey's words, her heart sank with compassion for Raymond. A wave of emotion swelled inside her, breaking her denial about his condition. She surrendered to what was about to happen to him.

She gripped his hand tightly. "What can I do?"

He let out a sputtering cough. Recovering, he examined her with a soft gaze. "Kemp, you let Father Anthony get you to the Underground. They'll keep you safe. Don't worry about me. I'm at peace as long as you get safely to them." He smiled again, and it was clear he meant that to be the last words of the conversation. It was his goodbye.

She stood, allowing a tear to roll down her cheek. Leaning over, she kissed him on the forehead and then kissed his hand still clenched in hers. Moving slowly toward the door, she paused to glance at him. He lay with his eyes closed, a gentle smile on his lips.

He is at peace. She envied him and promised she would learn that kind of peace.

The door shut behind her with a soft click, and she went to find Father Anthony. The Underground was about to inherit one ex-reporter-tool-of-the-Coalition who was determined to become something more. Despite what Raymond said about her, too many had given on her behalf. Too many had paid to protect her. She was going to stop hiding behind her words.

She owed it to Raymond.

She owed it to Audrey.

She owed it to herself.

Chapter Twenty-Six

Willis stood over the unconscious form of Jez. He remembered what she was like on the station with longer hair and a piercing gaze. In this state, she appeared so peaceful. Her short hair softened the appearance of her face, though the hard edges of her features were still there if he searched for them. The corners of her eyes were relaxed, and he imagined what they might appear like if she smiled—truly smiled. It wasn't something he could recall her ever doing on the station.

She'd been terrified. One recoding was all it was supposed to take. She lived every day with the knowledge that it could be her last. What would that do to someone? What would it make them do?

"She should be awake any second," Lydia said, bringing him out of his thoughts. "I administered a counter agent to the drug in her system a minute ago." Lydia picked up her gear and moved to his side. She studied him and then glanced at Jez. "You going to be all right?"

"Yeah." He nodded and smiled slightly. "I'll be fine."

She placed a hand on his shoulder. "We're right outside when you need us, understood?"

"Thanks."

She nodded and walked toward the door. Willis could see the team waiting anxiously in the hall, including Perryn who was busy biting through her lower lip. Lydia shut the door softly behind her leaving him alone in the tiny room with Jez. They agreed that Willis should be the first person she saw because of their history. Despite her attempt to kill him, Willis was still the best option. Jez hated Perryn and was always mistrusting of strangers. He was the lone member of the team that stood a chance to get a positive reaction.

He breathed a sigh of impatience and closed his eyes. He reminded himself he was the one who would need to help her adjust to her surroundings. Waking at the Underground instead of Solution Systems would shock anyone.

"Will?" Jez's drug-hindered voice creaked as she spoke his name, making him jump. She was the one person who called him Will, and the flood of emotion the name created made him shudder. He peered down and met her dark eyes. Her face wore a mix of bewilderment and concern.

"Hey, Jez." He kept his voice soft. He sat down on the side of the bed.

Her eyes darted around the space. "What? Where—where am I?"

"Someplace safe." The answer was vague, but he didn't want to give her too much information right away. He smiled to assure her.

Her eyes searched his face. "And you—you're here?"

"Yeah. I mean—yeah, I'm here."

"This isn't a hallucination of some kind?"

"No hallucination," he said.

Suddenly, she shot into a seated position and threw her arms around his neck. She squeezed him tighter than he believed she should be able to in her slightly drugged state. The movement startled him, and he forgot to push away. Instead, he sat there, arms limp.

"Uh—Jez?"

He waited for an answer, but none came. She simply started to shake. Confused, he looked down at her and realized what she was doing. She was crying—sobbing, in fact. The tears came with each heave of her shoulders, dampening his shirt, and yet she continued without shame. This was not the Jez he remembered.

Willis's heart broke, and he tried to imagine what she'd been through. He slowly brought his arms up to return the embrace. He'd never held Jez, and he was surprised at the slightness of her frame as it trembled with each sob.

Minutes passed, and her body settled with two long sighs. She pulled away slightly, not to break the embrace but to gaze at him. With one hand, she wiped her eyes and nose, still keeping one hand on his shoulder.

"I can't believe it's you," she said. "It was—that place—the things they did there—" Her thoughts burst in staccato phrases that didn't connect as if her mind jumped from one to the next as she spoke them aloud. She shook her head, and he envisioned her trying to clear some unpleasant memory out of her mind.

"Jez, it's going to be all right."

"No—no. It's not all right." Her normally piercing stare softened into a sad gaze.

He was not used to a softer Jez. Something inside him fluttered, out of fear or compassion, he couldn't tell. "What do you mean?"

"Will, what I did on the station, I was desperate." She shook her head again, glancing down. The tears returned. "I'm so sorry. I can't believe I was willing to do that."

I knew it. He let out an inward sigh, grateful that his suspicions had been correct. She'd survived her endless recodings. She was no longer afraid for her life, and that made all the difference. Could it be that this was the real Jez?

He brushed a rogue tear from her cheek. "Jez, I know. I can't imagine what you've been through, but you're safe here. We rescued you from the Coalition."

"We? Where am I? Who saved me?"

With that, he reached out and knocked on the door. Slowly at first, Lydia opened the door to reveal the team waiting outside. The painful surprise on Perryn's face reminded Willis that he still shared a partial embrace with Jez. Standing up, he broke his contact with her.

"Jez," he said nervously, "this is the team. Perryn and Kane you know. The others are Lydia, Chris, and Maria."

"'Sup?" Maria nodded upward, chomping on her gum.

"Thank you. All of you." Jez nodded to the group.

"So, I take it you two are okay with each other again?" Chris pointed at them.

"They know, Jez," Willis said. "It was fair they know."

"I understand." Her gaze found the floor. "I did many things on the station I'm not proud of."

Perryn stepped forward, her face twisted with contempt. "So, we're supposed to accept that you're a changed person? Like that?" She snapped her fingers.

"Yeah, I'm with my girl here." Maria pointed at Perryn with her thumb before crossing her arms. "How do we know you're not playing us?"

"The things the Alliance and Coalition did to me—they—they—" Jez choked on a sob, unable to finish her sentence. Composing herself, she started over. "Well, let's say it changes you to experience that. And no, Perryn, I don't expect you to trust me. Not right away. I hope you'll give me a chance in time." Jez gazed at Perryn with hopeful eyes.

Willis studied Perryn's expression to see if it would soften. It did, but only slightly. Maria stood behind Perryn, obvious that she stood with her friend. The rest appeared as though they might believe her, though Kane was impossible to read.

"I think we'll all agree that Jez needs to prove to us she's a changed person," Willis said. "But after what we saw in Solution Systems, I don't think there's any doubt that she's no friend of the Coalition. They were ready to—well—I can't imagine she'd want that."

Lydia nodded. "Agreed."

"Makes sense to me," Chris said.

Maria clicked her tongue. "She's not part of the Underground until she goes through the trials like the rest of us." She paused. "Rules are rules. No passes, no matter what you've been through." A murmur of agreement spread through the group.

"Also agreed," Lydia said.

Maria turned and gave Perryn a playful shove. "So, girl. Want to take your shot helping with the trials?"

Perryn glanced from Willis to Jez and back to Willis. She shook her head.

"No. I want no part in this." Her face contorted like she was holding in a scream, or tears, or something worse. Without another word, she turned and left the group. Willis stepped hesitantly, and then ran to follow her.

"Perr, wait up!" In a few strides, he was right behind her.

"No, Willis. I don't want to talk about it. Not here." She threw up a hand toward him, her neck growing red.

"Perr, please."

"I—I can't. Please don't follow me. I need some time."

With that, she ran off toward the women's barracks. Willis didn't follow.

Willis stood on the platform high above the training area next to Kane. They'd been surprised to see how quickly Jez recovered, and at her request, prepared for the trials only hours after she'd awakened. Below, a crowd gathered to welcome the newcomer with their traditional ceremony. Maria stepped from the crowd with her arms spread wide and waved them up and down to excite the crowd. Jez stood next to Lydia, who was whispering in her ear. No doubt getting the same instructions that he'd gotten with the trials. Seeing the ceremony from this perspective changed the experience. He could see its importance. The trials were not fair, but they weren't supposed to be. They tested if the new potential member would respond to a threat as the rest of the Underground would and had on countless occasions. Jez would be forced to react without knowing what was expected.

Hopefully, she figures this out a little faster than I did.

"Kane, will my mother need to pass the trials?" Willis hadn't thought about the possibility.

"She will if she wishes to join us long term, Boss," Kane said with a long breath. "For the time being, she is undecided, but no one feels threatened by her. Captain and I agreed that she could stay as our guest until she's sure. Eventually, she'll have to decide."

Willis breathed a sigh in relief. He couldn't imagine his mother having to go through this ceremony. She was tough. He had no doubt about that, but he wasn't sure he'd be able to watch.

She'd been through enough pain. And what about older members like the old woman who'd challenged the armored car or Barney, the older man he'd met on his arrival. What must it have been like for them to join?

He raised a brow at Kane. "Is Barney the oldest to have endured the trials?"

"No. He was with us from the beginning, before the trials existed." Kane smiled at the idea. "It was once we grew in number and people sought us out every other day that we decided some sort of initiation was necessary. People needed to fit in and become one of us, but the original members were already family and committed to the cause."

Willis nodded. He was impressed with how quickly the Underground had formed and become the community they were. He turned his attention to the platform below.

"So, little missy here needs to understand one thing." Maria was performing, more to the crowd than Jez. "She may be no friend of the Coalition, but she got to prove herself to become one of us."

The crowd roared their approval. Lydia stepped over and struck the box with her shock stick to demonstrate how the trial worked. As with him, she then struck Jez with the stick to prove its power. Jez screamed and retreated with her arms wrapped around her. Willis grimaced at the scene, the first he'd witnessed since his own trial. It was cruel to do this to Jez so soon after her treatment at Solution Systems, but there was no point in waiting. The rumors around Jez would best be dispelled if she was welcomed into the Underground. People trusted the initiated.

"She don't got it. She don't got it." Maria gave an exaggerated shake of her head, getting the crowd going with her jeers. Perhaps Maria felt responsible to represent Perryn, whom he hadn't seen for hours since she'd run off.

Four members, including Maria, surrounded Jez with their shock sticks ready. Jez took her place over the small cube and crouched slightly. Her hands were raised in a defensive position.

Figure it out, Jez. He willed his thoughts down to Jez's position. *Defend, don't fight.*

Lydia asked if she was ready, a question that would be hardly heard over the cheering and jeering onlookers.

Jez nodded, and the clock began.

Seconds passed and nothing happened. Then, the teenage boy in front of Jez leapt forward, jabbing his stick at her. As if expecting it, Jez sprang forward. To everyone's disbelief, she reached out and grabbed the end of the shock stick, allowing the energy to course through her. Her eyes narrowed as she fought the pain. A second later, her arm rose and struck the wrist of the teen boy. The maneuver broke his grip, and the stick ceased shocking Jez.

The other three, frozen by Jez's reaction, snapped to attention. Maria cried out as she swung her stick, and Willis expected the blow to immobilize Jez from behind. In a blur, Jez flipped her newly acquired weapon in her hand and whirled with a ducking motion. Maria's strike flew harmlessly over Jez's head, and Willis gritted his teeth as Jez jabbed her shock stick into Maria's exposed ribs. Maria screamed something unintelligible and fell to the ground holding her side.

The young girl to Jez's left fearfully poked at the cube, not wanting to engage Jez. Jez stepped on the handle of the shock stick, breaking it loose from the girl's hand. A moment later, she fell screaming as Jez struck her on the neck with a shock.

Straightening, Jez turned slowly to the fourth combatant and raised her shock stick to eye level. The crowd silenced and the two stared at each other. With a clatter that echoed off the walls, the boy dropped his stick and held his hands in surrender.

"Time." Lydia said the word in almost a whisper, still audible in the stillness of the room.

The entire crowd stood stunned as Jez stood motionless, stick still raised. Lydia slowly moved toward Jez, who finally lowered her weapon. She reached out and grabbed Jez's arm, raising it slowly as if unsure she should.

"Having passed the trial and proven steadfast in the face of overwhelming odds, I stand first to welcome a new sister to the Underground." Lydia's voice was flat and without the usual bravado. "Let all who agree sound off."

Murmured 'ayes' could be heard from the crowd. Several turned to leave quietly. Maria rose to her feet, her eyes still wide in shock.

"What—what was that?" She stumbled over the words. "Does that count?"

"She kept the box from being struck." Lydia still showed no emotion. Willis could see her give a worried glance toward Kane, whose grip tightened on the railing.

Willis waited for Kane to say something. "Does that count?"

Kane nodded without saying a word. It was clear that no one had ever passed the trials this way. Examining the space, Willis could see that the crowd had cleared except for Jez. No one was training. No one was congratulating her. Her eyes found Willis, and he watched her fierce stare melt. She broke their shared gaze, appearing lost as she scanned the area. She walked toward the exit, slowly at first. As she approached the stairs, she took off into a run.

"Boss, I think there's more to our teammate than we know. You'd better talk to her." Kane placed a hand on his shoulder.

"Me?" Willis drew back, surprised.

"Yes, you." Kane turned his head to nod in the direction Jez had run. "She needs Red Team Leader. It's the world she knows. It's time for you to coach your hurting teammate."

Willis followed Kane's gaze from the platform to the empty exit.

What did they do to her in that place?

Chapter Twenty-Seven

Perryn stared at the wall next to her cot. Her eyes stung, and the saltiness of tears still clung to her cheeks. It had been hours since she'd left Willis in the hallway. She'd hated to run from him like that, but she needed to collect her wits. The other women hadn't disturbed her, even when they hurried off to Jez's trials.

"You sure you don't want to come?" Maria had sat on her cot, the one brave enough to say anything. "I'm going to put a shock stick right in her spine for you."

"No, you go ahead," she'd said. With that, Maria had left her to her thoughts. The barracks sat silent, except when a few girls came in talking excitedly about something that'd happened. She couldn't make out what they were saying, and she didn't care.

I'm sure she passed. She closed her eyes in disappointment. Somewhere inside, Perryn realized she'd hoped Jez would fail and make this easier.

She couldn't bring herself to be mad at Willis—not truly. She understood the bonds that were created on the station, and nothing had happened that she should be upset about. Something unknown simply refused to stop gnawing at her insides.

Something is wrong. The notion echoed in her head for the thousandth time. *We storm into Solution Systems, and Jez is—there? And she's full of remorse?*

She'd watched Jez from afar too long on the station to believe her apologies. And yet, there was a part of her heart that yearned to welcome her into the fold. Jez was a broken person. Perryn had no doubt about that.

The Underground was a place for broken people. *What if—she's telling the truth?*

She chided herself for not giving Jez a chance. Of all people, she understood the desperation of coming close to death. Perhaps she'd been wholly unfair to Jez. Few people could understand the looming fear of a high recoding number. It was something they had in common. Willis had been able to move past the fact that she tried to kill him. Couldn't she? Breathing deeply to cleanse her spirit, she made a choice.

She rose, her legs stiff from sitting still for so long. She washed her face and examined her reflection in the mirror. *I'll reach out to her. I'll do it for Willis. If he can forgive her and give her a chance, then I can too.*

She headed off to find Willis.

Willis approached Jez slowly. She was seated on the floor in the hallway, far away from the training center. Her head and hands rested on her knees, and she stared at the wall in front of her. Stepping softly, he neared her and saw her tense as his approach became obvious. Turning his back to the wall, he slid down to the floor next to her.

She didn't move her eyes in his direction. Instead, she hid her face in her arms. "What did they do to me?"

He didn't know how to answer.

Her hands balled into fists. "They've transformed me into some sort of freak."

"I don't think—" he said.

"No. You do." She raised her head and waved a hand in the direction of the training center. "They all do. You saw what I did in there."

"But that doesn't make you a freak."

She glanced at him, a blend of anger and fear in her eyes. "Then why is it that I know you would favor your right side if you needed to defend yourself? Why do I know that there are three exits from this spot, and that the best one is the stairs to the left? Why do I sit here rehearsing how I could have defeated those four people in fewer moves instead of feeling bad for what I did?"

"I—I don't know." It was all he could say.

"Will," she said, turning to him. Her voice was low and

intense. "You don't remember being recoded. The things they do to you. They make you think things. They put things in your brain." She pointed at the side of her head.

He remembered the suggestions the chairman had put in his brain and tried to use against him in the Chase. He opened his mouth to tell her he understood but reconsidered and let her continue.

"They also take things out. Memories. Feelings. Abilities." She slumped against the wall.

"Well—I think it's obvious they added things to you. Seriously, we all saw what you can do—but that doesn't mean they took something away. Wouldn't you know?"

"I don't know." She slowly shook her head with the back of it resting on the wall. "What if I can never again be someone's friend? I'm sure that Maria hates me, which means Perryn might never give me a chance."

"I'd like to think we might still be friends," he said. "Or at least friends again."

"What if I can no longer—love someone?"

The question made Willis immediately uncomfortable, especially the words 'no longer.' His relationship with Perryn had to be obvious to Jez, so he wasn't sure what she was implying—if anything. On the station, she'd hinted at wanting more than a friendship, but he hadn't been sure.

"I'm sorry," she said. "That wasn't fair to ask."

He wasn't used to this soft, gentle version of Jez. She was so hard, so cold on the station. He couldn't think straight and tried to recover. "No. It's—it's fine." He sputtered nervously. "You're scared. I get it."

"No. It's not fine, Will." She pounded the floor on either side of her. "I don't remember much from the last few months, but in the moments I was conscious, I hated myself for what I did. I was so scared that if I ever saw you again, you'd hate me."

"I don't hate you, but I'll be honest that I'm not sure I know you. You're—different." She glanced away, and he regretted saying it.

"On the station,"—she kept her eyes turned away and wouldn't meet his—"I couldn't let anyone in. I was one recoding away from dying. I was scared, and that was easier to hide if everyone was scared of me. I made a point not to let anything or anyone keep me from being on the best team."

"You were good at that." He chuckled, trying to lighten the mood. She smiled. It was unexpected to see her brighten. He wasn't used to her smile, but he liked it. Her features were always striking, but she was beautiful when she smiled.

"Yeah. When I found out Amber learned my recoding number, I was terrified, so I tried to freak her out. That's when you saw me with her on the station. And when Jaden arrived, well— you were so drawn to him, I was afraid you'd replace me. Blacc even teased you about that if you remember."

Willis considered her history. It all fit. Amber, Blacc, Jaden. It all worked together to create one very terrified person who might be willing do anything to survive. A belief in Jez formed in his gut.

He had to ask her. "So, that's why you—?"

"Yes. I tried to kill you, Will. Let's say it like it is. But—" She hesitated.

"What?"

She turned to him and grabbed his hand. She stared into his eyes for a long minute. "I'm glad I failed."

"You are?"

"Yes. To know you made it. To see what you and Jaden did. To see you and Perryn—happy. It makes me glad I failed." She rested her head on his shoulder, clasping his hand in both of hers. "Thank you for being my one friend."

His stomach knotted with her leaning on him, but he didn't move. She'd been so honest, and he didn't want to ruin the moment by reacting to her. He wanted her to feel comfortable in her new setting. She needed to learn to be open with everyone, even if that meant starting with him. He opted to give things a minute and make an excuse to leave.

Down the hallway, Perryn sucked in a sudden breath. She couldn't believe she had the space for more sadness left in her soul, but neither could she believe what she was seeing. The months had been filled with heartbreak and sorrow, but seeing Jez lean into Willis that way shattered her. Even worse, Willis appeared to be doing nothing about it.

This can't be happening.

Willis faced away from her, so he hadn't noticed her approach. Jez, however, peered right at her, and the two of them stared at each other in silence.

Chapter Twenty-Eight

Not long after assuming the role of the Watcher, Sheila had arranged her own safehouse on the outskirts of the city. She needed to be certain she wasn't being followed by Penny's minions, so going straight to the Underground was out of the question. Giving away their position would make a bad situation much worse. The small apartment she'd rented under a false name was well supplied and could sustain her for a couple weeks if necessary. It was small, and the walls had several visible cracks. The barely usable kitchen was outdone by the stale odor of moldy carpet. The shower ran freezing cold when it worked, which wasn't often. It was far from glamorous accommodations, but it was safer than the streets.

Several days had passed, and she started to be hopeful that her getaway was complete. With morbid curiosity, she watched the broadcasts that displayed her picture and identified her as a disgraced reporter and hunted fugitive. She'd seen her face on television many times, but not like this. It unnerved her.

The screen shifted and showed a close-up of Penny, wearing more makeup than she'd ever seen her wear in a pre-recorded interview. The title 'Deputy Chairman of the Western Alliance' scrolled across the bottom of the screen.

"What we have here is a case of complete betrayal." Penny spoke to an off-screen journalist. "None feel it more than I do as we worked quite closely together. I took her in, trusted her, and showed her nothing but kindness. I believe in the goodness of our chairman, the Coalition, and, of course, the Law. I believe it is that Law that protects us, but also gives us hope. Sheila Kemp entered into our rehabilitation system, and I, for one, firmly believed that she was rehabilitated. However, that grace was unwarranted, and though I—rather we—showed her the greatest of kindness, she threw away her opportunity to serve the Coalition to instead help—well, terrorists."

"And does this mean the rehabilitation systems are flawed?" said the voice of the journalist.

Penny smirked and shook her head. "Certainly, not. The Law is perfect and good."

"So why did it not work for the fugitive Sheila Kemp?"

"The rebellious heart cannot accept grace." Penny feigned compassion. "Until they see the goodness of the Law, those who falsely claim their supposed freedom from it will never be able to receive its goodness. Frankly, it breaks my heart. What a horrible way to live."

Listening to the woman nauseated Sheila, and she was glad when the report broke away from the interview. Her momentary relief, though, changed to horror.

"The Deputy Chairwoman of the Western Alliance," said the reporter, "is living out her mission to bring the Alliance under the Law today as she appears live on the steps of Alliance headquarters."

The screen changed to a live shot of Penny standing behind a podium. The wind was blowing, and her perfect hair was tossed to one side. Sheila shook as she saw a couple the screen identified as Julio and Carmen Sanchez standing on the platform in handcuffs. She recognized them as members of the Underground intelligence network. Mr. Sanchez scanned out beyond the gathered crowd with a face that betrayed no emotion, but Mrs. Sanchez was unable to contain her tears. They wore orange jumpsuits, and both appeared like they'd been mistreated. What sickened Sheila even more were the Sanchez children who stood next to them. They, too, wore jumpsuits and handcuffs. Both couldn't control their quivering chins, and they kept searching their mother's face for comfort.

"Today represents a great victory for the Coalition," Penny announced. "The Law is truly good as it gives us a chance to end the cycle of terrorism that is gripping our city. Next to me stands a family that has openly stood against the Law and supported the violent acts around our city. I am pleased to say that our Law-keepers apprehended them last night, and their sentencing will see to it that their brand of chaos will not tear down our beautiful Coalition any longer. They stand guilty of not only helping the dissidents that cause chaos in our beautiful city, but also we have learned they personally helped assist the fugitives Willis Thomson and Perryn Davis."

The screen changed to an interview with Chairman DeGraaf. He sat in his traditional robes, his wire-rimmed glasses sparkling under the lights. He wore a grim expression upon his face like his heart was broken.

"Rebellion and violence come in many forms," he said. "The saddest of which can be found when parents train their children in the ways contrary to the goodness of the Law."

The screen shifted to a young, female journalist Sheila recognized as an intern in the Alliance office who must have had the unfortunate privilege of being Sheila's replacement. Behind her, Penny left the stage. With unfriendly jerks on their arms, Law-keepers escorted the Sanchez family out of sight. The journalist commented on the scene. "If there's one thing for certain, the Law remains, and the consequences are heavy for those who insist otherwise, no matter who they are."

Click!

Sheila couldn't watch any longer. She stood and gathered her few belongings. There were the items from her office and a bag of personal items she'd left in the apartment. She opened the bag and pulled out a small frame. The image of a young, healthy Audrey stared at her.

"Sis, no one is safe. I can't tell the world what I see anymore as the Watcher or as a reporter. I hope I make you proud doing something else for a while."

She closed her eyes and imagined Audrey's response. What she imagined filled her with determination. Locking the door to the apartment, she left for the Underground.

An hour later, she sat in Kane's office briefing him on her escape,

Raymond's sacrifice, and her assurance that she was careful not to be followed. He nodded and asked a few questions along the way, but mostly he appeared disappointed.

"Your intel as the Watcher kept us one step ahead of the Coalition, Ms. Kemp," Kane said. "We're not going to be as effective without you on the inside."

Sheila frowned. "I know. I'm sorry. I quietly downloaded what I could without being noticed over the last couple weeks at headquarters. Everything is encrypted, so I'm not sure what use it is."

"Leave that to my man, Chris." As if on cue, a knock came to the door, and a young man appeared.

"You sent for me, Chief?"

"Yes. Come in, Chris." Kane waved him inside. "You decrypt the files from Solution Systems yet?"

Chris nodded excitedly. "Broke through an hour ago. Lots of files to scroll through. Most are useless notes from the scientists from that place. Well—useless because no one here is likely to fully understand them. But—I'm still going through them to be thorough."

"Then take Ms. Kemp here with you. She has files that come from Alliance Headquarters. If we're lucky, the encryption is the same format. You can help her by opening the files. She can help you by weeding out the information that helps us."

"Any help would be amazing, especially from *The Watcher*." Chris smiled at Sheila, unable to hide his giddiness over meeting her. "I'll take you to where I'm set up if you're done here."

"Yes. We're done." Kane nodded at Chris.

"Thank you, Kane," she said. "Hopefully, something will come of all this."

Following Chris down the hallway, she inspected her latest surroundings. *I guess this is home.* Still, helping Chris sort through endless files, while tedious, was at least a way she could help. Information was her specialty.

Chris turned to her as they walked. "So, anyone tell you about how the Solution Systems raid went?"

"You can't be in this place without hearing about it. You got Brenda out, plus one. Who was the other?"

"Some friend of the Chief, Willis, and Perryn. Her name is Jez."

Sheila stopped in her tracks. "Jez?" She swallowed hard to choke down the news.

"Oh, yeah—you probably know her, don't you? You were on the station last year."

"Jez is here?" Sheila asked again to be certain she'd heard correctly.

"Yeah. Not sure what to make of her. She made quite a splash at the trials."

Sheila glanced around, puzzled. Something was off about Jez being here—something in her gut that set off alarms. Her thoughts were interrupted as they stepped into the mess hall.

"Sheila? Sheila Kemp?" The voice was pleasantly familiar.

Sheila turned to see Brenda and Perryn. They'd been talking in the corner when Sheila entered. Brenda smiled brightly, but Perryn didn't appear well. Still, they both rushed to hug Sheila.

"I can't believe you're here." Brenda hugged her again. "I'm so glad you're okay. How did you get away?"

"It's a long story." Sheila noticed Perryn's expression. "Everything all right?"

When Perryn hesitated, Brenda stepped forward. "Not exactly. I suppose you've heard of the other newcomer."

"I did. She causing trouble already?"

"That's what we're trying to figure out." Brenda put her arm around Perryn. It was clear Perryn didn't want to talk about it with Sheila.

"Brenda, about Max," Sheila said, changing subjects. "I—I'm sorry."

Brenda's eyes watered despite her attempt at a pained smile. "I miss him." She took a deep breath. "But I'm glad to be here with everyone."

"I hate to break this up, Ms. Kemp," Chris said bashfully, "but I could use your help. The sooner we crack these files, the better."

"You guys go." Brenda smiled a little bigger this time. "I'm glad for another familiar face around here. Still getting used to this place."

More hugs were exchanged. Brenda returned to her conversation with Perryn, and Chris led the way out of the mess hall. Two turns later, he opened a door to reveal his office. The space was a mess of computer screens, wires, and whirring hard drives. The center screen displayed a long list of scrolling file names.

"These are the files I downloaded at Solution Systems." Chris pointed to the screens. "There are a few thousand, so I'm having a hard time going through them quickly."

"Tell you what." She handed him a data disk. "You try decrypting this, and I'll see if I can narrow your search. Weeding the important details from the rest is what I've done for a long time."

He smiled, taking the disk from her. "Deal."

Chapter Twenty-Nine

Willis sat by himself in the mess hall poking at food he wasn't hungry enough to eat. He'd made his excuse and left Jez in the hallway. He searched the compound, wanting to ask Perryn if she would eat with him, but he couldn't find her anywhere. He breathed a sigh of relief. He needed to sort out his conversation with Jez before talking to Perryn anyway.

The interaction with Jez in the hallway confused him. The Jez he remembered on the station rarely showed emotion other than anger or frustration. She was someone to be feared, not someone who was afraid—much less showed affection.

But—his time with her in the hallway was different. She had changed, and he had to admit it was a good change. Even if it made him uncomfortable, he couldn't deny that he liked this version of Jez much better.

His mind fumbled over the pieces of information about Jez the way a child might approach a jigsaw puzzle that was missing the box. No matter how hard he tried, he couldn't see the bigger picture.

Jez was an exceptional Chase runner.

He'd recruited her the minute he saw her, knowing she would be an asset to Red Team. In time, they became more than teammates. They were good friends.

Meeting Jaden had changed his view of the world, and Jez couldn't understand that. Her loyalty to Willis had waivered. She hated Jaden for changing his motivation.

Did she hate Perryn? He stopped for a moment at this idea, unsure of how to answer. She expressed happiness about their relationship, but the rest of the conversation hadn't matched that sentiment.

Then Willis had found her on the autopsy table. She must have been an unexpected success, and the scientists at Solution Systems decided to discover everything they could to reproduce her results. He couldn't imagine all that she'd endured at their hands.

She was lost, alone, and afraid.

No, not alone. She has me. I'm still her friend.

Frustrated, he dropped his fork. The timeline made sense, no matter how many times he rehearsed it. Then why was he so bothered by it all?

He knew the answer, but he needed some advice first.

"Willis." Lydia startled him to attention with a hand on his shoulder. "Sorry to disturb your lunch, but Chief wants you."

"I wasn't hungry anyway." He pushed back from the table. "What does Kane want?"

"A mission. Thinks it will be good for our new recruit if she goes on an easy recon topside."

Willis grimaced before turning to her. He wasn't ready to see Jez again until he'd sorted this through. "Do *you* think it will be?" He bowed his head at Lydia, afraid to ask the question.

She pursed her lips before responding. "I think we need to find out."

"Makes sense," he said, lying. They walked together toward Kane's office.

———————◆⑨◆⑥◆———————

An hour later, Jez joined them atop a building overlooking a major road in the distance that led to the center of the city. They peered along the length of the road with binoculars, seeing nothing.

"What are we searching for again?" Willis cocked an ear toward Lydia.

"Intelligence predicts a massing of Law-keepers at Coalition headquarters after the escape of the Watcher," Lydia said. "We're here to verify any movement."

"Verify movement?" Willis couldn't hide his disbelief. It appeared a little redundant to him. Intelligence was rarely wrong on something as simple as troop movements.

"Yes." Lydia shot a glance at Jez and then glanced at Willis. "Verify."

He gave a slight nod to let her know he received the message. This was a dummy mission to see how Jez would perform in the field or if she would run the first chance she got. Jez had been scanning intently through her binoculars in silence the entire conversation, so it startled him when she spoke.

"What does it matter if Law-keepers move to headquarters? Doesn't that make it easier for us to move around out here?" Jez's question was perceptive, and Willis held his breath hoping she wouldn't put their real intentions together.

"It does, and that's why we want to know." Lydia frowned, clearly uncomfortable with the kind of questions being asked. Several minutes passed in silence.

"I see them! I see them!" Jez blurted as she stood, still gazing in the distance.

Lydia played along. "Where?"

"Way out there."

Willis peered through the lenses in the direction she was pointing. Sure enough, several black trucks with yellow insignias were driving the road in a single file line. While they couldn't see inside the trailers of the trucks, there was no doubt that troops and supplies were being transported somewhere.

"What do we do?"

Lydia bit her lip. "Get a count."

"One, two, three, four—" Jez counted aloud.

Slam! The three of them jumped at the sound of the ceiling access door opening. Turning, they saw two uniformed Law-keepers burst through the opening with their rifles at the ready.

"Halt right there!" one of the soldiers shouted.

Willis and Lydia turned slowly, raising their hands in the air. Jez slipped as she turned and fell seated by the edge of the roof, an expression of fear washing over her face. The Law-keepers rushed them, pointing their guns at Willis and Lydia.

"On your feet, traitor!" the soldier on the right shouted. He was about Willis's height, with broad shoulders, and a thin beard. The other soldier appeared much younger but with no less determination to intimidate them. His face was well-chiseled, and his head was clean shaven. "On your feet, I said."

Jez cowered in fear on the ground, and she raised her hands in front of her face as if afraid they might strike her. The younger Law-keeper shook his head in frustration and reached for her.

"Get up." He growled, grabbing the upper part of her arm and yanking her to her feet. As he did so, Jez's expression morphed from fearful to ferocious.

As soon as her feet were planted, she thrust herself upward with both legs. Curling her fingers, she drove her knuckles into the Adam's apple of the unsuspecting soldier. His grip loosened instantly, and he stepped backward gasping for air. Freed from his grasp, Jez didn't hesitate to move on the other Law-keeper.

Whirling to her left, she raised her left leg high in the air and brought her heel down on the trigger hand of the soldier. The rifle's barrel dropped, and a single bullet ricocheted harmlessly off the roof. The moment her left foot was planted, her right leapt upward connecting with the man's jaw. The soldier fell to the ground with a grunt. Jez's movement was a single fluid circle that allowed her to finish facing the first Law-keeper who was still attempting to force air into his lungs.

She screeched as she lunged at him. Grabbing the barrel of his rifle, she brought her knee upward into his chest, pulling on the rifle to double the power of her blow. Willis could hear something crack as the soldier cried out in pain, dropping his end of the firearm. Two hands on the barrel, Jez swung the rifle like a club and struck the man's temple. He crumpled to the ground, motionless.

Walking over to the older soldier, who was on his hands and knees trying to stand, she casually raised the rifle. The butt of the rifle stock collided with his head a second later. He, too, fell unconscious.

A long pause passed between the three of them.

"Jez?" Willis finally said quietly.

She stood silent. The one sound she made was her rapid panting as she tried to catch her breath.

He approached her slowly, his hand extended outward. "Jez?"

The rifle dropped from her hand, clattering to the ground. Standing straight, she looked slowly at Willis. Her eyes were wild, but not with the ferocity of moments earlier. Her lips curled into a slight smile, and she leapt at Willis.

"Ha ha!" She laughed as she lunged. Willis retreated backward, surprised by her advance, but not before she caught him. Throwing her arms around him, she let out another excited cry. Lydia stood frozen, taking in the whole scene.

"Uhh," Willis said, unable to get anything else out.

"Did you see what I did?" Jez was unable to contain her smile. She pulled away to gaze at Willis square in the face. She bounced in place like a child eager to get attention from their parent. "Did you see it?"

"Uhh. Um, yeah." He was babbling like an idiot, but he wasn't sure how to handle her reaction.

"I totally took them out." She punched Willis's arm.

Still dumbfounded, Willis remained silent. Jez let out an exasperated sigh and turned to Lydia.

"Come on." She smiled. "You of all people, Lydia, have got to be a little impressed."

"Yeah, sure." Lydia acted unconvinced or nervous or both. She attempted a smile.

"Seriously, how cool was that?" Jez stepped backward, releasing Willis. Her feet danced as she hopped in place, celebrating to herself. "It's like something took over, and I understood what to do. I knew. Somehow, I was sure those guys didn't stand a chance!" She examined her hands, turning them over and over. Closing her eyes, she danced again.

Willis shot a sideways glance at Lydia. "Yeah, pretty cool, Jez."

"Agreed." Lydia kneeled to check on the two Law-keepers. "That could have been pretty bad otherwise. They're alive, thank goodness. Kane will be happy to hear that."

Jez let out another gleeful yelp and hugged Willis tightly. The awkwardness of being held by Jez became too much, and he hesitantly returned the gesture. Then, he allowed his arms to hang limply at his sides. Lydia raised a knowing eyebrow, and he could feel himself blush.

"I think we got what we need. Let's get back before these guys are missed." Lydia nodded at Willis as she made the suggestion.

"Good idea." Willis saw his opportunity to step away from Jez.

Jez let out a long, satisfied sigh. "Yeah, let's get out of here. Maybe we'll run into more Law-keepers, and I can take them out too." She shadow-boxed the air a few times.

Willis hung back to walk behind the other two to collect his thoughts. They'd been out there to assess Jez and her readiness to be a part of the Underground. What had they learned? Not much. They'd guessed that she had some new fighting skills, but he hadn't expected her to be a trained killer.

He plodded along after them, trying to appear casual. Jez was happy, and he was certainly glad for it. Her jubilation forced a smile on his face as he reflected on it until his mind drifted to Perryn and what she would think of all this. He needed help, and there was one person he could think to talk to—one person who might give him the unbiased truth.

Chapter Thirty

Willis hadn't seen Barney since before the raid on Solution Systems, and he needed to find him wherever he was hiding. The old man had a way of calming him down, but he could be hard to find. His role in the Underground took him to the far reaches of the compound. He didn't get involved in the action outside headquarters, but down here was another matter.

Barney's primary job was to keep the place running and maintained. Willis laughed to himself. *He's probably head-first in a duct somewhere.*

He realized that he would have to talk to Perryn soon, but he needed to sort out his feelings first. Jez's presence confused him, not about his feelings for Perryn, but rather his feelings in general. He didn't question his love for Perryn. Where did Jez fit in, though? They'd been friends for so long that being around her was completely natural, and he liked the changes in her even more. He definitely needed to sort this out. Turning the corner, he could see Barney squatting in front of a panel with a frustrated frown on his face.

"Why is there power getting to that box over there, but not to this one?" Barney muttered to himself.

"Is it listening?" Willis enjoyed the slight startled jump from Barney.

"Willis! Good to see you, young man! I'm trying to figure out this here box. Almost appears tampered with. I guess rats got to it."

"Gross."

Barney gave him a smile that sent wrinkles through his entire face. "Yeah, welcome to my world. If you think that's gross, you should have seen the sewer pipe I fixed yesterday. What brings you down here?"

"Pass on the sewer pipe. Truth is—I need a friend," Willis said.

"A friend? Then you have one." Barney turned to sit with his back against the wall. Wiping his hands on an already dirty rag, he patted the floor next to him. "Sit down. I could use a break anyway."

"Thanks. So—" Willis hesitated, sucking a breath through his teeth.

"So—tell me about this new girl and why she's so taken with you." Barney raised an eyebrow. Willis must have given away his shock because Barney added, "It's amazing how much you hear when you're fixing things. Maintenance people always blend into the background. People forget I'm there when they're talking."

"So, people are talking?"

"After what she did in the trials? You bet."

Willis frowned. "Great. That's not going to help."

"Young man, let's cut to the chase. What's up with you?"

Willis considered the situation. "I don't know. I'm not honestly sure how I feel about Jez being here."

"You have feelings for this girl?"

"What? No!" He blurted the words out so quickly that even he thought it sounded defensive. "Maybe. I don't know. I don't think it's like that."

"Then what is it like?"

"She used to be my friend, until—"

"Until she tried to kill you?" Willis raised an eyebrow at the remark. Barney winked. "Again, word gets around."

"Yeah, until then, but—she's different. Or at least it feels that way." Willis's face fell. The more he said it out loud, the more confused he became.

"Well, that's good. Isn't it?"

"Yeah, it is."

"But—?" Barney could clearly see Willis was taking his time at getting to something, and he was forcing him to continue with the question. Willis took a deep breath before answering.

"Here goes. Perryn isn't thrilled that Jez is here. Jez acts way too affectionate. I love Perryn. I want to be Jez's friend. I'm not sure both can happen. Jez may want it to be more. I don't want to hurt anyone, but I'm not sure there's a way to avoid that." The sentences came out in a quick staccato—he was afraid he wouldn't get through them and would change his mind.

Barney stroked the gray stubble on his chin. "Hmm. That's a difficult one." Willis sat expecting more. "I'm nothing more than a tired, old man, but it sounds to me like the recent arrival of this young girl shouldn't be a threat to Perryn if she knows how much you love her."

"Yeah, well—" Willis started the thought, then cut himself off.

Barney nodded knowingly. "I see. Therein lies your problem, young man."

"Maybe."

"Willis, let me tell you a story." Barney began to finger a ring on his hand. Willis had never noticed it until that moment. "When I met Evelyn, she was the most beautiful woman I had ever laid eyes upon. Once I got to know her at the university, I discovered her inner beauty far exceeded her outward beauty—and that, my friend, is saying something. In short, she was the woman of my dreams. Did she know? Not a chance. I was too scared to say a word. Oh, we spent time together, for sure, but there comes a time when a couple needs to talk about how they feel—full out, no hesitating, and honestly talk about it. Then, Ronnie entered the picture."

"Ronnie?" Where was he going with this?

"He was an attractive young man from an influential family in the Alliance. Boy, did he have eyes for Evelyn. Their families spent time together, and well—as you can imagine—the writing was on the wall."

Willis examined Barney's ring again. "So, what happened?"

"Wouldn't you know," he said, "it was about a month after I had about given up that I ran into her at a Chase after-party on campus. Well, I don't know if I was excited about the Alliance winning the Chase or if I had enjoyed too much of the punch, but I couldn't help myself.

"I walked right up to her and said, 'Evelyn, I've loved you from the first day I met you. You're the woman I've dreamed of spending a lifetime with, and if you feel at all the same way, I thought one of us should say something.'"

"And?" Willis leaned in for the answer.

"What can I say? She stared right at me and said, 'It's about time.' Just like that. Crazy, huh?" Barney let out a soft chuckle. Willis nodded. "Well, we were married later that year and spent twenty-three amazing years together."

"What happened to her?"

Barney breathed a sigh of deep emotion. "Cancer. A beautiful creation of God had her life cut short."

"Why didn't you have her recoded? They can cure cancer that way."

"No access. You have to be wealthy to afford it unless you've access to facilities like the Underground has."

Willis straightened. "The Underground can recode someone?"

"Sure can! And they are much more cautious about how it's done than most. They're not interested in messing with someone's personality. Even so, they avoid using it except in the most extreme circumstances."

"Wow. I had no idea."

"All that's beside the point. Are you getting what I'm saying to you, young man?"

Willis nodded. "You think I should tell Perryn how I feel—how I honestly feel."

Barney patted him on the shoulder with an approving smile that again brought out every line on his face. "You got it. Tell her. Tell her before it's too late. If she feels the same way, it won't matter what this Jez girl does."

Willis glanced at Barney and smiled.

"Thank you, Barney."

"Thank you—for listening to an old man talk. But—you better get on unless you want to help me figure out this electrical panel.

If it was rodents, they did a number on it."

———————◆───————————

Perryn paced back and forth in front of Maria, arms crossed. She didn't have any more tears, and all she could feel was the anger that came in swells inside of her.

How could he?

"Girl, you gotta stop pacing. I'm getting a neckache watching you," Maria said.

"I think—how can he—what should I—?" Perryn couldn't put a coherent sentence together.

Maria pounded her fist into her hand. "I get it. Want me to punch her in the face for you?"

"No. She'd probably whoop your butt anyway from what I heard."

"I'll be ready next time, trust me." Maria appeared a little hurt by the comment.

Perryn turned to her friend. "I don't know what to do."

"Guess you're going to have to figure that out—and fast." Maria motioned with her chin behind Perryn. Turning around, she could see Willis on the other side of the mess hall scanning the room. He saw her and started in her direction.

"What do I say?"

"Tell him the truth," Maria said. "Might as well get it out in the open. And remember, the 'punch in the face' thing is still an option. Say the word, girl." With that, Maria rose and walked toward the barracks, leaving Perryn alone in the nearly vacant mess hall.

Willis appeared serious, like he was on a mission. Perryn wasn't sure how open he'd be to what she had to say.

"Hey, Perr. Can we talk?" Willis ran his hand through his hair nervously as he approached.

She bit the inside of her cheek. "I guess so."

"I've been thinking a lot—about us."

"It's about time." She hardly hid her annoyance. She'd meant to start in on him, but his expression at her response caught her. He was smiling.

"Perryn, we've been through a lot together over the last few months. At times, I've planned to tell you something important, but something always happens before I can get to it. My dad. The Underground. And then—"

"Jez." She couldn't hide the disdain in her voice.

Willis frowned. "I was going to say my mother's rescue."

"Are you sure?" She stepped toward him and pointed a finger at his chest. "I saw you, Willis. In the hallway, I saw you there— with her."

His eyes grew wide at the revelation, and they darted left and right as if searching for something to say. He took a step back and bit his lip. She glanced away to blink hard. She didn't want to cry, not in this conversation.

"I—I—oh man, I know how that must have appeared. You have to believe me that it was nothing."

"Nothing?" She mockingly smacked her forehead. She was trying hard not to act like a petty, jealous girl, but she couldn't help it. For months, Willis had shrunk backward from showing her his heart, and Jez had somehow broken down his walls in minutes.

"No, you're right. It wasn't nothing, but it wasn't me. Jez and I have been close friends for a long time, and it has always been clear she wanted something more. She's—"

"She's using you, Willis." Perryn gave him a shove. She couldn't contain her anger any longer, though she wasn't sure where her anger was most directed. "She has always used you— manipulated you. I watched on the station as she did whatever it took to control you, and it's no different this time. I don't know what she's planning—but it's all the same from where I'm standing."

Willis stood stunned by the outburst. He searched her face, and she resolved to hold her gaze and let the words hang in the silence between them.

Let it sink in, Willis. She's up to something.

He opened his mouth to speak and closed it again. He took a deep breath. "I—I think you're right. She's acting very strange, but it's beside the point."

"What is the point then?" She rolled her eyes. Still, some part of her was genuinely curious what he would say next.

"The point is that I need to tell you the truth."

"About?"

"About how I feel."

Somewhere inside, her anger cooled, and she allowed her heart to leap.

Chapter Thirty-One

"Not again!" Sheila exclaimed, slapping the table with her hand. She let out an exasperated sigh and rested her head on her hands. "Right when I think I'm on to something—" She never finished her thought, but Chris's sigh revealed he understood.

"I know," he said. "The doctors write about their theories, but then they simply include endless lists of drugs they are using on a specific patient. No conclusions. Countless charts of data."

She turned to him. "So. What do we know from what we've read?"

"People are being taken to Solution Systems against their will," Chris said with distaste in his voice. "I even read a set of notes on what was required to subdue a particularly unruly man they abducted."

Sheila nodded. "We know that those experimented on are all previously recoded."

"And there was that one doctor, Dr. Shepherd, that used the word 'improvement' and 'ultimate breakthrough' a lot."

"Ultimate breakthrough?" Sheila glanced at Chris suddenly.

"Yeah. I read three-in-a-row where he talked about his patients being close to the 'ultimate breakthrough' simply to have them die in the end. So morbid. I couldn't read anymore. Kept seeing the faces of the people we left behind there."

Sheila chewed on her lip, trying to piece the puzzle together in her mind. *What are they getting at?*

Sheila twirled her finger sideways in front of her. "Tell me, again, what you saw there."

"Room after room of sedated patients. A laboratory with doctors doing autopsies on deceased patients. And Jez."

"And you said they were going to—you know—to Jez?"

Sheila hesitated to say it.

"Cut her open? Yeah. That." He winced as he said it. "There was something else. We were opening doors, and the three of them, Willis, Kane, and Perryn, started checking behind the ears of the bodies."

Sheila shot up in her chair. "That's it." She snapped her fingers and started scanning files again.

"What's it?"

"The 'ultimate breakthrough.' The one-hundred barrier. Scientists have been trying to crack that for years." She raced through file names until she found the one she recalled. "Yes, here it is."

Chris leaned over her shoulder to read the notes:

Day 43

Dr. Shepherd

Patient 104 Notes

Patient 104 proved to be our greatest success in our search for the latest innovation in genetic recoding. Due to previous training to be an Alliance Chase runner, his recoding cycles were quite advanced in number. A 30-day regimen of drugs to stimulate the nervous system and brain function was administered prior to attempting the one-hundredth recoding. Patient underwent the genetic recode at 8am this morning. The consciousness took to the new body immediately, and healthy vitals were recorded for 5 hours and 3 minutes. This exceeds all previous attempts by more than three hours. Recommend all patients receive the same drug regimen. Consider checking for correlating data from Patient #1.

"So, someone was recoded the hundredth time and survived for a few hours? That's the breakthrough?" Chris scratched his head in confusion.

"Let's read another," Sheila said. The idea was forming in her mind, but she needed to be sure. For several minutes, they read through similar notes from Dr. Shepherd. Each time, he recorded a slightly modified set of procedures, and each time the patient survived a little longer than the previous one. A few went catastrophically wrong. The 'successful' ones all referred to

Patient #1.

Sheila snapped again. "I think I get it."

"I'm glad *you* do." Chris twisted his mouth in puzzlement.

"The Alliance has tried to break the one-hundred recoding barrier as long as they've been recoding people. However, they could rarely attempt it except when someone, usually Chase trainees, made it that high. Dr. Shepherd is using all of these abducted people to—"

Chris's eyes grew wide as he completed her words. "To systematically force people to their one-hundredth recoding to finally break the barrier."

"The Alliance is giving him an unlimited supply of people to recode."

"For the Chase?" Chris cocked his head to one side. "Half of the alliances don't even participate anymore. Sounds extreme when their odds are so high anyway."

Sheila shook her head. "No, it's got to be more."

But what?

"Who do you think Patient Number One is?" Chris cocked his head to one side.

On cue, the computer on the other side of the space chirped at the two of them. Chris hopped over to the screen, and he smiled.

"We're in luck. The encryption on Penny's files was the same as Solution Systems. I've managed to unlock them all."

"Scan to see if there are any references to 'recoding' or 'Patient #1' or even 'Project Rebirth.'" Sheila scooted her chair over behind Chris.

Chris entered the search parameters and crammed the enter key down. Scanning the filtered files, he selected one that included all the key words and opened it.

October 1st

To: Administrative Liaison to the Coalition Chairman

From: Dr. Ryan Shepherd

Re: Project Rebirth—Patient/Asset #1

Patient #1 continues to show incredible improvement with each recoding. Latest recoding has included combat training and advanced perception, which has remarkably reduced her reaction time in testing. Patient is completely loyal to the cause and will serve the chairman's goals well. She continues to be our greatest asset in Project Rebirth and the key to recoding your future army of enhanced soldiers. Recommend against autopsy at this time.

"That was dated a couple weeks ago." Chris pointed to the date.

Sheila lifted her chin toward the screen. "Open the next one."

October 2nd

To: Dr. Ryan Shepherd

From: Administrative Liaison to Coalition Chairman

Re: Project Rebirth—Patient/Asset #1

Due to timeline required by the chairman, you are hereby ordered to schedule the autopsy of Patient #1 once current tests are completed. Plans cannot proceed with a single enhanced soldier, and latest developments are minimal. More extreme measures must be taken to speed the development of final goals. Please advise when autopsy is to proceed.

The two of them sat dumbfounded as the picture formed in their minds. Solution Systems had been tasked with creating some sort of enhanced army. A female, known as Patient One, had undergone the enhancement, but the chairman was not content with a single successful case.

"You know who this Patient One sounds like?" Chris arched a brow, breaking the silence.

"Let's be sure. Click on the first file that references Patient One." She pointed to the file and Chris opened it. Scanning the document, it showed a list of various enhancements that'd been incorporated into the recoding process: increased strength, heightened endurance, weapons proficiency, hand-to-hand combat, problem-solving skills. It wasn't the list that drew most of their attention. That was reserved for the picture that sat in the upper right of the document. The fierce expression, dark eyes, and jet-black hair were unmistakable.

"Patient One is—" Chris trailed off as he spoke.

"Jez." Sheila's voice shook as she said the name. "It's Jez. She is the first of the Alliance super-soldiers."

"We have to warn—"

Chris's words were cut off when the ground shook. The explosion far away echoed through the tunnels of the Underground headquarters, and the lights and computers went dark. Emergency lights illuminated, creating an eerie glow with long shadows.

"It's too late for that," Sheila said, her flat tone contrasting with the fear in her eyes. "Come on!" She grabbed Chris's shirt and started pulling him toward the door.

Chapter Thirty-Two

Willis breathed deeply and opened his mouth to speak the long-awaited words. In moments, he would say what he should have long ago, and everything would become clear. Her response would tell him what he needed to know about them, about Jez—about everything. He could see the light glistening in her eyes and her hopeful stare.

Kaboom!

The explosion blasted through the far wall of the mess hall, the force of it pushing tables and chairs away from the blast and filling the area with debris. Instinctively, Willis threw himself toward Perryn, and the two crashed to the cold, hard floor. The lights extinguished, and they lay in complete darkness.

Emergency lights lit seconds later, and the air was thick with floating dust and smoke. He coughed on a lungful of the powdery air as he tried to stand, his legs shaking from the adrenaline rush. The sound of the blast still rang in his ears making the disorder around him appear dreamlike. Helping Perryn to her feet, his eyes burned from the particles in the air as he squinted at his surroundings.

Rattattatt. The sound of gunfire, still muffled in his ringing ears, could be heard coming from the direction of the explosion.

"What's happening, Willis?" Perryn's wide eyes searched his face. She appeared to be yelling, probably because her hearing was as muffled as his.

"I don't know," he said, equally stressed and taking her hand. "Let's get away from here."

They ran away from the area of the explosion, still choking on the unclean atmosphere. One hallway led to the next, each revealing panic-stricken members of the Underground. Some ran toward the explosion, dart guns already drawn. Others ran away in any direction they could. Willis and Perryn weaved their way through the swarming people.

Rattattatt. Rattattatt. The gunfire was spreading through the compound.

I have to find my mom and get to Kane. It was the one thing he could think to do.

Kaboom! Another explosion rocked the Underground facility. Willis stumbled. Running into him, Perryn's momentum took both to the floor again. His forehead smacked the concrete, and a flash of light filled his vision. Screams could be heard coming from every corner of the compound as frightened people fled. The emergency lights flickered, and then they finally went out. More screaming ensued in the darkness.

He placed a hand on the wound. It was wet with blood and full of gritty dirt. Clambering to all fours, he crawled forward to the next corner, Perryn following. The hallway they entered was quieter, empty of people. He sat against the wall and tried to collect himself.

The chaos quieted as people ran from the invasion, away from their position. Best he could tell, they were in a hallway that included storage closets, not an area to which anyone would be fleeing.

"Perryn, you hurt?" He glanced over at where she would be, but he could see nothing in the blackness of the tunnel.

She huddled next to him. "I don't think so. You?"

"Hit my head. We need to get out of here."

"The Coalition found us, didn't they?"

"I think so, but who tipped them off?"

"You haven't put that together, yet?" said a third voice.

A light illuminated, blinding the two of them. Willis raised his hand to shield his eyes. In front of them stood a figure shrouded in darkness behind the flashlight beam. The one distinguishing feature Willis could make out was the raised pistol, silhouetted against the light.

"Hello, Will," the voice said.

It was Jez.

Sheila and Chris darted between the escaping people. The emergency lights illuminated, but their strobing flicker made everyone's movement appear jerky and inhuman. Her breaths came in short heaves as she raced to find Willis. Men, women, and young people ran for their lives, making their way to several of the exits that led away from the compound. Turning a corner, she skidded to a halt.

Before them stood a wall of Law-keepers, each armed with semi-automatic firearms and dressed in riot gear. A flash from the barrel of the first Law-keeper was followed by the sting of stone debris hitting her cheek as the bullet hit the wall beside her.

"Get down!" Kane's voice boomed from behind.

She and Chris dropped to the floor as a cloud of tranquilizer darts flew over them. A few found their mark, and four of the Law-keepers dropped to the floor. The rest opened fire. A grunt behind them told her someone had been hit. Sneaking a peek, she could see the Underground perched in defensive positions, mostly out of sight. Another volley of well-aimed darts, and more soldiers fell. They were down to one in the small group that remained conscious.

Seeing his opportunity, Chris scrambled to his feet and rushed the Law-keeper. He wrapped his arms around the soldier's waist and tackled him, causing the man to grunt as they hit the ground. His weapon clattered to the floor a few feet away, and the two wrestled on the ground. Though he was larger than Chris, the young man's ferocity kept it an even match.

Sheila stood to her feet and ran to the soldier's weapon. Picking it up, she found herself surprised by its weight. Gripping it in both hands, she ran to the two struggling figures, and drove the butt of the rifle into the Law-keeper's head. He fell limp.

Kane leaped down from his perch and made his way over to them.

"Well done, Chris." Kane patted Chris on the shoulder.

"Thanks, Chief."

Sheila turned to Kane. "What's happening, Kane?"

"Law-keepers. Someone tipped off our whereabouts, and they are invading from the south entrance."

"I think we know who did it," Chris said, still breathless from the fight.

"Who?" Kane's face grew angry.

"Jez." Sheila spoke the name like she was spitting. "She's working for the Coalition. She's some kind of prototype soldier."

Chris nodded. "Guess that explains her performance in the trials."

Kane cursed under his breath. He scanned in all directions, listening to the screaming people fleeing the tunnels. A second explosion hit, followed by complete darkness. Small bits of debris fell from the ceiling, showering Sheila. Flashlights clicked on all around them as Kane's defensive group adjusted to the new darkness.

"We have to find Willis and Perryn." Sheila raised her eyebrows at Kane. "It's no accident she's been warming up to Willis since waking."

Kane's eyes narrowed, and he nodded. Motioning with his hand, he sent the rest of his group on to the next defensive position.

"Follow me," Kane said.

The three of them took off into the darkness.

<hr/>

Willis stood to meet Jez and gazed into the blackness where he guessed her face was. His head pounded as he did so, and he blinked hard to drive away the dizziness. She lowered the beam, and Willis could see her dark eyes staring at him. The thick shadows made her presence even more foreboding, and Willis slowly raised two hands to show her he wasn't armed.

"Jez, we don't have to do this again," he said, pleading.

"Oh? I think we do," she said through gritted teeth. "Kane isn't here to stop me this time."

"But why? Why do you hate me so much?"

"Because you stole everything from me!" she screamed,

jabbing the pistol in the air. A squeeze on his arm let Willis know that Perryn had taken a position next to him. "You stole my right to run in the Chase. It was mine—ours! I gave you everything I had, and you tossed me aside the first chance you had."

"I never planned to hurt you, Jez. Please, we don't have to do this."

"Do you know what they put me through? Huh?" She paused, a snarl appearing on her lips. "I've lived through hell, Will. I believed I was going to die when they hauled me away to recoding on the station. And you did nothing—*nothing*!"

"Jez—I—I'm sorry. At least you lived through it."

Jez's chin shook. "You think that was a good thing? I *wish* I had died on the station. When I woke from my recoding, it was in a cell."

"A cell?"

"Yes, a cell. Like an animal, they placed me in a cage to be studied. I went from earning my freedom to becoming a living science experiment. Every day for the last six months, I woke up wondering what horrible thing they were going to do to me." She was breathing heavily, the words escaping between breaths. The pistol shook in her hands, but Willis believed it more out of anger than fear.

"Jez—" Perryn said.

"Shut up. You, shut up!" Jez snapped. "You're one of the reasons he lost his way. You batted your little, brown eyes at him a few times and played that Blue Team damsel-in-distress act, and he came running, didn't he?"

Willis considered approaching her but hesitated. "Jez, please. I want to help you."

"It's too late for me." Her voice was softer this time.

The honesty of the statement gave Willis pause. "No, it's not. We can help." He lowered his own voice, forcing it to be calm.

"Will, it's too late. You see, that's the worst part of it." She brought the pistol to her head and tapped the side of it. "They're in there. Loyalty to the cause, coded permanently in my brain. I live to do their bidding, and there's nothing I can do about it. It's my living hell, every day knowing I want to escape—but my brain won't let me."

Willis's heart leapt. "You can overcome that."

"Oh please. Don't give me that. How do you think I spent the few waking hours I was permitted in that chop shop? Every day I planned my escape merely to have my brain switch into autopilot, so I would do whatever they asked. What would you know, anyway?"

"I did it."

For the first time, he saw the crack in her armor. She hadn't expected that answer, and he needed to keep her talking. Kane wouldn't leave without them, and he needed to keep her occupied until help arrived.

He took a step forward, and she pointed the pistol at him once again. Her hand was trembling worse this time.

"Look, when I went to the Chase, they activated something inside me. It was something they'd put into me as a child after my one recoding. I was supposed to win the Chase and do something to help the world, but their voice kept telling me to serve the Coalition. The chairman told me to pass a law giving him almost unlimited power, and everything in me planned to do it."

"And? Why didn't you?" She was curious, and that was good.

Connect with her, Willis. Help her see that you understand what she's going through.

"I—I broke through," he said. He didn't know how else to describe it.

Her lip curled. "Broke through? What is that supposed to mean?"

"I don't know. Somehow, I saw that following the chairman would harm those I loved. I realized that winning gave me little choice. I would pass the chairman's law if I won, but that didn't mean I didn't have a choice. I chose to lose the Chase."

She stared at him, considering his words.

"Jez," he said, this time daring a small step forward, "their suggestions are linked to triggers. Mine was winning the Chase, so by choosing not to win, I prevented the trigger from taking place. You can make a choice that lets you get around their suggestions, like I did."

Jez stood, her face stoic, but Willis could sense her churning inside. She was thinking about what he was saying. The pistol lowered an inch, and her gaze fell to the floor. For a minute, they all stood frozen in that state of tension.

"And what choice do I have?" Her voice was barely a whisper.

Chapter Thirty-Three

Sheila and Chris followed Kane's massive hulk through the darkness. The news about Jez and Willis had changed him, and his usually calm demeanor was replaced with a determined fury. He moved at surprising speed through the dark, cloudy hallways. More than once, Sheila stumbled over fallen debris that escaped her notice in the dim light of Kane's flashlight.

"They're not here either." Chris cursed as they reached the end of another tunnel.

Sheila went over their movements in her head, feeling completely lost in this maze.

Kane hit the wall with his hand in frustration and turned to head the way they'd come. "They must have been close to the south entrance. It's the one place that makes sense, or we would have found them already."

"That area is overrun with Law-keepers. They're either dead or captured." Chris frowned and shook his head.

Kane straightened and turned to them. "No," he whispered with fire in his eyes. "I won't let her finish what she started on the station. I should have ended her then. We keep searching."

Sheila placed her hand on Chris's shoulder to affirm it wasn't up for debate. He nodded, and they proceeded down the tunnel to the main passageway in that part of headquarters. As they neared the main hallway, someone yelled.

"Get down!" The voice belonged to Lydia.

Instinctively, the three of them dropped to the floor, and Kane turned off his light. A second later, a barrage of gunfire lit the dark hallway spraying bits of concrete as the wild bullets struck the walls. Light illuminated the tunnel from the left as the Law-keepers approached. Somewhere to the right, Lydia and whoever was with her must have been hiding. Small bursts of weapons fire from the Law-keepers echoed in the tunnels.

The three crouched in the shadows at the corner of the hallway. Sheila forced herself against the concrete, willing herself to become part of the wall. Chris, who took a position next to her, sounded like he was trying to control his breathing. Kane, however, didn't join them. Even in the dim light, she could see his silhouette kneeling in the shadow.

The first of the Law-keepers appeared in view. Turning, he peered down their tunnel to make sure it was secure. Instead, his light fell on Kane's face. He didn't even get a chance to react.

With the near-impossible speed developed as a Chase runner, Kane stood and wrapped his hand around the soldier's throat. Roaring like an enraged lion, Kane hurled the much smaller man backward. The thud that followed told Sheila that more than one Law-keeper had been knocked down.

Shots fired, and Kane still kept moving. A well-placed fist here and a kick there, and soldiers fell limp on the floor. Sheila dared to peer around the corner, and she saw Kane drop a Law-keeper to the floor with a single punch to the jaw. He then took the man's weapon and clubbed the final soldier, knocking him senseless.

Leaning out farther, she could see the bodies of six unconscious Law-keepers on the floor, their flashlights and rifles strewn around them. Kane stood above them, his shoulders heaving as he breathed. She stood and slowly approached him from behind.

"Kane?" she said softly.

He turned suddenly to her, his eyes wild with rage. Seeing her, his face softened, and his jaw unclenched. His legs wobbled, and he fell to one knee. He reached for his side.

Picking up a flashlight, Sheila shone it in Kane's direction. The blood was clearly visible on his shirt where a Law-keeper's shot had found its mark. Behind her, she could hear the Underground members approaching quickly.

"Chief, you okay?" Maria's body shook, and a tremble rocked her voice.

Lydia rushed to his side to check the wound, and he tried to wave her off.

"Chief, let me inspect it." She pulled at his arm. "It doesn't look good."

"No time." He grimaced with each word. He stood, appearing unsteady but determined.

"Why are you guys here?" Chris emerged from the hallway.

"We got separated from our group." Lydia pointed down the hallway.

Maria glanced down mournfully. "Yeah, what was left of them."

"We're trying to make it to Willis and Perryn," Sheila said. "Jez is a Coalition agent, which explains how they found us."

"If she finds my girl and her guy—" Maria started the statement, but she didn't need to finish.

"Then, let's find them." Lydia took a position next to Kane, a protective countenance on her face. Sheila understood she would stay by his side should he need assistance.

"South entrance," Kane said again. His breaths were coming in short gasps.

"Dear God. The south entrance?" Maria said.

"Let's stop wasting time and move," Lydia said, finishing the conversation. She waved her gun barrel. The five of them trotted at a moderate pace to allow Kane to keep up. He stumbled along with one hand on the wound. More than once, Lydia grabbed his arm as he appeared ready to fall. Still, they pressed toward the south entrance.

Jez stood frozen in front of Willis and Perryn. The pistol was still trained on Willis, but her eyes appeared to see beyond the two of them.

Perryn could see Jez thinking through Willis's words. *Keep it up, Willis. She's listening.*

Willis took a deep breath and tried to answer the question that still hung in the air between them.

"Jez, there's always another choice," he said, keeping his

voice calm. "We simply have to figure it out. We'll help you do that. I promise."

The hardness on Jez's face melted. "I don't know, Will. I've done everything they've programmed me to do so far," she said. She straightened as if catching her moment of weakness. "I was to infiltrate the Underground. That was easy enough when you invaded Solution Systems. Posing as a lab rat for the scientists there wasn't hard since that is what I was."

Willis winced at the statement, and Perryn could feel his muscles tense in anger. Jez had played all of them.

"Once you took me in, I was to alert them to your whereabouts, which wasn't hard to do. I even disabled an electrical panel that created the smallest crack in the security around this place."

"And since they're here?" Willis nodded to the hallway behind her. "What is your mission?"

Perryn didn't want the answer.

"I was supposed to deal with you. They've never forgiven you for what you did at the Chase."

The air hung thick with her statement. She had said it so matter-of-factly like it was a certainty.

"Was?" Perryn kept her voice soft, catching the tense of Jez's words. She found herself stepping forward to draw Jez's attention. She couldn't allow her to harm Willis.

"Are you rethinking your programming?" Willis raised his eyebrows.

"Yes." Her eyes welled with tears, and she added, "I don't want to kill you, Willis. Despite what you think of me, I've cared about you for a long time. I had hoped that we—" Her voice trailed off.

Perryn's insides soured at the confession. She tried not to show it in her expression. Even if the idea of Jez and Willis together was unthinkable, perhaps the hope of their relationship would be the crack in her armor they needed.

Go with it, Willis. Don't push her away.

As if sensing her thoughts, Willis spoke. "Jez, this is what I'm talking about. You can choose the life you want. There's a way around the Coalition's instructions. There has to be."

"I can't have you, Willis. I know that now. You forgave me for trying to kill you on the station, which was unbelievable. But— even you can't forgive me twice."

"Jez—"

"No!" she screamed. She raised the pistol again. "Don't say things you don't mean! I know what you're trying to do."

Perryn tensed at the outburst. She could sense Jez ready to act, and she resolved to act first.

"I'm trying to help you." Willis spread his hands outward in a non-threatening gesture.

"I know, but you can't." Jez's chin quivered, her tears returning. "I have no choice. They want you out of the picture."

"Jez, please." His voice caught, and she could hear the fear in his voice. "The programming can't be hindered, but it can be interpreted."

"Yes, it can. I believe you." She nodded, breathing deeply to compose herself. "They want you gone, ineffective, unable to serve as a symbol of defiance to the Coalition." She paused, considering her words. Perryn was ready to leap, sensing Jez had made a decision. "And there's more than one way to do that."

The pistol moved—in Perryn's direction. The muzzle flashed in a blinding brilliance.

The bullet ripped through the air and hit Perryn in the stomach. Fire filled her like a hot punch to the gut had expelled all the air from her lungs, and she was thrown backward against her will. Her body doubled over as the bullet moved through her, and she could feel her legs crumple beneath her. Falling to the floor hard, her vision went fuzzy as her head struck the concrete.

Chapter Thirty-Four

"No!" Willis screamed in terror. He rushed to Perryn's side but halted when Jez pointed the pistol back at him. "Why?" He searched Jez's face for an answer. None came.

"Don't worry," Jez said, eerily calm. "She won't die."

Willis gazed down at Perryn, who lay in a heap, her lip quivering as she peered at him. Her eyes were wide with shock. He glared at Jez, a mix of fury and fear on his face.

"What do you mean, she won't die?" Everything in him raged to leap at her, but he had to know what she meant.

"Her wound isn't fatal—not yet. With luck, you'll have time to get her to a recoding facility. I hear the Underground has access to one." Her voice took on an almost mocking tone as she spoke.

"So why, then?"

Jez smirked and tilted her head. "Oh, Willis, you wouldn't know, would you?"

"Know what?"

"What all those of us who have experienced countless recodings know too well—that the most powerful suggestion they can implant in your brain comes from the last thing you hear before being recoded."

He glanced at Perryn, and she was fading. Her eyelids fluttered as she struggled to remain conscious. Tears poured from the outside corner of her eyes. He fell to his knees and cradled her head in his hands, no longer caring about Jez's threat. "Hang in there, Perr." Tears flooded his own eyes and wet his cheeks.

"Willis?" Perryn's voice was weak.

"Don't speak. Focus on staying conscious. Stay with me."

"I—I love you." The words came as a barely audible whisper.

"I love you too." His long overdue confession came through

sobs. "And I should have said so a long time ago."

Jez stepped forward and crouched next to the two of them, pistol still trained on Willis. "Aww, how sweet. It finally comes out, but that's not the end of it. Remember, it's the last thing she hears, Will." She leaned forward and spoke softly in Perryn's ear. "It's not true, Perryn. He doesn't love you. He pities you. You were weak and pathetic, and like a wounded dog he couldn't help but pity you—but it's not love. It never was."

"What are you—?" Willis started, but it was too late. Jez jabbed her hand down on the bullet wound, and Perryn cried out from the pain. Her eyes rolled back into her head, and she slipped into unconsciousness.

Jez slowly stood, a smile spreading across her face.

"Thank you, Willis. You were right. I did have a choice. There's more than one way to destroy you, and I like this one better."

He glanced at Jez, feeling helpless. "What have you done?"

"I took what is most precious to you, and that will break you, once and for all." She paused. "I should know. It broke me."

"You lie!" he shouted.

"Goodbye, Will." Her smile softened. She backed away from him, pistol still raised.

Click! Her flashlight turned off, and darkness flooded the hall.

Willis sat there in the blackness, still holding Perryn. He could feel her growing weaker. Her trembling was barely perceptible to the touch. "Help me!" he shouted desperately in the darkness. "Someone help me!"

The rifle fire from the Law-keepers had died down as most of the surviving Underground must have fled the facility, so Sheila and the rest had clearly heard the single shot. They skidded to a halt, listening. Silence met them in the dim chamber.

"Where did that come from?" Maria scanned the faces of the others.

"Shh." Lydia held a finger to her lips and cocked an ear toward the hall in front of them.

They stood in the near darkness. Law-keepers could be heard closer to the mess hall, but that was it. Then, the screaming started.

"Help me!" The distant voice sounded desperate. "Someone help me!"

Chris pointed. "That's Willis."

"And if we heard him," Sheila said, "the Law-keepers did too."

Kane stepped forward and turned to the group. Then, he trotted off, drawing upon inhuman reserves to ignore his wound. The other four took his cue. Kane galloped ahead, following the screams, and it was all Sheila could do to keep up with his pace.

Tunnel after tunnel, they ran with abandon. It was a race to Willis and sneaking around would no longer serve them well. He'd apparently made his way east, away from the soldiers' entry point, and the group found no resistance.

The screams grew louder, telling them they were close. Kane turned a corner into a storage area, and he skidded to a stop. The screams stopped as the rest piled in behind Kane. Flashlights turned to illuminate the two figures on the floor.

Sheila stepped from behind the group and examined Willis. She covered her mouth with her hand when she saw him. His face was drenched with tears from his red and swollen eyes. Perryn's seemingly lifeless body lay in his arms. Blood soaked through her clothes and covered Willis as he desperately tried to keep his hands over her wound. More blood pooled in a tiny puddle on the floor around her.

Willis stared up at Sheila. "We have to save her." He whimpered and spoke to her, appearing like he couldn't see the rest of the group.

"Oh, please no." It was all she could say.

"No!" Maria shouted, stepping toward Perryn.

Lydia moved to intercede, but Kane threw a hand out to stop her.

"No time." Stooping, Kane grabbed Perryn's limp frame and picked her up. His huge arms dwarfed her body as they wrapped around her. "This way."

Sheila motioned to Chris, and they grabbed Willis off the floor. He swayed as though he could barely stand, much less run.

"Come on, Willis. She needs you to move forward." Sheila whispered in his ear. He sucked in a breath, and she could feel him accepting the weight of his body on his own legs.

Oh, God. Let us make it in time. Sheila prayed silently.

Kane rushed down the hallway and crashed through a door to the right. Inside the empty storage space, he kicked at what came across as a solid wall. Lydia joined him, and a crack, almost perfectly straight, started to appear in the stone. Suddenly, the wall gave way to reveal a hidden door that'd been cleverly disguised with a thin coat of concrete.

The tunnel beyond was black, and their flashlights revealed a small hover cart that sat waiting in the tunnel. Kane collapsed onto the cart, still holding Perryn. He held his hands over the entry and exit wounds of the bullet. Lydia jumped to the controls and had it moving the instant the rest were aboard.

"Where are we going?" Sheila gave the others a questioning glance. She sat cradling Willis who had crumpled in her arms. He was barely moving, his glassy eyes staring blankly into the dark tunnel.

"There's a recoding facility sympathetic to the Underground," Lydia said over the soft hum of the hovering cart. "We can get there from here. It's not far."

"Recode her? Are you certain?" Sheila couldn't hide the shock in her voice.

"She has minutes to live. It's that or let her die."

"Won't they follow us there?" Maria glanced backward the way they had come.

"No. I programmed that door myself to electronically lock behind whoever used it," Chris said, still catching his breath. "By the time they find it and get through it, we'll be long gone."

"And what about—" Sheila hesitated to continue, not wanting to upset Willis more. "What about Brenda?" Willis's chest expanded under her grip with a sudden breath, but otherwise he didn't move.

"No idea." Lydia shook her head. "I last saw her in the women's barracks, which was the farthest from the explosion. If anyone had time to make it out without being captured, she did."

I hope she's right.

Kane grunted from the pain of his injury, but he wouldn't move his massive hand from Perryn's wound. In the dim light, Sheila could still see she'd grown pale, and her breathing was shallow. Sheila closed her eyes and whispered another silent prayer.

The group sat in silence listening to the echoing hum of the cart as they traversed the tunnels under the city with surprising speed.

Chapter Thirty-Five

Morning. Willis's eyes burned as they opened, the salt of the previous night's tears still clinging to the corners. The light coming in the window was dim, and he guessed that the sun had barely risen. He rubbed his eyes and scanned his surroundings.

There were few objects in the room other than the metal and canvas cot on which he lay. The stone walls were a bland gray, and a single phone by the door blinked as lines were answered. In the corner, two metal filing cabinets sat next to a small wooden table and chair. The fluorescent glow of the ceiling light washed everything in a pale glow broken by a streak of yellow sunlight on the wall next to the window. A medicinal odor filled the air.

He couldn't remember where he was and tried to remember how he'd gotten there. That's when the memory of what happened struck him like a punch in his gut. His insides turned, and his breathing quickened.

Is Perryn all right? Is she alive? Where is my mother? Did she make it out? His mind raced. He sat up in a panic, and a bolt of pain shot through his head. He fell back to his pillow and gave the headache a second to dull. He recalled what he could remember of the night they'd experienced.

The cart had brought them far down the length of the tunnel to an unassuming door, on which Lydia had pounded several times in code. A nervous attendant dressed in scrubs had emerged, and after a few exchanged words with Lydia, ran inside. A couple seconds later, he emerged with another assistant and a gurney. Loading Perryn, they took off down the hallway. He hadn't seen her since. Last he could remember was Lydia giving him an injection saying it would help him sleep for a while.

He lay awake with a post-drug headache and the realization

that the night hadn't been a nightmare. Bile rose into his mouth as images of Jez and the flash of the pistol returned to his mind's eye.

He took a deep breath and slowly turned to his side. Pushing with his arms, he raised himself to a seated position, moving carefully this time. His feet hit the floor, and the cold tile sent a shudder through his spine. He bent over to reach his shoes, which lay next to the cot, and cried out with the surge of his headache. What felt like hours later, he finally had his shoes on and pushed himself into a standing position.

The heavy door opened with surprising ease, and he shuffled into the hallway. It was quiet except for a murmur coming from behind a door near the end of the hallway. The walls and floors gleamed white under the lights, and he squinted as he moved toward the soft sounds. He had to keep one hand braced against the wall to prevent him from falling over.

"Hello?" His voice creaked when he spoke. He cleared his throat and tried again. "Hello?"

The murmur went silent. The door at the end of the hallway opened.

"Willis? You're awake?" The voice was his mother's as she stepped out of the doorway. She rushed to him, and he welcomed the assistance of her arms as she embraced him. "They said you wouldn't awaken for a few more hours."

"Mom? What—how?"

"Oh, my son." She pulled back to study his face as her eyes glistened. "What have you been through?"

He searched her face. "How are you here? Where is everyone?"

"Most are still asleep. It's still quite early. You've been asleep for more than a day." He must have appeared shocked because she immediately kept going. "They gave you drugs to sleep. You were a wreck when they got you here, and they needed you to rest. As for how I got here, well, let's sit first. You're swaying like you're ready to pass out."

She placed her arm around him and helped him walk the remainder of the length of the hallway. Turning into the door she'd emerged from, he was welcomed with the sight of Lydia, Sheila, and a man wearing a priest's collar who he didn't recognize. Brenda helped him sit in the closest chair.

"Sorry, Willis." Lydia offered an apologetic smile. "This facility uses some strong drugs, so I'm sure you've had a wicked headache since waking."

"It's fine," he said. It was far from the truth, but he didn't want her to feel bad.

"Son," Brenda said, pointing at the man in the collar, "this is Father Anthony. He was kind enough to bring me here when we received word of what happened to your group."

"It's good to meet you, Willis." Father Anthony extended his hand. Willis took it, noting his eyes, which appeared filled with compassion.

"Willis, he's a friend of the Underground." Sheila winked at Father Anthony. "He operates several safe houses in the city, which is where your mother and a group of other members escaped to during the invasion. He has helped me more than once, and you can trust him."

"It's my small part to do what is right for those who are free," Father Anthony said.

Willis examined the faces in the group, and his eyes landed on his mother. He scrunched his eyebrows together.

"Yes, son. She's alive." Brenda sensed his worry.

Willis's lip quivered, and sobs of relief threatened to overcome him. He might have let them, but he had too many questions. His breath shuddered a couple of times as he tried to calm himself.

She made it. She's so tough—far tougher than me.

Willis cleared his throat, but it didn't help. His mouth felt as dry as plaster. "Can I see her?"

Lydia shook her head. "I wouldn't advise it. We need to give the process sufficient time. I've been in regular communication with the doctors here, and while this was an extremely rushed recoding, they are confident that the process took. This place is state-of-the-art, and they can produce the physical copy of the body quickly here. They are asking for patience to ensure we don't disrupt the process of letting her consciousness settle into her body."

Willis nodded, a little deflated.

"How about everyone else?"

Sheila spoke for the room. "Kane is recovering from his injuries. He did himself no favors carrying Perryn through the tunnels, but he'll be fine. Chris and Maria are resting. They'll be eager to know that you're awake."

"In truth," Lydia said, "we're all a bit shell-shocked after what happened. From what we can figure, about half our people are dead or captured. The rest are scattered among safe houses all over the city. Father Anthony is working to move people farther outside the city until we can regroup."

Father Anthony nodded in agreement. "We need to keep everyone safe at this point. It'll be a long while before we can regain the level of organization we had."

"Willis, is there anything you can remember?" Lydia turned to him. "Did Jez tell you anything that might give away what the Coalition's next move is?"

Willis studied the floor trying to remember all that'd transpired. He mentally walked through the explosion, their flight to the storage hallway, Jez's appearance, and finally her words. It wasn't much to go on.

"They wanted me out of the picture," he said.

Sheila raised a brow. "They? You mean the Coalition?"

"I guess so. Whoever was in charge of her recode programming planned to have me removed. She said I was a 'symbol of defiance' and had to be destroyed."

Brenda scrunched her face in confusion. "So why shoot Perryn?"

To destroy me. Willis said the words silently, but he wasn't ready to share those details. He wasn't ready to admit that his insides were torn to pieces and held together on the slim hope that Jez had been wrong.

"Because she feels—something—towards me." He avoided

meeting the eyes of the group. The idea made his stomach lurch. The disgusted frowns around the circle when he did look told him he wasn't alone with this reaction.

"I think everyone's thinking it. Can I say it?" Sheila grimaced. "That's messed up—really messed up."

Lydia didn't waver and continued her questioning. "Is that all she told you?"

"Yes," Willis said. It was all he would say at this point.

"Very well. Why don't you rest then? I'll let you know when Perryn is ready to see you." Lydia nodded to Brenda who took the cue to stand. She placed her hand on Willis's shoulder, and he joined her.

<hr />

Willis and his mother sat staring out a third-floor window of the recoding facility. The city appeared gray under the cloudy sky, and the morning fog still clung to the streets between the buildings where it could hide from the rising sun. Brenda sat to his right with her legs curled under her so that she leaned toward him. He could smell the herbal tea in her hand. The pleasant aroma warmed his soul, and he took a deep breath.

Sitting there, he realized how long it'd been since they'd sat and enjoyed being a family. His heart was split, overwhelmed with gratitude to have his mother safe again but aching over the empty chair to his left that should have been filled by his father.

"Mom?" He turned to her.

"Yes, son?"

"Tell me about Dad."

Brenda gave him a soft smile. "What would you like to know?"

"Anything, really. I barely had a few months with him. There's so much I don't know." Willis paused thoughtfully and said, "How did you first meet?"

Brenda laughed gently, and Willis noticed the joy in her eyes as she remembered his father. "The truth is, I didn't think much of Max when I first met him."

"What do you mean?"

She smiled as she spoke. "He was so cocky. He was a fantastic racer, but that wasn't the problem. The problem was that he loved it." She sighed. "He believed he could beat anyone at anything. That is, until I came along."

"What happened?"

"I beat him."

Willis let a single laugh escape his lips. "Beat him? At what?"

She smiled again at the memory and turned to him. "Do they still play the chair game at the Lake Placid training center?"

Willis, too, smiled, remembering the numerous times the young trainees had challenged each other. The game was simple—squat in a seated position with your back against the wall and see who could hold the position the longest. He remembered beating out several of his friends during his years there. It required incredible leg and core strength to remain for more than a minute.

"Yeah," he said, chuckling. "They still did when I was there."

"Well," Brenda said, "one day at lunch, he was being extra loud and boasting about the race he'd run that day, to the point that I'd had enough. I walked right over to him and challenged him to the chair game with the condition that he shut up if I beat him."

Willis laughed again, imagining the scene. "What did he say?"

"He wanted to know what he'd get out of it if he won."

"And?"

"I told him I would wash his uniform for a week, which was saying something. Your father could sweat profusely during training. He agreed, and a crowd gathered to watch this girl who had challenged the best racer at the center. Well, after about a minute and half, my legs were shaking so badly, all I could think about was how gross his uniform was after each training run. I refused to have to wash anything of his, so I set my mind to it and kept going."

Willis was smiling from ear to ear. "What did Dad do?"

"That was the best part. After about three minutes, he kept glancing at me like he was scared. His friends started harassing me, so I closed my eyes to focus. Suddenly, everyone screamed, which startled me. I slipped and fell to the floor. I believed I'd lost until I saw Max. He was lying on the floor, catching his breath with all his friends laughing at him. They'd shouted because *he* had fallen first."

"I bet he hated that."

"You know—it wasn't like that. He got up, brushed himself off, and offered me a hand. Once I was standing, he asked me a question." She stopped and stared out the window again as if to remember the next part of the story. Her eyes glistened.

He gave her a respectful moment. "What was the question?"

She smiled, still gazing out the window. "He said to me, 'Before I shut my mouth for the rest of lunch, can I ask you your name?' I told him it was Brenda, and he'd better not forget it. I'll never forget his response." Willis waited for her to continue. "'No, I won't. I definitely won't,' he'd said. A month later, he was called up to the space station. It was another year until I saw him again."

Willis smiled and imagined his father as a cocky, young racer. It was another way his life had mirrored his father's, and it helped him feel closer to him. He imagined his father sitting in the chair to his left shaking his head with a smile at the embarrassing story. Willis stared out the window, silently drinking in the images in his mind.

"Son, what is eating at you?" Brenda leaned toward him, apparently noticing his blank stare.

"I don't know. I guess I'm worried." It was a vague answer, but he wasn't sure he was ready to talk about it. No amount of discussion could change things. Either Jez was right—or she was wrong.

"She's going to be all right you know. There's nothing to worry about, I'm sure." It astounded him how his mother could read his mind.

"I hope so, but I can't help feeling—" He paused, unable to finish.

"Responsible?" Mind reader—totally in his head.

"Yes," he said. "I made the choice to bring Jez back with us. Everything that has happened is my fault."

"You can't believe that, son."

"I can, and I do. Without Jez, the Coalition would never have found us. So many would still be alive. And Perryn—well, she'd be fine. *We'd* be fine."

Brenda studied him, reading his face. *She can sense I'm keeping something from her.*

She reached out an touched his hand. "Willis, I don't think Perryn is going to blame you. You didn't pull the trigger. Jez did."

"No. It's not that." He pulled away before he could stop himself.

His mother frowned. "What is it, then?"

Willis wrung his hands in his lap so hard that one of his knuckles popped. He wished he could tell her about Jez's words. He longed to admit his fear of how Perryn would be when she awoke.

He opened his mouth and then closed it.

"I never got to tell her how I feel. I was about to—when the Coalition bomb when off. I'm afraid I won't get another chance." It was as close as he could get to the truth without breaking down.

Brenda smiled lovingly and placed her hand on his forearm this time. "Son, that chance will come. She is here, and she's alive. We can be grateful for that."

"I am." He was thankful. Perryn could be dead, and he could never live with himself if that had happened.

They resumed staring out the window. The clouds were beginning to part, and the fog had lifted from some of the brighter streets.

Brenda leaned into whisper to him. "I think you're going to see that everything is going to be all right." She smiled and took a sip of her tea.

"Yeah. Maybe you're right." For the first time since waking, Willis allowed a flutter of hope to rise in his chest. Maybe, his mother grasped something he didn't.

Slowly, the darkness gave way to an awareness of her surroundings, and Perryn could sense that others were nearby. Her eyelids fluttered and cracked open slightly. Blinding light intruded on her vision, and she winced. Trying again, she managed to open them.

She was lying on a hospital bed with several monitors beeping her vitals nearby. A nurse stood in the corner, oblivious to her newly conscious patient.

Please, no. She cried inwardly, realizing what had happened. *No, no, no. Not again.*

She was alive and could feel her heart pounding inside of her. She tried to move her fingers, which responded, but she couldn't escape the feeling that they were not hers. A tear leaked out the corner of her eye. Such was the feeling of waking from a genetic recoding—alive, but in a body not your own.

No, no, no! Her mind remembered the dozens of previous recodings she'd experienced, and the horror was always the same. It was a feeling she'd grown to hate. She shuddered as sadness threatened to overwhelm her.

"Well, well." the nurse said cheerfully. She walked over and checked Perryn's vitals on the monitors. "Welcome back to the land of the living. Everything appears right as rain here. Are you feeling anything unusual?"

Perryn stared.

"I know. It's a hard feeling to wake to, but you're alive, and that's what matters most."

Is it? The flood inside of Perryn made her want to cry or shout or run from the room all at once.

"Take a second to gather yourself." The nurse continued her encouragement in practiced form. She'd clearly seen more than her share of recovering recoding patients. "Practice a few small movements—fingers, toes, turning your head—and then we'll see about sitting up for the first time."

Perryn lay still, unmoving.

"Take your time—whenever you're ready. I'll inform the doctor that you're awake."

Perryn's lip quivered, and she stared at the ceiling.

My name is Perryn. I was a Chase runner for the Western Alliance. I survived training and joined the Underground. I was shot by Jez. I was prepared to die for Willis.

"Willis," she said in a whisper. The tears finally overtook her. The others would be here soon, and she needed to let them out.

Chapter Thirty-Six

Willis stood in the hallway outside the recovery area. He could hear the joyful sound of greetings as the others stopped in to see Perryn. Her waking had lifted everyone's spirits, and the group had hurried to her bedside as soon as they heard the news. Making an excuse, he held back while the rest rushed to her side.

He needed to see how she was before going in.

Peering inside, he could see the others gathered around Perryn's bed. She was sitting, still dressed in a hospital gown. Maria was at the head of the bed smiling and smacking her gum excitedly and talking to Sheila. Kane and Lydia stood a respectful distance, whispering to each other, probably about which safehouse they would use or some other Underground business. A joke from Chris got everyone laughing, including Kane. At the moment, though, Perryn and Brenda were in a long, tight embrace.

Willis could see the joyful tears gathering in his mother's eyes as she pulled back from Perryn. She brushed Perryn's hair out of her face and held her face in her hands. The smile on Perryn's face was everything he remembered, and he was overcome with his love for her. She appeared so happy and glad to see everyone. She was Perryn.

"Thank you, God." He prayed quietly.

He planned to allow everyone to have their chance to greet her, and so he waited until his mother glanced around for him.

"Willis?" Brenda circled, scanning the group.

He appeared in the doorway, smiling. Hope rose in his chest, yet his insides twisted with uncertainty. Thoughts of rushing to her side or declaring his love right there were checked as he remembered all the witnesses. He simply moved forward purposefully. He would hold her—and he wouldn't let go.

Perryn was laughing at one of Chris's jokes, her eyes creasing with the joy of seeing everyone. She threw a playful punch at Maria before turning her head to see Willis approaching.

He loved her smile. Her face was beautiful, but never as much as when her smile spread from ear to ear. Her whole spirit lighted a room when she laughed. Seeing her this way made all his fears melt. The pain and trauma of the previous days drifted away in the long moment when their eyes locked, and they smiled at each other.

Then, she stopped smiling.

Willis's heart halted at the sight, but he was too close. He stepped in for an embrace, to which she complied. He held her tightly, but she didn't return the hug, instead lightly patting his shoulders twice, her back tensing. He took the cue and pulled away.

Her expression was flat, but noticing the others, she quickly forced the corners of her mouth upward. No one else saw except Brenda, whose own smile was gone as she glanced from Perryn to Willis. Her eyes pled with him for an explanation. Willis opened his mouth to whisper to her.

"So, what's a girl got to do to get something to eat around here?" Perryn got the joke out before he could speak. The others laughed and moved to exit. Maria grabbed Perryn's arm to walk with her.

"Come on, girl. You can't eat in that nasty gown. Let's get you some clothes." The two exited the room, followed by the rest of the group. Brenda remained with Willis.

"Willis, what is going on?" Brenda stepped toward him, placing a hand on his upper arm. "That isn't how I pictured that would happen."

Willis simply stood frozen, staring at the door where Perryn had left. His mother tried again to speak to him.

"Son, talk to me."

Jez was telling the truth. Perryn doesn't believe I love her and never will, no matter what I say. The realization sank into his heart as he repeated it over and over. *She'll never believe me.*

Somewhere inside of him, deep down, a crack formed in his soul. The icy fingers of sorrow reached into his spirit and tore it in both directions. The crack became a cavern, and his body shook. His breath left him, and he sat down hard on the bed.

His insides shattered.

"Willis," his mother pleaded worriedly, "please say something."

He raised his eyes from the floor to see his mother's face, her forehead creased with concern. He longed to cry, but the tears wouldn't come. A numbing wave had taken over his body, and he couldn't feel anything other than the soul-wrenching pain of what had happened.

Brenda stepped forward and placed her hands on either side of her son's face. Studying his eyes, she repeated her statement silently. He stared. He opened his mouth to speak and found it dry.

"She doesn't love me." He could barely get the words out.

"Son, that's nonsense," Brenda said. "I happen to know full well how she feels about you. I wasn't supposed to say, but she talked to me about you. That young woman is madly in love with you and already knows how much you love her. I'm sure it will come to her. She's barely woken. Give her a minute."

Willis closed his eyes and shook his head slightly. He wished he could believe his mother, but the truth was plain. Jez's words to Perryn had taken root in the recoding. When she saw him, she didn't see a young man who would do anything to prove his love to her. She saw a man who pitied her, thinking her pathetic and needy. No matter what he said or did, she would doubt his intentions.

Without opening his eyes, the confession finally came. "I wanted to tell you, but I was afraid—afraid that if I said it, it would come true. Jez was the last person she heard. She passed out right after. Jez told Perryn I didn't love her."

Brenda's eyes grew wide at the realization. She raised her hands together to cover her mouth as she sucked in a deep breath.

"Oh, dear." Tears rimmed her eyelids. "Willis, I'm so sorry."

She stepped forward and wrapped her arms around him,

holding him tightly like she hoped to somehow absorb her son's burdens. He could feel her hand stroking his hair to comfort him, but no comfort came. No tears. No hope. All that remained was a soul-less existence that he couldn't see beyond.

I can't be here. I can't wake every day knowing that the Perryn I remember is gone. And trying to persuade her that she loves me feels wrong.

As if sensing his resignation, Brenda spoke softly through tears. "Give it time, son. Your heart will heal. I promise. This won't hurt forever."

He wished he could believe her, but his heart recognized the truth. And that created a wound that would never heal.

Chapter Thirty-Seven

How could he do that to me? Perryn was disgusted and crinkled her nose at what had happened. Willis had tried to hug her in front of everyone. He understood the truth. He grasped that she had learned the truth.

Everything fit in Perryn's mind. She could remember every detail of her relationship with Willis. Every moment, every stolen glance, every shared experience—all were stored away in her memory and at her beck and call. However, each was laced with a new realization. None of it was real.

She could remember Jez's words, but they rang as true in her mind. Each time she recalled an image from her history with Willis, she could find a crack in the façade—a moment here where he forgot what she said or a second there where he hadn't been quite as quick to return an embrace. She was foolish for not seeing it sooner. In fact, everything in recent memory had a lot to do with Willis and very little about her. His father had died. His mother was captured and rescued. He chose to seek out the Underground and ultimately save Jez. Then, there had been that scene in the hallway with Jez. The truth had been in front of her face all along, but she'd been too lost in infatuation to see it.

Even his words of love were nothing more than pity for a dying girl.

She hated Jez, but she owed her this—she'd helped Perryn see clearly. Willis had always avoided talking about their relationship. He'd taken every convenient excuse to avoid the topic. She guessed he didn't want to have to admit the truth.

She sat eating food brought by Father Anthony with Maria, who was giving her all the details of the Coalition invasion and their escape through the tunnel. She winced at Maria's description of finding Willis with her and would need to tell Maria later not to talk about Willis with her yet.

In truth, she was happy to be reunited with everyone. They were her family. Even Brenda, who had been more of a mother to her in these months than anyone prior in her life, brought her joy to see again. She was grateful for all of them.

But how could she see Willis every day? Their friendship— their relationship if it could be called that—was a farce. She wouldn't play his game anymore.

"Girl? Hello, girl? You listening?" Maria waved her hand in Perryn's face, and she realized she hadn't heard a word for the last several minutes. "Seriously, you spaced for a second there."

"Sorry. Got a lot on my mind," she said truthfully.

"Yeah, I can see that. But—don't spill your food on those clothes. They were all I could find." Maria had scrounged up a pair of jeans and t-shirt out of a pile of clothes from previous recoding patients. The t-shirt was a little too big, but Maria had insisted that was all that was remotely her size. She hated to think why the families of the recoded hadn't taken these clothes with them.

She took a bite of her sandwich and tried to ignore the feeling that she was chewing with someone else's teeth. Even swallowing felt foreign, as though she could feel her food traveling into a stomach outside of her. Still, she was thankful for the food, and a full stomach always helped after waking from recoding.

"Perryn?" Sheila approached from behind her. Glancing up, she could see Sheila smiling at her. "Can I talk with you for a moment—in private?"

"Umm." She glanced at Maria who winked and got up with her meal. "Okay, sure."

"Later, girl," Maria said with a mouthful of food. Sheila waited until Maria was a good distance away and sat down next to Perryn.

"I spoke with Brenda." She paused. "She noticed what happened upstairs."

"I'm not sure I want to talk about it." Perryn *was* sure she didn't want to talk, but she didn't want to hurt Sheila's feelings.

She supposed that this was a time to retain as many friends as she could. When the truth came out, people might take sides, and that could get ugly.

"You don't need to talk. I'm asking you to listen."

Perryn nodded.

"Do you remember that night between the two days of the Chase? The night when Willis suggested giving everything to the chairman?"

Perryn nodded again, curious where this was going.

"The Coalition put that idea in his head as an infant and activated it before the Chase. It was a powerful suggestion that he almost didn't overcome."

Perryn dropped her eyes to the floor, guessing where Sheila was going. She was unsure she could stand to hear this.

Sheila continued. "I brought Willis's parents to him to try to jog his memory. All it took was a reminder of the past, the true past, to give him a fighting chance. After that, the suggestion was still there, but he was able to fight it."

"So, you're suggesting I need to fight what Jez said to me." Perryn rolled her eyes. The course of this conversation annoyed her. Why couldn't they leave her alone? She'd barely woken, and already everyone was trying to tell her what to think.

"I'm suggesting that maybe you can't today. I'm merely asking that you be open to the idea that you may feel differently later—if we can think of something to break through the suggestion."

The idea made sense to her. It was logical, but she didn't feel like being logical. "Listen. I woke in this *body* minutes ago." She motioned to herself with two fingers, sickened by the word. "My memory is clear about what feels, smells, and tastes like the truth, and you want me to question my own sanity?" She was raising her voice and regretted it. Sheila was a friend, and she had no reason to yell at her.

Sheila offered a shy smile. "Perryn, I know it must feel like that's what I'm asking, but I watched the same battle happen in Willis a few months ago. You watched it. He was as convinced as you feel, but we all knew the truth."

Perryn shook her head trying to clear her thoughts. She remembered thinking Willis was crazy that evening of the Chase, and she'd been relieved to know that it'd been an implanted suggestion. This, though, sat so right—so true.

Is this how it was for Willis?

She fixed her eyes on her plate as she spoke. "Sheila, I know you and everyone here care, but this is something I need to figure out on my own."

"No, it's not. That's my point." Sheila paused, and Perryn looked up to find Sheila gazing intently at her. "You're not alone."

Perryn sighed and nodded, grateful for Sheila's words. A ball of sorrow formed in her gut, and she worried it would burst out of her.

"Thank you. Let us in so we can help. That's all we want." Sheila put her arm around Perryn's shoulders and squeezed her. Perryn leaned in and rested her head on Sheila's shoulder.

No, I'm not alone, but they'll see the truth. Willis doesn't love me. He never did.

———————◆✦◆———————

A few minutes later, Sheila and Brenda walked together toward Willis's quarters. Perryn had agreed to their help, and Sheila delivered the news to a much-relieved Brenda. They planned to tell Willis the good news and perhaps give him a little hope.

"He's so broken. You can see it in his eyes," Brenda said, unable to hide her sadness from Sheila. She gripped Sheila's arm with both her hands like a child afraid of their first day of school.

"I know, but we have to believe this can happen. He won't believe it if we don't." Sheila patted Brenda's hand.

"You're right." Brenda blotted at her eyes with her sleeve and took a couple of deep breaths. "Losing Max nearly killed me. I can't lose Willis, too. If he crawls into a shell, I may never get him back."

Approaching the door, Sheila turned to Brenda and put her hands on her shoulders. She gave her a reassuring nod, which Brenda returned.

"You ready?" Sheila said. "Here goes."

She turned and knocked on the door to Willis's room. Stopping to listen, they couldn't hear anything coming from inside. Sheila knocked again—more silence. She tried the handle, surprised to find it was unlocked.

"Willis?" Sheila said softly as she pushed the door open a crack. Seeing lights on, she pushed it all the way open.

Inside the room, the bed was a rumpled mess with the blanket hanging halfway on the floor. The desk sat empty, every drawer open. The chair lay on the floor as if knocked over in haste and not returned to its feet. Walking over to the desk, Sheila noticed a piece of paper with a few lines scribbled on it:

Mom,

Please know that I love you very much. I'm so glad you're safe and with people who will take care of you. I have decided to leave the Underground and avoid causing people to choose sides—including you. Please don't come after me. I need to figure this out on my own and give Perryn the space she needs.

Your loving son,

Willis

"Where—where is he?" Brenda sounded like she was out of breath.

Sheila stared at the mess and put the pieces together. She could sense Brenda's eyes searching the side of her face for answers. Nothing in the room said he was coming back. He hadn't left hoping they would chase him down. He meant to leave for good.

"Brenda, he's gone." Sheila handed the note to her.

"Gone?" Her eyes drifted down to the piece of paper.

"He's left us. He's left Perryn, and I don't think he means to return."

Brenda stared in disbelief at the words. Her throat caught in a choked gasp, and she collapsed to her knees. Leaning her head against the frame of the bed, she covered her trembling lips with her hand. "My boy. My beautiful son." Sheila knelt and held Brenda as she lost her son a second time.

Chapter Thirty-Eight

Willis stared ahead at the sun setting on the horizon. He faced westward down the street, and the sun nestled perfectly between the columns of buildings to bathe them in a golden glow on either side. He closed his eyes and allowed the heat to warm his face.

Slung over his shoulder was a bag with the few belongings he had on him when they escaped the tunnels. He'd included the clothes he'd worn that day, but disposed of the shirt, which was still stained with Perryn's blood. He also swiped a couple of the sandwiches from the supplies Father Anthony had brought.

He'd considered writing a note to everyone but changed his mind at the last second. They would eventually understand why he left once word got around about Perryn and him. The last thing he'd done with this mother was to hug her, and he believed that was the best goodbye he could offer. He realized leaving a note would hurt her, but he couldn't risk having her try to stop him. He needed to leave before anyone noticed.

He'd also considered writing Perryn. *What would that accomplish?* It would simply wound her each time she read it, so he'd decided against it.

Where would he end up? He had no idea. Coming to Central City had been to save his mother, and she was with people who would keep her safe. There was no reason for him to stay here.

The best plan he could invent on short notice was to travel south to the next alliance. Maybe there would be a way to start a fresh life there and one day have his mother join him. Regardless, getting out of the city was a wise first move.

The decision to leave had been a relatively easy one. He would never be allowed to love Perryn the way he wanted. After Jez's words, she would forever doubt that anything he did was genuine.

Resentment would grow, and it would ultimately divide their group. Perryn viewed the Underground as her family and destroying that would do her more harm. Leaving was the one option. It was the most loving thing to do.

"If I can't love her by being with her, I'll love her by leaving," he said quietly. The words sounded like nonsense when he said them aloud, but it made perfect sense in his head.

Staying would be selfish.

The air blew coolly on his face, and he realized the sun had completely disappeared beyond the horizon. Finding a place to stay for the night was a priority, and he couldn't travel to the usual places one might stay for an evening, even if he had the credits to afford them. He chided himself for leaving without a better plan, or at least more time to figure one out before nightfall.

That's when he smelled the fire.

A smoky aroma singed his nose, and he searched around for the source. In the distance to his left, he could see the flickering light of a small fire. Squinting, he could see several figures huddled around the flames to warm themselves as the evening cool settled.

Walking the three blocks, he noticed several children among the larger figures. From the best he could tell, the group was made up of three families. The fire was coming from a large barrel that'd been placed underneath a highway leading to the center of the city. In the shadow of the bridge, blankets and boxes had been assembled into makeshift shelters.

One of the men, a thirty-something with a prematurely graying beard, had been watching his approach. As Willis got closer, the man whispered something to the woman next to him. Quickly, she moved to huddle the children out of sight. The other two mothers did the same. The man, joined by the other adult male, started walking in his direction.

"Hey, mister. We don't want any trouble." The first man stepped out from their little community.

"Yeah, but we can sure dish it if we have to," the second man said. He was older by a few years, balding, and appeared as though he'd worked in a factory for most of his life. His hands were already balled into fists, ready to pummel Willis if needed.

Willis put up both hands. "I don't bring trouble. I'm searching for a place to stay tonight that's safe. I'm not wanting to cause any problem. A chance to stand by your fire and lay down for a night is all I need."

The first man scanned him up and down. "Empty the bag."

Willis took off his bag and turned it over. His few belongings—a pair of pants, socks, the sheet from his bed, a screwdriver he'd found, and the two sandwiches—fell to the sidewalk. He glanced and could see the second man staring at the food. Noticing Willis, he turned to gaze at the place where the children were hidden.

"Where'd you get those?" The younger man nodded at the food.

"Brought them with me for the journey." It was best to be vague.

His eyes stared beyond Willis. "You running from someone?"

"That matter?"

"Maybe." The second man eyed him suspiciously.

"Son, maybe we can work a trade." The first man placed a hand on his friend's shoulder calming him.

"A trade? For what?" Willis gazed down at the small pile of his possessions. There wasn't much.

"Food is hard to come by for us. Maybe the sandwiches for a night by our fire?"

Willis's heart sank. He'd been hoping to ration the food he had for as long as possible, or at least until he was able to resupply. He glanced at the bridge and could see a small face peering from behind the blankets. A hushed whisper came from his mother who pulled him out of sight.

"But mommy, he has food." The boy protested. His mother hushed him again.

"Okay," Willis said, thankful at least that some of the food was going to help children. "Sandwiches for a night by the fire."

"Agreed," the first man said. He tapped the shoulder of his friend.

"Fine." The second man shrugged his shoulders, relenting.

Willis picked up the sandwiches and presented one to each man. The rougher fellow turned and ran to the bridge. He ducked behind the blanket, and Willis guessed that he was already splitting the food with those behind it.

"Sorry about Ben. He struggles with trusting others," the first man said. "My name is Scott." He extended a hand toward Willis.

"I'm Willis." He shook Scott's hand, his stomach already grumbling at the loss of his food. "Thank you for taking me in."

Scott stooped to help Willis pick up the rest of his belongings. He carefully collected a photo from the ground and stared at it. He handed it to Willis. "Who are they? Your family?"

Willis sighed at the sight of the picture. His father smiled back at him with his arm around his mother. Perryn beamed next to him as her hands cradled his arm. It was the one personal item he'd taken from the cabin. The edges were tearing from living in his pocket, but he never travelled without it.

"My mother and father," he said. "I lost my father to the Coalition."

"And the girl?" Scott pointed to Perryn.

Willis took a deep breath. "I lost her too."

Scott sighed and stood up. He motioned to the photo. "Son, we've all lost someone. The Coalition has taken almost everything from people like us. You're in good company."

Willis smiled and nodded. Placing the photo in his bag, he walked with Scott over to the bridge.

Willis sat huddled under a blanket next to the barrel fire. Introductions had been brief. Scott's wife, Janet, had been the first to emerge from the blanket, holding the hand of a young girl who couldn't have been more than seven years old. They sat next to him, Scott picking at the portion of the sandwich he saved for himself.

He'd learned that Ben had, indeed, worked in a factory, but as a slave rather than a paid worker. It explained why he was slow to trust anyone else. His wife, Rebecca, held on tightly to two children. The first was the boy Willis had seen, and he couldn't take his eyes off Willis, except to ask his mother, "Does the stranger have any more food, Mommy?" Willis's heart broke seeing the girl. Not more than five years old, she appeared emaciated. Her hair was missing in patches, and she stared blankly at the fire. The third woman said very little. She cradled a toddler in her arms and made soft *shhh* noises to calm her child. Scott had introduced her as Sandra, but that's all Willis learned about her. They pressed him for his story, and he'd offered enough details to satisfy them without giving too much away. He left out his ties to the Underground to be safe.

"That's when I left the Alliance office I worked for," Scott said. He'd been telling the story of their life since Jaden's law change. "I believed our family needed to be free, but I didn't know the consequences. I recognized employment would be tough to find, but we were certain we could make it a while."

"So how did you find yourself out here?" Willis motioned to the makeshift shelter behind them.

"One day," Janet said with a small voice, "the Law-keepers showed up at our door. They demanded we make a choice. We could show our allegiance by giving our child to train for the Chase or lose our home." Willis shivered at the notion that children were still being forcefully taken from homes into training.

Scott shook his head in disgust. "There was no choice to make. We've been on the streets ever since."

"I'm sorry." Willis frowned.

"He's sorry," Ben said sarcastically. "Wait until you're on the streets for a month. Then, you'll know what sorry is. I would think a famous Chase runner would be smarter than that." Ben paused to glare at Willis. In fact, everyone, including Sandra was studying him. "That's right. I recognize you."

"Ben, come on—" Scott started to raise a hand to stop Ben.

"No." Willis waved Scott off. "You're right, Ben. I've been pretty well taken care of most of my life. I can't imagine what it's like to live like this."

"Mommy, are you sure he doesn't have any more food?" The

boy peeked at Willis again.

"Quiet, son," Ben snapped. He pointed an angry finger at Willis. "Look you—"

"No, Ben." Sandra interjected in a soft tone, breaking off Ben's statement. Her voice startled the entire group into silence. She rocked her sleeping boy as she spoke, staring at the fire. "He can't imagine our lives. He can't imagine being thrown to the streets, but he has experienced loss. You lost your father, is that right?"

Willis nodded. "Coalition killed him."

"See, Ben? We've all lost someone. Me, I lost my husband. We were kids when we married, barely seventeen, but it was love. And there was the baby that was coming." She paused when her child stirred. "One day, a man broke into our home threatening to harm us, and my husband did what a man should do for his family. He defended us. He killed the intruder with his bare hands. As it turns out, the man was the son of a high-ranking Alliance official who couldn't afford the scandal. He turned the whole story around to say my husband attacked his son. He was taken away from me and sent to prison for murder. But it was self-defense, I tell you."

The group sat silently listening to Sandra's story.

"It wasn't long after I was told that he died in prison. They said he was killed by another prisoner in a fight, but my husband doesn't lose in fights. It didn't make sense to me, but I believed I was alone. I did my best to raise my boy on my own. And that's when it happened."

"What happened?" Willis studied her face. He was entranced by her story.

"I saw him. My husband. He was there on the broadcast, lined up to run the Chase last year—alive. It was like he returned from the dead. He didn't die like they said. They stole him to run in that Chase." Her chin quivered, but she pursed her lips, not allowing the emotion to get the better of her. "That's why I'm here in this city. I heard he came here after the riots, and I'm searching for him. But they must've told him we were dead like they told me because he doesn't appear to be seeking us. I had almost given up hope—

until you, Willis Thomson."

Sandra gazed at him and let his name hang in the air between them. Her story slowly connected in his mind, and he realized what she was saying. *How could it be? He has a family?* He stared at her in stunned silence. The fire glistened off the hopeful tears welling in Sandra's eyes.

"Please, Willis Thomson, do you know where my husband is? Have you seen my Kane?"

Willis's lip trembled with emotion. Kane had a family, one he'd gone to prison for, and he didn't even know they still existed. He searched for the right words, but all that came out was, "Yeah, I have."

As if afraid to break the silence, the group stared, their glances alternating between Willis and Sandra. Even the children acted frozen. Someone shuffled their feet, but Willis didn't pay any attention. He met Sandra's gaze and realized she was waiting for more.

"Umm—he's here. In the city."

"He's—here?" Her voice shook as she spoke the words. "Where? Can you take me?"

"Yes. He leads the Underground." Willis winced at giving away the information in his excitement. Willis started to stand. "I've been with him for weeks. He's—"

"Hold on," Ben said loudly. Willis jumped at his intrusion. "It's nighttime, and you all know better than to wander off into the dark. We're not alone living on these streets. This far away from Alliance headquarters, there aren't enough Law-keepers to stop the violent gangs. Young man, you can do whatever you want, but Sandra is staying here. Even a Chase runner couldn't make it with a mother and child in tow. They would find you and kill you for the clothes on your back—or worse."

"What do you mean?" Willis began to protest.

"Everyone please settle down," Scott said calmly. "Ben is right. No one should be wandering away from camp tonight. We're safer together, so we'll travel tomorrow to reunite Sandra with her husband."

"But, I—"

"Willis, please. I'm glad you're so willing to help, but we know what we're talking about. You aren't in charge here. I am."

Sandra sniffed, and both men turned to her.

Scott's voice softened. "Sandra, you know I'm right."

Sandra nodded, clearly feeling impatient.

"There, that settles it. Willis can help reunite Sandra with her husband tomorrow. We'll leave first thing in the morning and celebrate together."

Willis fumed, unable to disguise his frustration.

Scott stood, effectively announcing the end of the evening. "And I think it's time we all turn in. That's enough excitement for one night."

On cue, everyone started to move toward the various makeshift shelters. Scott directed Willis toward a corner with hanging blankets on either side as his wife herded their son to bed. After brushing some gravel from the spot, he lay down using his bag as a pillow. To his right, he could hear Scott whispering to Sandra, offering her words of comfort as she reluctantly retired to her box.

Scott was clearly a good man—a protector and leader. He resolved to mention Scott to Kane. The Underground could use someone like him. Ben, however, could use some work. He let out a satisfied sigh at the thought of reuniting Sandra and her son with Kane the next day. He would have to explain himself, but this reunion couldn't be avoided. Kane had no idea his family was searching for him, and Willis owed Kane so much more than even this could repay.

"Mr. Scott, could you turn on the radio?" The voice was that of Ben's daughter. "I'm scared."

"Sure thing, sweetheart," he said with a smile in his voice. A click brought the slow fade of a voice over the radio. It was mid-sentence, but the announcer was saying something about a special announcement from Alliance Headquarters. That's when a woman's voice began speaking:

"This is the Alliance Deputy Chairwoman, calling upon all

citizens loyal to the Western Alliance and World Coalition. Today marked a great achievement in Coalition intelligence. Alliance Law-keepers were able to infiltrate and neutralize the terror agency known as the Underground. Key members were arrested and will face the consequences of their actions. However, a few leaders are still at large and are believed to still be in the limits of Central City. Anyone with information on the whereabouts of these fugitives are urged to show their loyalty by contacting authorities right away. As your Deputy Chairwoman, I promise that you and your family shall forever have the gratitude of the Alliance. The Law is good.

The announcement finished, and the radio announcer changed to discussing the various team possibilities for the Chase that year.

Ben grunted. "I guess we know where our new friend comes from." He scoffed, and Willis could hear him roll over.

Willis closed his eyes, hoping sleep would find him. He had to leave this city.

Chapter Thirty-Nine

Willis awoke to find himself wrapped in the sheet he'd taken and huddled near one of the hanging blankets. His nose was ice cold, and he could see his breath in the cool morning air. He rubbed his eyes as he examined the space around him. A gray morning light lit parts of the walls under the bridge, and he guessed it was cloudy.

His muscles complained as he sat up. Sleeping on the ground hadn't done his back any favors, and he was stiff as he tried to stand. Emerging from behind the blanket, he could see a small tendril of smoke rising from the barrel with a low flame in the center. Ben was busy tending to it.

"Good morning," Willis croaked. He stretched to get the blood in his body moving.

Ben glanced in his direction. "I see you're an early riser too. Keep your voice down. Don't want to wake the others. Think you can help me with this fire?"

"Sure." He grabbed a stack of papers and started rolling them tightly, so they would burn slower. He needed to make peace with this man. "Ben, I didn't mean to offend you last night."

Ben stopped working and placed his hands on the edge of the still-cold barrel. He stared at the small flame with his lips pursed. Taking a deep breath, he finally spoke. "Listen. I got a family to take care of. I don't trust you. I don't trust any outsiders. My family will always come first, you got that?"

Willis gazed at Ben, hurt that he was still being harsh with him. *Why does he hate me so much? Overprotective is one thing, but this goes further.*

"Yeah, I got that," Willis said. He was starting to have his doubts about leading this man to members of the Underground, a group that was built on trust.

"Good. Then, maybe you'll understand that what I do next I do for my family."

Willis saw movement out of the corner of his eye. Turning to where it came from, he saw the end of a gun barrel poking out from behind a bush near the bridge. The gun was held in the hands of a Law-keeper in urban camouflage. Two others flanked the officer. Willis turned to run when a pinch stabbed at the side of his neck.

Reaching up, he fingered the metal tranquilizer dart protruding from his skin. He opened his mouth to call out, but the world around him began to spin. His vision blurred and went black. His head struck the concrete, and it throbbed for a second until he lost consciousness.

Chapter Forty

Sheila threw her last couple of items in her bag. The administrator of the recoding facility was getting nervous after the previous night's announcements, and everyone had agreed that they should move on to prevent putting the facility in danger.

The team had taken the news of Willis's departure with mixed feelings. Brenda quietly wept as Sheila told everyone. Kane had been devastated, sitting and placing his head in his hands. Chris and Lydia had simply shaken their heads as she recounted what happened. Maria, caught up to speed by Perryn, smacked her gum with her arms crossed as she stood defiantly by her friend.

It was Perryn's expression that'd baffled Sheila the most. She'd stared down and scanned the floor over and over as if reading several of her own thoughts. Sheila couldn't tell if her face communicated shock, disappointment, or relief.

Perhaps it was a mix of all three.

They were packing to move to a safe house that Father Anthony had directed them to. Several of the other Underground were staying there. A van was promised to transport them, but it was more than an hour late.

"You think they forgot about us?" Sheila turned, startled to see Lydia standing in the doorway. Her feet shuffled nervously. They were all on edge and eager to leave.

"I hope not. Whatever the reason, I'm sure there's an explanation. Father Anthony hasn't let me down yet," she said.

"He'd better have one. This team is a mess. I think you and I are the last sane ones left capable of leading."

Sheila raised her eyebrows in surprise. "What do you mean?"

"All due respect to the Chief, but he's not himself. The invasion was enough to mess him up physically, but Willis's departure got in his head. He keeps whispering to himself about 'failing his family again,' and frankly, I don't know what to do about it."

"He shouldn't take it personally. Willis made his choice, and it had nothing to do with him."

Lydia crossed her arms and leaned on the door frame. "You obviously don't know what kind of leader Kane is. Everything is personal to him."

"I see." A long pause passed between them, and Sheila pretended to check the contents of her bag.

Lydia continued as if she hadn't stopped. "Brenda can't hold it together. No surprise there. Perryn's moody, and Maria can't see past her best friend. Chris is too young to lead, so that leaves you and me."

"I suppose." Sheila paused to think. "Maybe things will get better when we get to the safehouse. Seeing so many other people from the Underground might encourage everyone."

Lydia stepped into the room and shut the door. "What I want to know is, why did he do it? Why leave?"

Sheila sighed. She suspected she was going to get this question a lot.

"I mean, I know Perryn's brain is all muddled and confused, but to leave her right after saving her doesn't make sense."

"Because he loves her."

Lydia stopped and gazed at Sheila, caught off guard by her response.

"Because he loves her?"

"Yeah." Sheila half-smiled as she nodded. "He loves her, so he left."

Lydia tilted her head and raised one eyebrow. "Maybe I'm alone in being the sane one."

"Don't you see it? Her reprogramming has her doubting everything that's ever happened between them. If he'd stayed, it would serve to divide us all as we took sides between them. Did you notice Maria? She's already made her choice. Imagine the pressure we would all feel. Perryn loves the Underground, so he left. He didn't want to destroy the one thing she still loved."

Lydia shook her head, in disbelief or disgust, Sheila couldn't tell. Sheila had never seen Lydia this rattled about anything.

"All I know," Lydia said, "is we need the Chief in one piece, so this had better get straightened out." She sat down hard on the edge of Sheila's bed and rested her head in her hands.

"Are you okay, Lydia?"

Lydia breathed deeply, but her cool demeanor was no more than partially restored. "We had a good thing going, Sheila. We were the Underground. You were the Watcher. We were doing good for the Liberated, and what have we become? A decentralized mess scattered across the city. We have to pull everyone together, and the one who has kept everyone working together is currently a headcase. And it's all because of two kids who can't get their relationship straight."

Sheila couldn't help but smile. Saying it out loud made it sound ridiculous. *But it's the truth. Maybe oversimplified, but the truth.*

"And Kane." Lydia pointed toward the door. "He's watched over all of us through his leadership. We need him to be right. I— I need him to be right." She barely got the final words out, and Sheila stepped toward her. She wasn't sure she'd meant to let Sheila in on her secret, but it was clear what she meant.

"Does he know how you feel about him?" Sheila smiled shyly. Lydia opened her mouth to respond, already shaking her head.

A knock at the door brought Chris's face peering in the door. "Chief says the van is here." He disappeared before they could answer. In truth, they all itched to get out of there. The safe house and more people would be a welcome change over these empty hallways. Sheila walked over to Lydia and grabbed her hand.

"Lydia, we'll figure it out. The Underground isn't dead, and the Watcher has a few more tricks up her sleeve." She offered a playful smirk to emphasize the last words, and it drew a smile from Lydia.

"Fine." Lydia sighed as she stood. "But I'm holding you to it."

An hour later, they pulled up to the safe house. It had once been a school building, long since out of use. The building was made of brick, crumbling after years of neglect, and it stood way on the outskirts of the Central City metro area. The windows were boarded on the front side and the grass was several feet tall. From the street, it still appeared like an abandoned facility.

"It's perfect." Lydia stared out the van window.

"How?" Chris curled his lip. "Looks like a dump to me."

"That's why it's perfect. You can't even tell anyone is here, but there are already about a hundred. It's the perfect place for us to regroup."

True. Sheila could see no signs that so many people had already taken residence there. The van pulled to the backside of the building. Without a word, a service door opened, and the van pulled inside.

Staring in wonder, Sheila couldn't help but grin. The building may have appeared old and abandoned from the outside, but inside was a beehive of movement. Training rings had been set around the room. Offices were located on the other side of the space where they'd pulled in. Even a medic station occupied one corner.

The Underground hadn't stopped. It was very much alive.

Lydia reached forward and patted Kane's shoulder. He gazed out the window stoically, and Sheila longed to know what was going on inside his head. She hoped desperately that he was encouraged by what he saw.

Pulling to the middle of the space, the van stopped. The door opened, and Father Anthony met them with a smile on his face. Sheila jumped out of the van and walked briskly to him, throwing her arms around him before he could protest.

He laughed. "I take it you approve."

"You set all this up?" Sheila stared in awe at the scene as she let him go.

"No, not alone. They mostly did this themselves, but I'll take the credit for the fun of it."

The rest of the team piled out of the van, scanning their surroundings. Maria still flanked Perryn like a protective mother hen over her chick. Father Anthony laughed as they appeared lost, taking in the flurry of activity around them.

"We avoid the outside front rooms," he said. "It keeps the façade of an abandoned building intact. No one ever drives down this road, but it's best not to risk it."

"Where do we stay?" Chris twirled a finger in the air to motion to the room.

"Men are on the second floor. Women are on the third. You'll find there's plenty of space. Chris, you'll be interested in the technology and computer systems which are located in the basement. Lydia, I see you've already noticed the training center."

"How many are here?"

"We've relocated about one hundred fifty already, with more to come." His face took on an apologetic expression. "Oh, and I'm sorry for my delay in getting to you today. I hope it didn't worry you. Our Deputy Chairwoman's announcements brought a few of the Liberated to our other safehouses, and I needed to be sure they were taken care of first."

Kane stepped forward and extended a hand, which Father Anthony shook with a smile. "Thank you, Father," Kane said. He smiled, the first Sheila had seen in days.

"My son, I'm glad it pleases you, but I'm not finished. There's one person who came to us today that I simply had to relocate here right away."

Sheila tilted her head to the side. "Who?"

"Oh, it's someone quite notable we picked up. I understand he's been missing a while. Follow me."

Willis? They found Willis? Thank God for Father Anthony. It was the one explanation that made sense. Somehow, they'd discovered Willis and convinced him to return. It would be a strange dynamic with what happened to Perryn, but they would figure it out.

Father Anthony led them through several corridors. Either side of the hallway had rooms that used to be occupied with students prior to the Alliance's abandonment of traditional education for what it deemed 'more practical skill training.' Still, the walls held onto the yellowed remains of projects and posters completed by children long ago.

Halfway down, the hall opened to a larger foyer that used to serve as the entrance to the school. A giant painting of a dog's head biting down ferociously on a bone gazed down upon them with the emblem "Go Fighting Bulldogs!" emblazoned beneath it.

A wide stairwell led to the second floor, upon which sat a young man with his back to the group. He was reading a book that he must have discovered in the abandoned school library. He had brown hair that'd grown long enough to touch his collar, each strand slightly curling at the end. What was unmistakable was his physique. He had the build of a racer.

Sheila studied the back of his head for several moments, and it clicked. The gasp from Perryn confirmed her suspicions, and she glanced at the team to see Kane and Perryn were as wide-eyed as she.

"My son, your friends have arrived," Father Anthony said, not trying hard to hide his smile. "You might like to greet them before they settle in."

The figure straightened and slowly closed the book. He turned to meet them, and his mouth broke into a huge smile that reached all the way to his brown eyes. Jumping from his seat, he ran to them and threw his arms around Perryn, who appeared frozen for a moment before returning the embrace. He pulled away and smiled at her, and then to Kane and Sheila. Perryn's face was flushed and her mouth hung open.

"How? How?" Perryn stuttered.

"Oh, you know me," he said. "I love to surprise."

"Son, some of these people you know, but might I introduce the rest to you." Father Anthony pointed. "From your left, we have Maria, Chris, Lydia, and Brenda."

"Hey, everyone. It's good to meet you. My name is Jaden."

Epilogue

Willis could feel the headache before his eyes opened. The drugs from the dart were wearing off, but his limbs still lay like lead weights. They wouldn't move, no matter how hard he focused.

Stay calm, Willis. Let's at least get your head straight. What happened?

He fought through the haze in his head to rehearse what happened. He'd spent the night with three homeless families to be betrayed and captured by Law-keepers the next morning.

What had Ben said? Maybe then you'll understand? Understand what?

The truth occurred to him. Ben had given in to the promise of 'gratitude' from the Deputy Chairwoman's announcement and sold him out. He must have gone during the night and arranged for his arrest without waking the others. Had they'd even seen what happened, or did they wake to simply find him missing? Then, *she* came to mind.

"Sandra!" he said aloud. *She'll think I abandoned her. I was going to reunite her with Kane, and she'll assume I ran out on her.* He shot up in bed—or at least he tried to. Despite his effort, his body jerked back toward the bed he was on. He tried again with the same effect. Shaking his head, he tried to clear his vision.

He glanced down and gasped in horror. His arms and legs wouldn't move, but not because of the drugs. Thick leather straps crossed his wrists, biceps, chest, waist, thighs, and ankles. He thrashed to loosen himself, but they wouldn't budge.

He panted in fear.

Where am I? What is this? His mind raced with the possibilities.

The room was illuminated with the pale glow of fluorescent

lights. Next to the bed were several machines connected to various intravenous tubes that protruded from his veins. Otherwise, the space was blank and quite small. The door was blank, save for a small window.

A man, with round wire-rimmed glasses, stared at him through the glass. He gazed at Willis with emotionless eyes. Occasionally, he glanced down, and the movement of his shoulder suggested he was writing something.

"Who are you?" Willis screamed. "Where am I?"

Glasses didn't flinch.

"I demand you tell me where I am and what you're doing to me? Let me out of here!"

More notes.

Willis was desperate. He could feel the fear gripping his heart with its talons. His screams turned to pleading.

"Please. Please let me go."

More notes.

"I know you think I'm the one causing all the problems, but I'm not. Please, I promise I won't be any more trouble. Please let me go."

The man raised his eyes from his notes to someone apparently approaching from the side. The sounds of muffled voices could be heard.

"Is he awake?" Willis could hear the voice was female. Willis couldn't understand why, but it sounded familiar.

"Yes, ma'am," Glasses said. "He's come to, but I'm not sure he's ready to be interviewed."

"Oh, I will decide that. Thank you. Please unlock the door, Doctor."

Willis could hear the beeping of the electronic combination being entered and the *thwack* sound of the latch opening. The handle turned, and the doctor entered holding the door for the other person.

The woman was wearing a burgundy skirt with matching suit top. A gold Alliance insignia was pinned to her lapel, and it glinted as she entered the bright lighting. On her arm, Willis counted ten bracelets which clattered as she clasped her hands together.

"Mr. Thomson, how are you this morning?"

Willis was unsure she wanted an answer, so he stayed silent.

She sighed. "I see. I suppose circumstances would leave you with mixed feelings. I'll grant you that. It is my hope that this will not always be our arrangement, though."

He finally managed to speak. "Who—who are you?"

She huffed in annoyance. "Well, I suppose your previous accommodations did not permit you to view a screen broadcast. I am the Deputy Chairwoman of the Western Alliance and *personal friend* of the Chairman of the World Coalition, but you can simply call me Penny." She smiled and tilted her head slightly, implying her words should help him be more comfortable around her.

"I—I—" He stammered. "Why have you brought me here?"

"Young man, you have been a bit of a thorn in our side, haven't you?" Her tone was sickeningly sweet.

"What do you mean? What have I—?"

She sighed again, interrupting him. "I understand. It must be so difficult to see the world clearly after all that you have been through. I speak of you and your fellow rebels. You seek to undermine our efforts to bring peace and harmony to the World Coalition."

Willis's faced darkened at her language.

"I see you don't approve. Well, in time, that may change. I hope that we can work well together."

"Why would I ever want to work with someone like you?" Willis's courage was suddenly back, and his fearful stutter disappeared.

"Because you are about to become the greatest asset of the Coalition. Your efforts will help reunite the supposed 'Liberated' with the glorious Law."

Willis almost laughed. What she was proposing was ridiculous. *I'd rather die.* He considered saying it out loud, but the tug of the leather straps made him think otherwise.

"I'm not sure that I want to do that," he said carefully.

"In time you will. You will choose to help us before long."

This time he did laugh out loud. He laughed so hard that the straps cut into his wrists as his body attempted to double over. He took a breath to calm himself and saw that Penny was enraged. Her tone changed.

"Mr. Thomson, laugh all you want, but the truth is this." The skin of her neck started to flush red. "You belong to the World Coalition. You have since the day you were born. Your parents' relationship was a fabrication. Your birth was planned. Your destiny has always been ours for the choosing. If you think we are so small-minded to think one shot at the Chase is the reason we poured so much time and effort into your programming, you need to think again. We *own* you."

Willis glared at her. He wanted to curse aloud, but he wouldn't give her the pleasure.

"My parents' marriage was not fabricated." He wanted to stab her with each word.

She clenched her teeth. "Believe what you want. When we're done with you, you'll think otherwise. You are not the first asset we've procured and put to good use." She turned to the door. "Come in and show our guest what I mean."

Appearing in the doorway, a face Willis had come to hate in the last few days appeared. Jez stood there, arms crossed, with a murderous glare.

"Hello, Will." Her lips curled into a smirk.

"You see, young man," Penny said. "You are not above our influence. We have the capability to make anyone do anything we please."

"I don't think using me to infiltrate the Underground will work this time," he growled. "After that one over there, they'll be far more careful." He glared daggers at Jez, who t'sked with annoyance.

"Young lady, you may leave. It is clear you are upsetting the patient." Penny waved her out the door.

"Goodbye, Will." Jez smirked. She waved mockingly as she disappeared.

"Mr. Thomson, let me tell you a little about what is going to happen. You will agree to help us, because we have no intention of doing anything less than transforming you into our greatest creation. Your friend who was here—she was the beginning, the prototype. However, you will be our masterpiece. When we are finished, you will stand as the shining example of the new wave of Law-keeping for the future."

Penny crouched until her head was level with his at the edge of the bed.

"You know the words, don't you, Willis. The Law protects us all. The Law is good. It preserves us all. And, yes, the Law remains." She lowered her voice to a whisper. "And because of you, the Law will once again save us all. All will declare that the Law is good."

Penny smiled sweetly and stood.

Willis was certain that she wasn't kidding. They were going to do whatever it took to change him into their pawn.

"Well, there we have it." Penny resumed her sweet tone as if flipping a switch in her mind. She moved toward the doorway. "Oh, and in case you hold out hope that your friends will be able to get in here again to rescue you, the last time was no more than a ruse. We let you in last time, so our young lady friend could join you, and we could oust the Watcher. No one gets in here or out of here—ever."

Willis shot a glare at her. "Again?" He glanced around the room for a clue as she moved for the door. "Get in here again?"

"Welcome to Solution Systems, Mr. Thomson. I hope you enjoy your stay." Penny smiled and walked out, her bracelets jingling as she went. The doctor closed the door, and Willis could hear the lock latch in place.

Author's Note

Honestly, after finishing *The Chase*, the next chapter of the series was very difficult for me to write. The initial story of Willis and Perryn and Jaden came as inspiration and seemed to jump from my head to the page. This book felt more like a mystery, one that I had to uncover clue by clue. All I knew was that Willis and Perryn would be in hiding and that Sheila would be in prison. From there, the story took on a life of its own, and I was along for the ride.

I had to tell this story, though, because I felt I knew these characters so well. I wanted to know what their life would be like outside of the space station and in a world where the Law had been ended. I also took inspiration from *The Empire Strikes Back* to believe that the second part of a series can actually outdo the first. (We all know Episode V is the best of the entire Star Wars saga. I dare you to change my mind!) Established characters were fun to work with, and I only had to figure out how to get them back together. At times the story surprised me. The fate of Max happened suddenly, and I struggled with it for a while. I can remember the moment when I realized who they would find inside Solution Systems, I stopped typing and had to digest it for a moment. Then, I couldn't stop until those chapters were written. And when I realized what would happen to Willis and Perryn in the end, I scrambled to get started on the third installment.

The title, *The Choice*, reminds me of when life has thrown me into 'no-win' scenarios far more often than I'd like. The choice to leave my ministry career during burnout was a choice to save my family or save my church. Family, hands down, won that debate, but the choice still involved incredible loss. As Willis learned, choices have consequences, and the negative ones cannot always be avoided. It is our character amid that pain that determines whether we shrink from or grow into the person God created us to be. God does not always remove the thorns we carry (see 2 Corinthians 6), but that doesn't mean we've missed out on His best for us. His grace is ALWAYS sufficient for the moment.

I would love to connect with you to find out if you resonated with the position that Willis was put in. Did you see the ending coming? Which characters are you rooting for and what do you hope will happen in the third installment? If you haven't already, sign up for my newsletter to get the latest news on book releases, book recommendations, and get your own free copy of my prequel *Kane: A Chase Runner Story* to learn how our favorite leader of the Underground made it to the space station in the first place.

Here's how to connect with me:
Website/Newsletter/Free book - *BradleyCaffee.com*
Facebook - *Facebook.com/bradleycaffeeauthor*
Instagram - *@bradleycaffeeauthor* (tag me in a picture of you with *The Choice!)*

Most of all, PLEASE LEAVE ME A REVIEW AND TELL YOUR FRIENDS. Authors' success can live or die by reviews and referrals. If you loved *The Choice*, please consider saying so on Amazon and Goodreads and telling another reader about the series.

Thanks for reading, friend.

And Now, a Sneak Peek at Book Three in
The Chase Runner Series

Chapter One

My name is Willis Thomson, and I am free from the Law.

"Patient 842, are you still with us?" The voice blared in the velvety darkness. Willis stared into the blackness without responding. "Patient, we aren't asking much of you. Is it really worth all this?"

My name is Willis Thomson, and I am free from the Law.

"Patient 842, your rehabilitation will be much smoother if you accept your position here. We only need a token response from you of your openness to the process. Just four words." Silence fell over the chamber as the voice waited for his response. Willis's breath came in gasps as he managed his panic. Sweat beaded upon his forehead and rolled down his face, joining with the involuntary tears that quietly seeped from the corners of his eyes. "The law is good. That's all. Just four words. You can do it—and this can end."

My name is Willis Thomson, and I am free from the Law. He repeated the phrase over and over in his mind. It was the one thing keeping him sane. His wide eyes scanned the darkness for what seemed like the millionth time in the days and weeks he'd been kept here. *Or has it been months?*

"Patient 842—"

I won't do it. I can't.

"Four simple words."

No. No. No.

"Don't make us do this to you."

I won't.

"We can help you. Give us a chance."

Liars!

"Patient, this only ends one of two ways. Don't make this harder on yourself."

I can't.

"You can accept this or resist, but eventually you'll give in. Why drag it out?"

Please don't.

An audible sigh could be heard as if the voice forgot to mute itself.

"Last chance."

"The—" Willis began.

"There you go."

"The Law—" Willis paused for a long breath.

"Come on. You've got this!"

"The Law is—GONE!" Willis shouted into the dark void.

Pain. The electrical impulse coursed through his body, white flashes filling his vision despite the darkness of the room. His back arched involuntarily off the table. His wrists pulled at the restraints, reopening the raw wounds on his skin that hadn't been able to heal properly. He screamed to the point his voice broke.

The shock ended, and his body slammed back onto the table. Sobs began to well up inside him, and he clenched his eyelids shut.

"You disappoint us, Patient 842. It doesn't have to be this way."

Willis's lips trembled as he sucked in a breath. He searched the suffocating blackness as if looking for an explanation he could give the voice.

"Why—why don't you just recode me and get it over with?" Willis asked, his voice hoarse and barely audible.

"All in good time, 842. For now, we suggest you work with us."

Willis breathed deeply and set his jaw. He looked upward at the supposed ceiling and willed his tears to end. *I can't let them break me. I can't. I can't.*

Another audible sigh could be heard. "Okay, Patient 842. Let's begin again." The voice paused. "Just four words."

My name is Willis Thomson, and I am free from the Law.

CPSIA information can be obtained
at www.ICGtesting.com
Printed in the USA
BVHW041318050222
628167BV00013B/405